THE LIGHT OF DAY

Eric Ambler

With an Introduction by
MARTIN EDWARDS

This edition published 2016 by
The British Library
96 Euston Road
London NW1 2DB

Originally published in 1962 by William Heinemann

Copyright © Eric Ambler Literary Management Ltd
Introduction copyright © Martin Edwards 2016

Cataloguing in Publication Data

A catalogue record for this book is
available from the British Library

ISBN 978 0 7123 5650 3

Typeset by Tetragon, London

Printed and bound by
CPI Group (UK) Ltd, Croydon CR0 4YY

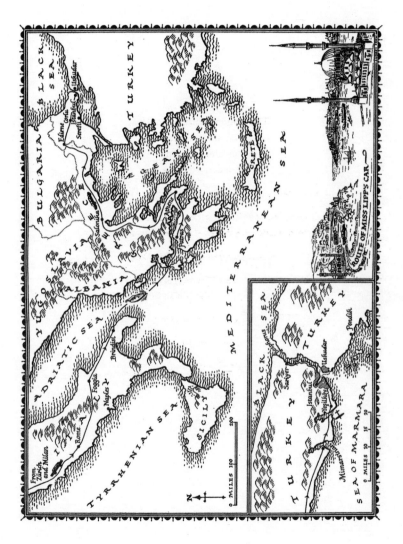

ROUTE OF MISS LIPP'S CAR

INTRODUCTION

The Light of Day is a wonderfully enjoyable thriller about the unlike-liest of spies. Arthur Abdel Simpson, part-British, part-Egyptian, recounts the story of his misadventures as a reluctant agent for the Turkish secret police. He is acting under duress after being caught at the wheel of a Lincoln Continental in which guns and ammu-nition have been hidden. When interrogated by Major Tufan, of the Turkish counter-intelligence department, the Second Section, he protests his innocence, but to no avail. Whilst it is true that he did not know about the secret cargo he was transporting, Arthur is not an innocent; he is merely naive. Although he calls himself a journalist, in truth he is a petty criminal, preying on people even more gullible than he is.

The reason Arthur has made his journey to Istanbul from Athens is that he has been blackmailed by a man who calls himself Harper, whom Arthur has unwisely tried to rob. The attempted theft back-fired, one of many occasions in the book when it is painfully evident that Arthur is much less clever than he thinks he is. Arthur leeches on wealthy tourists, but Harper is not what he seems. He is a villain, in cahoots with a glamorous mistress called Elizabeth Lipp, the owner of the Lincoln. As the story develops, the pair's disdain for Arthur becomes clear, and he determines to pay them back—a habit that he developed as a schoolboy in England, when he was bullied by fellow pupils and teachers. Arthur's weaknesses make him a natural victim, but his determination to retaliate, coupled with his lack of conscience, make him a surprisingly formidable adversary.

Neither Arthur nor Tufan are clear about what Harper and Elizabeth are up to. Are they political conspirators, planning some form of attack on the Turkish regime, or are their motives rather different? Arthur comes up with more than one theory, but his detective work is fallible. Ambler drops a hint for the alert reader during a scene when Arthur assumes the role of Elizabeth's tour guide, but only towards the end of the book is it made plain exactly what Harper and his lover are plotting.

As Arthur tries to keep tabs on Harper and Elizabeth, his thin skin and inflated ego keep landing him in trouble. Towards the end of the story, in a rare and rueful moment of self-awareness, he remarks, "I have a unique capacity for self-destruction." The burning question for the reader is whether Arthur will be saved from the consequences of his own folly by a primitive but powerful survival instinct which has overcome suicidal thoughts in the past, and on which he depends to keep the conspirators from discovering his duplicity.

Arthur is superbly characterized, and he has been compared—for example by Ambler's biographer, Peter Lewis—to Shakespeare's Falstaff. Ambler demonstrates his skill as a novelist by allowing the reader to see through Arthur's feeble attempts to blame everyone but himself for his misfortunes, and yet nevertheless hope—however reluctantly—that he will manage to find a way to keep Tufan happy without betraying himself to Harper and Elizabeth. Although he never comes on to centre stage, a sinister figure lurks menacingly in the background throughout the book. This is Tufan's boss, the ruthless Haki, who a generation earlier featured memorably in

Ambler's most famous novel, *The Mask of Dimitrios* (also known as *A Coffin for Dimitrios*).

Eric Ambler (1909–98) was already established as the leading British writer of espionage fiction by the time he started work on *The Light of Day* in 1961, although a writer with a very different approach to the genre, Ian Fleming, would shortly make a breakthrough when his James Bond books were filmed with Sean Connery in the lead role. Ambler's work on the novel was interrupted when a fire at his home in California destroyed both his unfinished manuscript and his research material. Undaunted, he completed the novel, and its success prompted him to contemplate an "Arthurian trilogy" featuring the same anti-hero. A change of publisher derailed this plan, although Arthur returned five years later in *Dirty Story*.

The engaging plot of *The Light of Day* guaranteed interest from film-makers, and Jules Dassin, who had made his name with *Rififi*, directed *Topkapi*, a caper movie based on Ambler's book in 1964. Peter Ustinov was cast as Simpson (whose middle name was changed from Abdel to Simon) and Melina Mercouri as Elizabeth. Robert Morley played Cedric Page, who does not appear in the book at all, while Maximilian Schell took the role of Harper. It has been said that Peter Sellers was the director's first choice for the part of Simpson, but was reluctant to work with Schell. In the event, Ustinov's performance earned him an Academy Award for best supporting actor. This was a curious achievement, because Simpson is a central figure in the film, as in the book. Schell later theorized that the servile aspects of Simpson's personality meant that the actor who took the part was not perceived as a suitable candidate for the Oscar for best actor. The film dispensed with the element of mystery and surprise about the villains' plan, and its humour was less subtle than that of the book, but it enjoyed success at the box office, and to this day remains very watchable. *The Light of Day* has, perhaps, stood the test of time even better. It is a splendid addition to the list of British Library Classic Thrillers.

MARTIN EDWARDS
www.martinedwardsbooks.com

CHAPTER ONE

I T CAME DOWN TO THIS: IF I HAD NOT BEEN ARRESTED BY THE
Turkish police, I would have been arrested by the Greek police. I
had no choice but to do as this man Harper told me. He was entirely
responsible for what happened to me.

I thought he was an American. He looked like an American—tall,
with the loose, light suit, the narrow tie and button-down collar, the
smooth, old-young, young-old face and the crew cut. He spoke like
an American, too; or at least like a German who has lived in America
for a long time. Of course, I now know that he is not an American,
but he certainly gave that impression. His luggage, for instance, was
definitely American: plastic leather and imitation gold locks. I know
American luggage when I see it. I didn't see his passport.

He arrived at the Athens airport on a plane from Vienna. He
could have come from New York or London or Frankfurt or Moscow
and arrived by that plane—or just from Vienna. It was impossible to
tell. There were no hotel labels on the luggage. I just assumed that
he came from New York. It was a mistake anyone might have made.

This will not do. I can already hear myself protesting too much,
as if I had something to be ashamed of; but I am simply trying to
explain what happened, to be completely frank and open.

I really did not suspect that he was not what he seemed. Naturally,
I approached him at the airport. The car-hire business is only a
temporary sideline with me, of course—I am a journalist by profession—but Nicki had been complaining about needing more new
clothes, and the rent was due on the flat that week. I needed money,
and this man looked as if he had some. Is it a crime to earn money?

The way some people go on you would think it was. The law is the law and I am certainly not complaining, but what I can't stand is all the humbug and hypocrisy. If a man goes to the red light district on his own, nobody says anything. But if he wants to do another chap, a friend or an acquaintance, a good turn by showing him the way to the best house, everyone starts screaming blue murder. I have no patience with it. If there is one thing I pride myself on it is my common sense—that and my sense of humour.

My correct name is Arthur Simpson.

No! I said I would be completely frank and open and I am going to be. My correct *full* name is Arthur Abdel Simpson. The Abdel is because my mother was Egyptian. In fact, I was born in Cairo. But my father was a British officer, a regular, and I myself am British to the core. Even my background is typically British.

My father rose from the ranks. He was a Regimental Sergeant-Major in the Buffs when I was born; but in 1916 he was commissioned as a Lieutenant-Quartermaster in the Army Service Corps. We were living in officers' married quarters in Ismaillyah when he was killed a year later. I was too young at the time to be told the details. I thought, naturally, that he must have been killed by the Turks; but Mum told me later that he had been run over by an army lorry as he was walking home one night from the officers' mess.

Mum had his pension, of course, but someone told her to write to the Army Benevolent Association for the Sons of Fallen Officers, and they got me into the British school in Cairo. She still kept on writing to them about me, though. When I was nine, they said that if there were some relative in England I could live with they would pay for my schooling there. There was a married sister of Father's living at Hither Green in south-east London. When the Benevolent

Association said that they would pay twelve-and-six a week for my keep, she agreed to have me. This was a great relief to Mum because it meant that she could marry Mr Hafiz, who had never liked me after the day I caught them in bed together and told the Imam about it. Mr Hafiz was in the restaurant business and as fat as a pig. It was disgusting for a man of his age to be in bed with Mum.

I went to England on an army troop-ship in care of the sick-bay matron. I was glad to go. I have never liked being where I am not wanted. Most of the men in the sick bay were V.D. cases and I used to listen to them talking. I picked up quite a lot of useful information, before the matron, who was (there is no other word) an old bitch, found out about it and handed me over to the P.T. Instructor for the rest of the voyage. My aunt in Hither Green was a bitch, too, but I was wanted there all right. She was married to a book-keeper who spent half his time out of work. My twelve-and-six a week came in very handy. She didn't dare get too bitchy. Every so often, a man from the Benevolent Association would come down to see how I was getting on. If I had told him the tale they would have taken me away. Like most boys of that age, I suppose I was what is known nowadays as 'a bit of a handful'.

The school was on the Lewisham side of Blackheath and had a big board outside with gold lettering on it:

CORAM'S GRAMMAR SCHOOL
For the Sons of Gentlemen
Founded 1781

On top of the board there was the school coat of arms and motto, *Mens aequa in arduis*. The Latin master said it was from Horace; but the English master liked to translate it in Kipling's words: 'If you can keep your head when all about you are losing theirs... you'll be a Man, my son.'

It was not exactly a public school like Eton or Winchester—there were no boarders, we were all day boys—but it was run on the same lines. Your parents, or (as in my case) guardian, had to pay to send you there. There were a few scholarship boys from the local council schools—I think we had to have them because of the Board of Education subsidy—but never more than twenty or so in the whole school. In 1920 a new Head was appointed. His name was Brush and we nicknamed him 'The Bristle'. He'd been a master at a big public school and so he knew how things should be done. He made a lot of changes. After he came, we played rugger instead of soccer, sat in forms instead of in classes and were taught how to speak like gentlemen. One or two of the older masters got the sack, which was a good thing; and The Bristle made all the masters wear their university gowns at prayers in the morning. As he said, Coram's was a school with a good tradition, and, although we might not be as old as Eton or Winchester, we were a good deal older than Brighton or Clifton. All the swotting in the world was no good if you didn't have character and tradition. He made us stop reading trash like the *Gem* and *Magnet* and turn to worthwhile books by authors like Stevenson and Talbot Baines Reed.

I was too young when my father was killed to have known him well; but one or two of his pet sayings have always remained in my memory; perhaps because I heard him repeat them so often to Mum or to his army friends. One, I remember, was 'Never volunteer for anything', and another was 'Bullshit baffles brains'.

Hardly the guiding principles of an officer and a gentleman, you say? Well, I am not so sure about that; but I won't argue. I can only say that they were the guiding principles of a practical, professional soldier, and that at Coram's they worked. For example, I found out very early on that nothing annoyed the masters more than untidy handwriting. With some of them, in fact, the wrong answer to a question neatly written would get almost as many marks as the right answer badly written or covered with smears and blots. I have always written very neatly. Again, when a master asked something and then said 'Hands up who knows', you could always put your hand up even if you did not know, as long as you let the eager beavers put their hands up first, and as long as you smiled. Smiling—pleasantly, I mean, not grinning or smirking—was very important at all times. The masters did not bother about you so much if you looked as if you had a clear conscience.

I got on fairly well with the other chaps. Because I had been born in Egypt, of course, they called me 'Wog', but, as I was fair-haired like my father, I did not mind that. My voice broke quite early, when I was twelve. After a while, I started going up to Hilly Fields at night with a fifth-former named Jones iv, who was fifteen, and we used to pick up girls—'square-pushing' as they say in the army. I soon found that some of the girls didn't mind a bit if you put your hand up their skirts, and even did a bit more. Sometimes we would stay out late. That meant that I used to have to get up early and do my homework, or make my aunt write an excuse note for me to take to school saying that I had been sent to bed after tea with a fever-ish headache. If the worse came to the worst, I could always crib from a boy named Reese and do the written work in the lavatory. He had very bad acne and never minded if you cribbed from him; in fact I think he liked it. But you had to be careful. He was one of the book-worms and usually got everything right. If you cribbed from him word for word you risked getting full marks. With me, that would make the master suspicious. I got ten out of ten for a chemistry paper once, and the master caned me for cheating. I had never really liked the man and I got my revenge later by pouring a test-tube of sulphuric acid (conc.) over the saddle of his bicycle; but I have always remembered the lesson that incident taught me. Never try to pretend that you're better than you are. I think I can fairly say that I never have.

Of course, an English public-school education is mainly designed to build character, to give a boy a sense of fair play and sound values, teach him to take the rough with the smooth and make him look and sound like a gentleman.

Coram's at least did those things for me; and, looking back, I suppose that I should be grateful. I can't say that I enjoyed the process, though. Fighting, for instance: that was supposed to be very manly, and if you did not enjoy it they called you 'cowardy custard'. I don't think it is cowardly not to want someone to hit you with his fist and make your nose bleed. The trouble was that when I used to hit back I always sprained my thumb or grazed my knuckles. In the end, I found that the best way to hit back was with a satchel, especially if you had a pen or the sharp edge of a ruler sticking out through the flap; but I have always disliked violence of any kind.

Almost as much as I dislike injustice. My last term at Coram's, which I should have been able to enjoy because it *was* the last, was completely spoiled.

Jones iv was responsible for that. He had left school by then, and was working for his father, who owned a garage, but I still went up to Hilly Fields with him sometimes. One evening he showed me a long poem typed out on four foolscap pages. A customer at the garage had given it to him. It was called 'The Enchantment' and was supposed to have been written by Lord Byron. It began:

Upon one dark and sultry day,
As on my garret bed I lay,
My thoughts, for I was dreaming half,
Were broken by a silvery laugh,
Which fell upon my startled ear,
Full loud and clear and very near.

Well, it turned out that the laugh was coming through a hole in the wall behind his bed, so he looked through the hole.

A youth and maid were in the room,
And each in youth's most beauteous bloom.

It then went on to describe what the youth and maid did together for the next half-hour—very poetically, of course, but in detail. It was really hot stuff.

I made copies and let some of the chaps at school read it. Then I charged them fourpence a time to be allowed to copy it out for themselves. I was making quite a lot of money, when some fourth-form boy left a copy in the pocket of his cricket blazer and his mother found it. Her husband sent it with a letter of complaint to The Bristle. He began questioning the boys one by one to find out who had started it, and, of course, he eventually got back to me. I said I had been given it by a boy who had left the term before—The Bristle couldn't touch *him*—but I don't think he believed me. He sat tapping his desk with his pencil and saying 'filthy smut' over and over again. He looked very red in the face, almost as if he were embarrassed. I remember wondering if he could be a bit 'queer'. Finally, he said that as it was my last term he would not expel me, but that I was not to associate with any of the younger boys for the rest of my time there. He did not cane me or write to the Benevolent Association, which was a relief. But it was a bad experience all the same and I was quite upset. In fact, I think that was the reason I failed my matric.

At Coram's they made a fetish out of passing your matric. Apparently, you couldn't get a respectable job in a bank or an insurance company without it. I did not want a job in a bank or an insurance company—Mr Hafiz had died and Mum wanted me to go back and learn the restaurant business—but it was a disappointment all the same. I think that if The Bristle had been more broad-minded and understanding, not made me feel as if I had committed some sort of crime, things would have been different. I was a sensitive boy and I felt that Coram's had somehow let me down. That was the reason I never applied to join the Old Coramians' Club.

Now, of course, I can look back on the whole thing and smile about it. The point I am making is that persons in authority—headmasters, police officials—can do a great deal of damage simply by failing to understand the other fellow's point of view.

How could I have possibly known what kind of man this Harper was?

As I explained, I had simply driven out to the Athens airport looking for business. I spotted this man going through customs and saw that he was carrying his ticket in an American Express folder. I gave one of the porters two drachmas to get me the man's name from his customs declaration. Then I had one of the uniformed airline girls give him my card and the message: 'Car waiting outside for Mr Harper.'

It is a trick I have used lots of times and it has almost always worked. Not many Americans or British speak demotic Greek; and by the time they have been through the airport customs, especially in the hot weather, and been jostled by the porters and elbowed right and left, they are only too ready to go with someone who can understand what they're talking about and take care of the tipping. That day it was really very hot and humid.

As he came through the exit from the customs I went up to him.

'This way, Mr Harper.'

He stopped and looked me over. I gave him a helpful smile which he did not return.

'Wait a minute,' he said curtly. 'I didn't order any car.'

I looked puzzled. 'The American Express sent me, sir. They said you wanted an English-speaking driver.'

He stared at me again, then shrugged. 'Well, okay. I'm going to the Hôtel Grande Bretagne.'

'Certainly, sir. Is this all your luggage?'

Soon after we turned off the coast road by Glyfada he began to ask questions. Was I British? I side-stepped that one as usual. Was the car my own? They always want to know that. It is my own car, as it happens, and I have two speeches about it. The car itself is a 1954 Plymouth. With an American I brag about how many thousands of miles it has done without any trouble. For the Britishers I have a stiff-upper-lip line about part-exchanging it, as soon as I can save enough extra cash, for an Austin Princess, or an old Rolls-Royce, or some other real quality car. Why shouldn't people be told what they want to hear?

This Harper man seemed much like the rest. He listened and grunted occasionally as I told him the tale. When you know that you are beginning to bore them, you usually know that everything is going to be all right. Then, you stop. He did not ask how I happened to live and work in Greece, as they usually do. I thought that would probably come later; that is, if there were going to be a later with him. I had to find out.

'Are you in Athens on business, sir?'

'Could be.'

His tone as good as told me to mind my own business, but I pretended not to notice. 'I ask, sir,' I went on, 'because if you should need a car and driver while you are here I could arrange to place myself at your disposal.'

'Yes?'

It wasn't exactly encouraging, but I told him the daily rate and the various trips we could take if he wanted to do some sight-seeing—Delphi and the rest.

'I'll think about it,' he said. 'What's your name?'

I handed him one of my cards over my shoulder and watched him in the driving mirror while he read it. Then he slipped it into his pocket.

'Are you married, Arthur?'

The question took me by surprise. They don't usually want to know about your private life. I told him about my first wife and how she had been killed by a bomb in the Suez troubles in 1956. I did not mention Nicki. I don't know why; perhaps because I did not want to think about her just then.

'You did say you were British, didn't you?' he asked.

'My father was British, sir, and I was educated in England.' I said it a little distantly. I dislike being cross-examined in that sort of way. But he persisted just the same.

'Well, what nationality *are* you?'

'I have an Egyptian passport.' That was perfectly true, although it was none of his business.

'Was your wife Egyptian?'

'No, French.'

'Did you have any children?'

'Unfortunately no, sir.' I was definitely cold now.

'I see.'

He sat back, staring out of the window, and I had the feeling that he had suddenly put me out of his mind altogether. I thought about Annette and how used I had become to saying that she had been killed by a bomb. I was almost beginning to believe it myself. As I stopped for the traffic lights in Omonias Square I wondered what had happened to her, and if the gallant gentlemen she had preferred to me had ever managed to give her the children she had said she wanted. I am not one to bear a grudge, but I could not help hoping that she believed now that the sterility had been hers not mine.

I pulled up at the Grande Bretagne. While the porters were getting the bags out of the car Harper turned to me.

'Okay, Arthur, it's a deal. I expect to be here three or four days.'

I was surprised and relieved. 'Thank you, sir. Would you like to go to Delphi tomorrow? On the week-ends it gets very crowded with tourists.'

'We'll talk about that later.' He stared at me for a moment and smiled slightly. 'Tonight I think I feel like going out on the town. You know some good places?'

As he said it there was just the suggestion of a wink. I am sure of that.

I smiled discreetly. 'I certainly do, sir.'

'I thought you might. Pick me up at nine o'clock. All right?'

'Nine o'clock, sir. I will have the concierge telephone to your room that I am here.'

It was four-thirty then. I drove to my flat, parked the car in the courtyard and went up.

Nicki was out, of course. She usually spent the afternoon with friends—or said she did. I did not know who the friends were and I never asked too many questions. I did not want her to lie to me, and, if she had picked up a lover at the Club, I did not want to know about it. When a middle-aged man marries an attractive girl half his age, he has to accept certain possibilities philosophically. The clothes she had changed out of were lying all over the bed and she had spilt some scent, so that the place smelt more strongly of her than usual.

There was a letter for me from a British travel magazine I had written to. They wanted me to submit samples of my work for their consideration. I tore the letter up. Practically thirty years in the magazine game and they treat you like an amateur! Send samples of your work, and the next thing you know is that they've stolen all your ideas without paying you a penny-piece. It has happened to me again and again, and I am not being caught that way any more. If they want me to write for them, let them say so with a firm offer of cash on delivery, plus expenses in advance.

I made a few telephone calls to make sure that Harper's evening out would go smoothly, and then went down to the café for a drink or two. When I got back Nicki was there, changing again to go to work at the Club.

It was no wish of mine that she should go on working after our marriage. She chose to do so herself. I suppose some men would be jealous at the idea of their wives belly-dancing with practically no clothes on in front of other men; but I am not narrow-minded in that way. If she chooses to earn a little extra pocket money for herself, that is her affair.

While she dressed, I told her about Harper and made a joke about all his questions. She did not smile.

'He does not sound easy, Papa,' she said. When she calls me 'Papa' like that it means that she is in a friendly mood with me.

'He has money to spend.'

'How do you know?'

'I telephoned the hotel and asked for him in room two-three-two. The operator corrected me and so I got his real room number. I know it. It is a big air-conditioned suite.'

She looked at me with a slight smile and sighed. 'You do so much enjoy it, don't you?'

'Enjoy what?'

'Finding out about people.'

'That is my newspaper training, *chérie*, my nose for news.'

She looked at me doubtfully, and I wished I had given a different answer. It has always been difficult for me to explain to her why certain doors are now closed to me. Reopening old wounds is senseless as well as painful.

She shrugged and went on with her dressing. 'Will you bring him to the Club?'

'I think so.'

I poured her a glass of wine and one for myself. She drank hers while she finished dressing and then went out. She patted my cheek as she went, but did not kiss me. The 'Papa' mood was over. 'One day,' I thought, 'she will go out and not come back.'

But I am never one to mope. If that happened, I decided, then good riddance to bad rubbish. I poured myself another glass of wine, smoked a cigarette and worked out a tactful way of finding out what sort of business Harper was in. I think I must have sensed that there was something not quite right about him.

At five to nine I found a parking place on Venizelos Avenue just round the corner from the Grande Bretagne, and went to let Harper know that I was waiting.

He came down after ten minutes and I took him round the corner to the car. I explained that it was difficult for private cars to park in front of the hotel.

He said, rather disagreeably I thought: 'Who cares?'

I wondered if he had been drinking. Quite a lot of tourists who, in their own countries, are used to dining early in the evening start drinking *ouzo* to pass the time. By ten o'clock, when most Athenians begin to think about dinner, the tourists are sometimes too tight to care what they say or do. Harper, however, was all too sober. I soon found that out.

When we reached the car I opened the rear door for him to get in. Ignoring me, he opened the other door and got into the front passenger seat. Very democratic. Only I happen to prefer my passengers in the back seat where I can keep my eye on them through the mirror.

I went round and got into the driving seat.

'Well, Arthur,' he asked, 'where are you taking me?'

'Dinner first, sir?'

'How about some sea-food?'

'I'll take you to the best, sir.'

I drove him out to the yacht harbour at Tourcolimano. One of the restaurants there gives me a good commission. The waterfront is really very picturesque, and he nodded approvingly as he looked around. Then I took him into the restaurant and introduced him to the cook. When he had chosen his food and a bottle of dry Patras wine he looked at me.

'You eaten yet, Arthur?'

'Oh, I will have something in the kitchen, sir.' That way my dinner would go on his bill without his knowing it, as well as my commission.

'You come and eat with me.'

'It is not necessary, sir.'

'Who said it was? I asked you to eat with me.'

'Thank you, sir. I would like to.'

More democracy. We sat at a table on the terrace by the water's edge and he began to ask me about the yachts anchored in the harbour. Which were privately owned, which were for charter? What were charter rates like?

I happened to know about one of the charter yachts, an eighteen-metre ketch with twin diesels, and told him the rate—one hundred and forty dollars U.S. per day, including a crew of two, fuel for eight hours' steaming a day and everything except charterers' and passengers' food. The real rate was a hundred and thirty, but I thought that, if by any chance he was serious, I could get the difference as commission from the broker. I also wanted to see how he felt about that kind of money; whether he would laugh as an ordinary salaried man would, or begin asking about the number of persons it would sleep. He just nodded, and then asked about fast, sea-going motor-boats without crew.

In the light of what happened I think that point is specially significant.

I said that I would find out. He asked me about the yacht-brokers. I gave him the name of the one I knew personally, and told him the rest were no good. I also said that I did not think that the owners of the bigger boats liked chartering them without their own crewmen on board. He did not comment on that. Later, he asked me if I knew whether yacht charter parties out of Tourcolimano or the Piraeus covered Greek waters only, or whether you could 'go foreign', say across the Adriatic to Italy. Significant again. I told him I did not know, which was true.

When the bill came, he asked if he could change an American Express traveller's cheque for fifty dollars. That was more to the point. I told him that he could, and he tore the fifty-dollar cheque out of a book of ten. It was the best thing I had seen that day.

Just before eleven o'clock we left and I drove him to the Club.

The Club is practically a copy of the Lido night-club in Paris, only smaller. I introduced him to John, who owns the place, and tried to leave him there for a while. He was still absolutely sober, and I thought that if he were by himself he would drink more; but it was no good. I had to go in and sit and drink with him. He was as possessive as a woman. I was puzzled. If I had been a fresh-looking young man instead of, well, frankly, a pot-bellied journalist, I would have understood it—not approved, of course, but understood. But he was at least ten to fifteen years younger than me.

They have candles on the tables at the Club and you can see faces. When the floor-show came on, I watched him watch it. He looked at the girls, Nicki among them, as if they were flies on the other side of a window. I asked him how he liked the third from the left—that was Nicki.

'Legs too short,' he said. 'I like them with longer legs. Is that the one you had in mind?'

'In mind? I don't understand, sir.' I was beginning to dislike him intensely.

He eyed me. 'Shove it,' he said unpleasantly.

We were drinking Greek brandy. He reached for the bottle and poured himself another. I could see the muscles in his jaw twitching as if with anger. Evidently something I had said, or which he thought I had said, had annoyed him. It was on the tip of my tongue to mention that Nicki was my wife, but I didn't. I remembered, just in time, that I had only told him about Annette, and about her being killed by a bomb.

He drank the brandy down quickly and told me to get the bill.

'You don't like it here, sir?'

'What more is there to see? Do they start stripping later?'

I smiled. It is the only possible response to that sort of boorishness. In any case, I had no objection to speeding up my programme for the evening.

'There is another place,' I said.

'Like this?'

'The entertainment, sir, is a little more individual and private.' I picked the words carefully.

'You mean a cat-house?'

'I wouldn't put it quite like that, sir.'

He smirked. 'I'll bet you wouldn't. How about *"maison de rendez-vous"*? Does that cover it?'

'Madame Irma's is very discreet and everything is in the best of taste, sir.'

He shook with amusement. 'Know something, Arthur?' he said. 'If you shaved a bit closer and had yourself a good haircut, you could hire out as a butler any time.'

From his expression I could not tell whether he was being deliberately insulting or making a clumsy joke. It seemed advisable to assume the latter.

'Is that what Americans call "ribbing", sir?' I asked politely.

This seemed to amuse him even more. He chuckled fatuously. 'Okay, Arthur,' he said at last, 'okay. We'll play it your way. Let's go to see your Madame Irma.'

I didn't like the '*your* Madame Irma' way of putting it, but I pretended not to notice.

Irma has a very nice house standing in its own grounds just off the road out to Kifissia. She never has more than six girls at any one time and changes them every few months. Her prices are high, of course, but everything is very well arranged. Clients enter and leave by different doors to avoid embarrassing encounters. The only persons the client sees are Irma herself, Kira, the manageress who takes care of the financial side, and, naturally, the lady of his choice.

Harper seemed to be impressed. I say 'seemed' because he was very polite to Irma when I introduced them, and complimented her on the decorations. Irma is not unattractive herself and likes presentable-looking clients. As I had expected, there was no nonsense about my joining him at *that* table. As soon as Irma offered him a drink, he glanced at me and made a gesture of dismissal.

'See you later,' he said.

I was sure then that everything was all right. I went in to Kira's room to collect my commission and tell her how much money he had on him. It was after midnight then. I said that I had had no dinner and would go and get some. She told me that they were not particularly busy that night and that there need be no hurry.

I drove immediately to the Grande Bretagne, parked the car at the side, walked round to the bar, and went in and ordered a drink. If anyone happened to notice me and remember later, I had a simple explanation for being there.

I finished the drink, gave the waiter a good tip and walked through across the foyer to the lifts. They are fully automatic; you work them yourself with push-buttons. I went up to the third floor.

Harper's suite was on the inner court, away from the noise of Syntagmaios Square, and the doors to it were out of sight of the landing. The floor servants had gone off duty for the night. It was all quite easy. As usual, I had my pass-key hidden inside an old change purse; but, as usual, I did not need it. Quite a number of the sitting-room doors to suites in the older part of the hotel can be opened from outside without a key, unless they have been specially locked, that is; it makes it easier for room-service waiters carrying trays. Quite often the maid who turns down the beds last thing can't be bothered to lock up after her. Why should she? The Greeks are a particularly honest people and they trust one another.

His luggage was all in the bedroom. I had already handled it once that day, stowing it in the car at the airport, so I did not have to worry about leaving fingerprints.

I went to his briefcase first. There were a lot of business papers in it—something to do with a Swiss company named Tekelek, who made accounting machines—I did not pay much attention to them. There was also a wallet with money in it—Swiss francs, American dollars and West German marks—together with the yellow number slips of over two thousand dollars' worth of traveller's cheques. The number slips are for record purposes in case the cheques are lost and you want to stop payment on them. I left the money where it was and took the slips. The cheques themselves I found in the side pocket of a suitcase. There were thirty-five of them, each for fifty dollars. His first name was Walter, middle initial K.

In my experience, most people are extraordinarily careless about the way they look after traveller's cheques. Just because their counter-signature is required before a cheque can be cashed they assume that only they can negotiate it. Yet anyone with eyes in his head can copy the original signature. No particular skill is required; haste, heat, a different pen, a counter of an awkward height, writing standing up instead of sitting—a dozen things can account for small variations in the second signature. It is not going to be examined by a handwriting expert, not at the time that it is cashed anyway; and usually it is only at banks that the cashier asks to see a passport.

Another thing: if you have ordinary money in your pocket, you usually know, at least approximately, how much you have. Every time you pay for something, you receive a reminder; you can see and feel what you have. Not so with traveller's cheques. What you see, if and when you look, is a blue folder with cheques inside. How often do you count the cheques to make sure that they are all there? Supposing someone were to remove the *bottom* cheque in a folder. When would you find out that it had gone? A hundred to one it would not be until you had used up all the cheques which had been on top of it. Therefore, you would not know exactly *when* it had been taken; and, if you had been doing any travelling, you probably would not even know *where*. If you did not know when or where, how could you possibly guess *who*? In any case you would be too late to stop its being cashed.

People who leave traveller's cheques about *deserve* to lose them.

I took just six cheques, the bottom ones from the folder. That made three hundred dollars, and left him fifteen hundred or so. It is a mistake, I always think, to be greedy; but unfortunately I hesitated. For a moment I wondered if he would miss them all that much sooner if I took two more.

So I was standing there like a fool, with the cheques right in my hands, when Harper walked into the room.

CHAPTER TWO

I WAS IN THE BEDROOM AND HE CAME THROUGH FROM THE sitting-room. All the same he must have opened the outer door very quietly indeed or I would certainly have heard the latch. I think he expected to find me there. In that case, the whole thing was just a cunningly planned trap.

I was standing at the foot of one of the beds, so I couldn't move away from him. For a moment he just stood there grinning at me, as if he were enjoying himself.

'Well now, Arthur,' he said, 'you ought to have waited for me, oughtn't you?'

'I was going back.' It was a stupid thing to say, I suppose; but almost anything I had said would have sounded stupid at that point.

And then, suddenly, he hit me across the face with the back of his hand.

It was like being kicked. My glasses fell off and I lurched back against the bed. As I raised my arms to protect myself he hit me again with the other hand. When I started to fall to my knees, he dragged me up and kept on hitting me. He was like a savage.

I fell down again and this time he let me be. My ears were singing, my head felt like bursting and I could not see properly. My nose began to bleed. I got my handkerchief out to stop the blood getting all over my clothes, and felt about among the cheques lying on the carpet for my glasses. I found them eventually. They were bent a bit but not broken. When I put them on, I saw the soles of his shoes about a yard from my face.

He was sitting in the armchair, leaning back, watching me.

'Get up,' he said, 'and watch that blood. Keep it off the rug.'

As I got to my feet, he stood up quickly himself. I thought he was going to start hitting me again. Instead, he caught hold of one lapel of my jacket.

'Do you have a gun?'

I shook my head.

He slapped my pockets, to make sure, I suppose, then shoved me away.

'There are some tissues in the bathroom,' he said. 'Go clean your face. But leave the door open.'

I did as I was told. There was a window in the bathroom; but even if it had been possible to escape that way without breaking my neck, I don't suppose I would have tried it. He would have heard me. Besides, where could I have escaped to? All he would have had to do was call down to the night concierge, and the police would have been there in five minutes. The fact that he had not called down already was at least something. Perhaps, as a foreigner, he did not want to get involved as a witness in a court case. After all, he had not actually lost anything; and if I were to eat enough humble pie, perhaps even cry a bit, he might decide to forget the whole thing; especially after the brutal way in which he had attacked me. That was my reasoning. I should have known better. You cannot expect common decency from a man like Harper.

When I came out of the bathroom, I saw that he had picked up the cheque folder and was putting it back in the suitcase. The cheques I had torn out, however, were lying on the bed. He gathered them up and motioned me towards the sitting-room.

'In there.'

As I went in, he moved past me to the door and bolted it.

There was a marble-topped commode against the side wall. On the commode was a tray with an ice-bucket, a bottle of brandy and some glasses. He picked up a glass then looked at me.

'Sit down right there,' he said.

The chair he motioned to was by a writing table under the window. I obeyed orders; there did not seem to be anything else to do. My nose was still bleeding, and I had a headache.

He slopped some brandy into a glass and put it on the table beside me. For a moment or two I felt encouraged. If you are going to have a man arrested you don't sit him down first and give him a drink. Perhaps it was just going to be a man-to-man chat in which I told him a hard-luck story and said how sorry I was, while he got dewy-eyed over his own magnanimity and decided to give me another chance.

That one did not last long.

He poured himself a drink and then glanced across at me as he put ice in the glass.

'First time you've been caught at it, Arthur?'

I blew my nose a little to keep the blood running before I answered. 'It's the first time I've ever been tempted, sir. I don't know what came over me. Perhaps it was the brandy I had with you. I'm not really used to it.'

He turned and stared at me. All at once his face was neither old-young nor young-old. It was white and pinched and his mouth worked in an odd way. I have seen faces go like that before and I braced myself. There was a metal lamp on the writing table beside me. I wondered if I could possibly hit him with it before he got to me.

But he did not move. His eyes flickered towards the bedroom and then back to me.

'You'd better get something straight, Arthur,' he said slowly. 'That was just a little roughing-up you had in there. If I really start giving you a going-over, you'll leave here on a stretcher. Nobody's going to mind about that except you. I came back and caught you stealing. You tried to strong-arm your way out of it and I had to defend myself. That's how it'll be. So cut out the bull, and the lies. Right?'

'I'm sorry, sir.'

'Empty your pockets. On this table here.'

I did as I was told.

He looked at everything, my driving licence, my *permis de séjour*, and he touched everything. Finally, of course, he found the pass-key in the change purse. I had sawn off the shank of it and cut a slot in the end so that I could use a small coin to turn it, but it was still over two inches long, and heavy. The weight gave it away. He looked at it curiously.

'You make this?'

'Not the key part. I just cut it down.' There seemed no point in trying to lie about that.

He nodded. 'That's better. Okay, we'll start over. We know you're a two-bit ponce and we know you heist traveller's cheques from hotel rooms when you get the chance. Do you write the counter-signature yourself?'

'Yes.'

'So that's forgery. Now, I'm asking again. Have you ever been caught before?'

'No, sir.'

'Sure?'

'Yes.'

'Do you have any sort of police record?'

'Here in Athens?'

'We'll start with Athens.'

I hesitated. 'Well, not exactly a police record. Do you mean traffic offences?'

'You know what I mean. Quit stalling.'

I sneezed, quite unintentionally, and my nose began bleeding again. He sighed impatiently and threw me a bunch of paper napkins from the drink-tray.

'I had you pretty well figured out at the airport,' he went on; 'but I didn't think you'd be quite so stupid. Why did you have to tell that Kira dame that you'd had no dinner?'

I shrugged helplessly. 'So that I could come here.'

'Why didn't you tell her you'd gone to gas up the car? I just might have bought that one.'

'It didn't seem important. Why should you suspect me?'

He laughed. 'Oh brother! I know what that car you have sells for here, and I know that gasoline costs sixty cents a gallon. At the rates you charge you couldn't break even. Okay, you get your pay-offs—the restaurant, the clip joint, the cat-house—but they can't amount to much, so there must be something else. Kira doesn't know what it is, but she knows there's something because you've cashed quite a few traveller's cheques through her.'

'She told you that?' This really upset me; the least one can expect from a brothel-keeper is discretion.

'Why shouldn't she tell me? You didn't tell her they were stolen, did you?' He drank his brandy down. 'I don't happen to like paying for sex, but I wanted to find out a bit more about you. I did. When they realized that I wasn't going to leave without paying, they were both real friendly. Called me a cab and everything. Now, supposing *you* start talking.'

I took a sip of brandy. 'Very well. I have had three convictions.'

'What for?'

'The charge in each case was representing myself as an official guide. In fact, all I did was to try to save one or two clients from those boring archaeological set speeches. The official guides have to learn them by heart before they can pass the examination. Tourists like to know what they are looking at, but they do not want to be bored.'

'What happened? Did you go to jail?'

'Of course not. I was fined.'

He nodded approvingly. 'That was what Irma thought. Now you just keep on playing it straight like that and maybe we can keep the police out of this. Have you ever been jailed anywhere, to serve time I mean?'

'I do not see why I should…'

'Okay, skip it,' he broke in. 'What about Turkey?'

'Turkey? Why do you ask?'

'Have you been there?'

'Yes.'

'Any police record there?'

'I was fined in Istanbul for showing some people round a museum.'

'Which museum?'

'The Topkapi.'

'Were you posing as an official guide that time?'

'Guides must be licensed there. I did not have a licence.'

'Have you ever driven from here to Istanbul?'

'Is that a criminal offence?'

'Just answer. Have you?'

'Occasionally. Some tourists like to travel by road. Why?'

He did not answer. Instead he took an envelope from the writing desk and began to scribble something in pencil. I desperately needed a cigarette, but was afraid to light one in case it might look as if I were no longer worried. I *was* worried, and confused, too; but I wanted to be sure I looked that way. I drank the brandy instead.

He finished his scribbling at last and looked up. 'All right, Arthur. There's a pad of plain paper there and a pen. I'm going to dictate. You start writing. No, don't give me any arguments. Just do as I tell you.'

I was hopelessly bewildered now. I picked up the pen.

'Ready?'

'Yes.'

'Head it, *"To the Chief of Police, Athens"*. Got that? Now go on. *"I, Arthur A. Simpson of—"* put in your address—*"do hereby confess that on June fifteenth, using an illegal pass-key, I entered the suite of Mr Walter K. Harper in the Hôtel Grande Bretagne and stole American Express traveller's cheques to the value of three hundred dollars. The numbers of the cheques were..."'*

As he felt in his pocket for the loose cheques, I started to protest.

'Mr Harper, I can't possibly write this. It would convict me. I couldn't defend myself.'

'Would you sooner defend yourself right now? If so, I can call the police and you can explain about that pass-key.' He paused and then went on more patiently: 'Look, Dad, maybe you and I will be the only ones who will ever read it. Maybe in a week's time it won't even exist. I'm just giving you a chance to get off the hook. Why don't you take it and be thankful?'

'What do I have to do for it?'

'We'll get to that later. Just you keep writing. *"The numbers of the cheques were P89.664.572 through P89.664.577, all in fifty-dollar units. I intended to forge Mr Harper's signature on them so that I could cash them illegally. I have stolen, forged and cashed other cheques in that way."*

Shut up and keep writing! *"But now I find I cannot go through with it. Because of Mr Harper's great kindness to me during his visit to Athens and his Christian charity, I feel that I cannot rob him. I am, therefore, sending the cheques I stole from him back with this letter. By taking this decision, I feel that I have come out of the darkness into the light of day. I know now that, as a sinner of the worst type, my only chance is to make restitution, to confess everything, and to pay the penalties the law demands. Only in this way can I hope for salvation in the world to come."* Now sign it.'

I signed it.

'Now date it a week from today. No, better make it the twenty-third.'

I dated it.

'Give it to me.'

I gave it to him and he read it through twice. Then he looked at me and grinned.

'Not talking any more, Arthur?'

'I wrote down what you dictated.'

'Sure. And now you're trying to figure out what would happen if I sent it to the police.'

I shrugged.

'All right, I'll tell you what would happen. First they'd think you were a nut. They'd probably think that I was some kind of a nut, too, but they wouldn't be interested in me. I wouldn't be around anyway. On the other hand, they couldn't ignore the whole thing, because of the cheques. Three hundred dollars! They'd have to take that seriously. So they'd start by getting on to the American Express and finding out about all the cheque forgeries that have been traced back to accounts in Athens banks. Then they'd pull you in and grill you. What would you do, Arthur? Tell them about me and what really happened? You'd be silly to do that, wouldn't you? They'd throw the book at you. No, you're too smart for that. You'd go along with the reformation jazz. That way, you'd have a real defence—voluntary confession, restitution, sincere repentance. I'll bet you'd get away with just a nominal sentence, maybe no more than a year.'

'Thank you.'

He grinned again. 'Don't you worry, Arthur. You're not going to do any time at all.' He waved the paper I had written and the cheques. 'This is just a little insurance.' He picked up the brandy bottle and refilled my glass. 'You see, a friend of mine is going to trust you with something valuable.'

'What?'

'A car. You're going to drive it to Istanbul. You'll be paid a hundred bucks and expenses. That's all there is to it.'

I managed to smile. 'If that's all there is to it, I don't see why you have to blackmail me. I would gladly do the job every week for that money.'

He looked pained. 'Who said anything about blackmail? I said insurance. This is a seven-thousand-dollar Lincoln, Arthur. Do you know what it's worth now in Turkey?'

'Fourteen thousand.'

'Well, then, isn't it obvious? Supposing you drove it into the first garage you came to and sold it.'

'It wouldn't be so easy.'

'Arthur, you took a hell of a risk tonight for just three hundred dollars. For fourteen thousand you'd do pretty well anything, now, wouldn't you? Be your age! As it is, I don't have to worry, and my friend doesn't have to worry. As soon as I know the car's delivered, that little confession 'll be torn up and the cheques 'll go back in my pocket.'

I was silent. I didn't believe a word he was saying and he knew it. He didn't care. He was watching me, enjoying himself. 'All right,' I said finally; 'but there are just one or two questions I'd like to ask.'

He nodded. 'Sure there are. Only that's the one condition there is on the job, Arthur—no questions.'

I would have been surprised if he said anything else. 'Very well. When do I start?'

'Tomorrow. How long does it take you to drive to Salonika?'

'About six or seven hours.'

'Let's see. Tomorrow's Tuesday. If you start about noon you can spend the night there. Then Wednesday night in Edirne. You should make Istanbul Thursday afternoon. That'll be okay.' He thought for a moment. 'I'll tell you what you do. In the morning, you pack an overnight bag and come here by cab or streetcar. Be downstairs at ten.'

'Where do I pick up the car?'

'I'll show you in the morning.'

'Whatever you say.'

He unbolted the door. 'Good deal. Now take your junk and beat it. I have to get some sleep.'

I put my belongings back in my pockets and went to the door.

'Hey!'

As I turned, something hit me in the chest and then fell at my feet.

'You've forgotten your pass-key,' he said.

I picked it up and left. I didn't say good-night or anything. He didn't notice. He was finishing his drink.

The worst thing at school was being caned. There was a ritual about it. The master who had lost his temper with you would stop ranting, or, if it was one of the quiet ones, stop clenching his teeth, and say: 'Take a note to the Headmaster.' That meant you were for it. The note was always the same, *Request permission to punish*, followed by his initials; but he would always fold it twice before he gave it to you. You were not supposed to read it. I don't know why; perhaps because they didn't like having to ask for permission.

Well, then you had to go and find The Bristle. Sometimes, of course, he would be in his study; but more often he would be taking the sixth form in trigonometry or Latin. That meant you had to go in and stand there until he decided to notice you. You would have to wait five or ten minutes sometimes; it depended on the mood he was in. He was a tall, thick man with a lot of black hair on the backs of his hands, and a purple face. He spoke very fast while he was teaching, and after a while little flecks of white stuff would gather at the corners of his mouth. When he was in a good mood, he would break off almost as soon as you came in and start making jokes. 'Ah, the good Simpson, or perhaps we should say the insufficiently good Simpson, what can we do for you?' Whatever he said, the sixth form always rocked with laughter, because the more they laughed the longer he would go on wasting time. 'And how have you transgressed, Simpson, how have you transgressed? Please tell us.' You always had to say what you'd done or not done—bad homework, lying, flicking ink pellets—and you had to be truthful, in case he asked the master later. When he had made some more jokes, he initialled the note and you went. Before that 'Enchantment' business I think he rather liked me, because I pretended not to be able to help laughing at his jokes even though I was going to be caned. When he was in a bad mood he used to call you 'sir', which I always thought a bit stupid. 'Well, sir, what is this for? Cribbing under the desk? A pauper spirit, sir, a pauper spirit! Work for the night cometh! Now get out and stop wasting my time.'

When you returned to the form-room you gave the master the initialled note. Then he took his gown off, so that his arms were free, and got the cane out of his desk. The canes were all the same, about thirty inches long and quite thick. Some masters would take you outside into the coat lobby to do it, but others would do it in front of the form. You had to bend down and touch your toes and then he would hit you as hard as he could, as if he were trying to break the cane. It felt like a hot iron across your backside, and if he happened to hit twice in exactly the same place, like a heavy club with spikes on it. The great thing was not to cry or make a fuss. I remember a boy once who wet himself after it and had to be sent home; and there was another one who came back into the room and threw up, so that the master had to send for the school porter to clean up the mess. (They always sent for the porter when a boy threw up, and he always said the same thing when he came in with his bucket and mop—'Is *this* all?'—as if he were disappointed it wasn't blood.) Most boys, though, when they were caned, just got very red in the face and tried to walk back to their places as if nothing had happened. It wasn't pride; it was the only way to get any sympathy. When a boy cried you didn't feel sorry for him, merely embarrassed because he was so sorry for himself, and resentful because the master would feel that he had done something effective. One of the most valuable things I learned at Coram's was how to hate; and it was the cane that taught me. I never forgot and never began to forgive a caning until I had somehow evened the score with the master who had given it to me. If he were married, I would write an anonymous letter to his wife saying that he was a sodomite and that he had been trying to interfere with young boys. If he were a bachelor, I would send it as a warning to one of the other boys' parents. Mostly I never heard what happened, of course; but on at least two occasions I heard that the parents had questioned their boys and then forwarded my letters to The Bristle. I never told anyone, because I did not want the others copying my idea; and as I was very good at disguising my writing the masters never knew for certain who had done it. Just as long as they had a suspicion they could not prove, I was satisfied. It meant that they knew I could hit back, that I was a good friend but a bad enemy.

My attitude to Harper was the same. He had given me a 'caning'; but instead of wallowing in self-pity, as any other man in my position might have done, I began to think of ways in which I could hit back.

Obviously, there was nothing much I could do while he had that 'confession'; but I knew one thing—he was a crook. I didn't yet know what kind of a crook—although I had some ideas—but I would find out for certain sooner or later. Then, when it was safe to do so, I would expose him to the police.

Nicki was in bed when I got back to the flat. I had hoped that she would be asleep because one side of my face was very red where he had hit me, and I didn't want to have to do any explaining; but she had the light on and was reading some French fashion magazine.

'Hullo, Papa,' she said.

I said hullo back and went to the bathroom to get rid of the handkerchief with all the blood on it. Then I went in and began to get undressed.

'You didn't stay long at the Club,' she said.

'He wanted to go on to Irma's.'

She did not like that, of course. 'Did you find out any more about him?'

'He is a business man—accounting machines, I think. He has a friend who owns a Lincoln. He wants me to drive it to Istanbul for him. I start tomorrow. He's paying quite well—a hundred dollars American.'

She sat up at that. 'That's very good, isn't it?' And then, inevitably, she saw my face. 'What have you done to yourself?'

'I had a bit of an accident. Some fool in a Simca. I had to stop suddenly.'

'Did the police come?'

She had a tiresome habit of assuming, just because I was once accused (falsely) of causing an accident through driving while drunk, that every little traffic accident in which I was involved was going to result in my being prosecuted by the police.

'It wasn't important,' I said. I turned away to hang up my suit.

'Will you be long away?' She sounded as if she had accepted the accident.

'Two or three days. I shall come back suddenly by air and surprise you with a lover.'

I thought that would amuse her, but she did not even smile. I got into bed beside her and she put the light out. After a few moments she said: 'Why does a man like Mr Harper want to go to a house?'

'Probably because he is impotent anywhere else.'

She was silent for a time. Then she put up a hand and touched my face.

'What really happened, Papa?'

I considered telling her; but that would have meant admitting openly that I had lied about the accident, so I did not answer. After a while, she turned away from me and went to sleep.

She was still asleep, or pretending to be, when I left in the morning.

Harper kept me waiting ten minutes; just long enough for me to remember that I had forgotten to disconnect the battery on my car. It did not hold its charge very well anyway, and the electric clock would have run it down by the time I returned. I was wondering if I would have time to telephone Nicki and tell her to ask the concierge to disconnect the battery, when Harper came down.

'All set?' he asked.

'Yes.'

'We'll get a cab.'

He told the driver to go to Stele Street out in the Piraeus.

As soon as we were on the way, he opened the briefcase and took out a large envelope. It had not been there the night before; of that I am certain. He gave it to me.

'There's everything you'll need there,' he said: '*carnet de tourisme* for the car, insurance Green Card, a thousand Greek drachmas, a hundred Turkish lira, and fifty American dollars for emergencies. The *carnet* has been countersigned authorizing you to take it through customs, but you'd better check everything out yourself.'

I did so. The *carnet* showed that the car was registered in Zürich, and that the owner, or at any rate the person in legal charge of it, was a Fräulein Elizabeth Lipp. Her address was Hotel Excelsior, Laufen, Zürich.

'Is Miss Lipp your friend?' I asked.

'That's right.'

'Are we going to meet her now?'

'No, but maybe you'll meet her in Istanbul. If the customs should ask, tell them she doesn't like eight-hundred-and-fifty-mile drives, and preferred to go to Istanbul by boat.'

'Is she a tourist?'

'What else? She's the daughter of a business associate of mine. I'm just doing him a favour. And by the way, if she wants you to drive her around in Turkey you'll be able to pick up some extra dough. Maybe she'll want you to drive the car back here later. I don't know yet what her future plans are.'

'I see.' For someone who had told me that I wasn't to ask questions, he was being curiously outgoing. 'Where do I deliver the car in Istanbul?'

'You don't. You go to the Park Hotel. There'll be a room reservation for you there. Just check in on Thursday and wait for instructions.'

'Very well. When do I get that letter I signed?'

'When you're paid off at the end of the job.'

Stele Street was down at the docks. By an odd coincidence there happened to be a ship of the Denizyollari Line berthed right opposite; and it was taking on a car through one of the side entry ports. I could not help glancing at Harper to see if he had noticed; but if he had he gave no sign of the fact. I made no comment. If he were simply ignorant, I was not going to enlighten him. If he still really thought that I was foolish enough to believe his version of Fräulein Lipp's travel needs and arrangements, so much the better. I could look after myself. Or so I thought.

There was a garage half-way along the street, with an old Michelin tyre sign above it. He told the cab-driver to stop there and wait. We got out and went towards the office. There was a man inside, and when he saw Harper through the window he came out. He was thin and dark and wore a greasy blue suit. I did not hear Harper address him by any name, but they appeared to know one another quite well. Unfortunately, they spoke together in German, which is a language I have never learned.

After a moment or two, the man led the way through a small repair shop and across a scrap yard to a row of lock-up garages. He opened one of them and there was the Lincoln. It was a grey four-door Continental, and looked to me about a year old. The man handed Harper the keys. He got in, started up and drove it out of the garage into the yard. The car seemed a mile long. Harper got out.

'Okay,' he said. 'She's all gassed up and everything. You can start rolling.'

'Very well.' I put my bag on the back seat. 'I would just like to make a phone call first.'

He was instantly wary. 'Who to?'

'The concierge at my apartment. I want to let him know that I may be away longer than I said, and ask him to disconnect the battery on my car.'

He hesitated, then nodded. 'Okay. You can do it from the office.' He said something to the man in the blue suit and we all went back inside.

Nicki answered the telephone and I told her about the battery. When she started to complain that I had not wakened her to say good-bye, I hung up. I had spoken in Greek, but Harper had been listening.

'That was a woman's voice,' he said.

'The concierge's wife. Is there anything wrong?'

He said something to the man in the blue suit of which I understood one word, 'adressat'. I guessed that he had wanted to know if I had given the address of the garage. The man shook his head.

Harper looked at me. 'No, nothing wrong. But just remember you're working for me now.'

'Will I see you in Istanbul or back here?'

'You'll find out. Now get going.'

I spent a minute or two making sure that I knew where all the controls were, while Harper and the other man stood watching. Then, I drove off and headed back towards Athens and the Thebes-Larissa-Salonika road.

After about half a mile I noticed that the taxi we had used on the drive out there was behind me. I was driving slowly, getting used to the feel of the car, and the taxi would normally have passed me; but it stayed behind. Harper was seeing me on my way.

About five miles beyond Athens I saw the taxi pull off the road and start to turn around. I was on my own. I drove on for another forty minutes or so, until I reached the first of the cotton fields, then turned off down a side road and stopped in the shade of some acacias.

I spent a good half-hour searching that car. First, I looked in the obvious places: in the back of the spare-wheel compartment, under the seat cushions, up behind the dashboard. Then I took off all the hub-caps. It's surprising how big the cavities are behind some of them, especially on American cars. I knew of a man who had regularly smuggled nearly two kilos of heroin a time that way. These had nothing in them, however. So I tried the tank, poking about with a long twig to see if any sort of a compartment had been built into or on to it; that has been done, too. Again I drew a blank. I would have liked to have crawled underneath to see if any new welding had been done, but there was not enough clearance. I decided to put the car into a garage greasing-bay in Salonika and examine the underside from below. Meanwhile, there was an air-conditioner in the car, so I unscrewed the cover and had a look inside that. Another blank.

The trouble was I did not have the slightest idea what I was looking for—jewellery, drugs, gold or currency. I just felt that there must be something. After a bit, I gave up searching and sat and smoked a cigarette while I tried to work out what would be worth smuggling into Turkey from Greece. I could not think of anything. I got the *carnet* out and checked the car's route. It had come from Switzerland, via Italy and the Brindisi ferry to Patras. The counter-foils showed that Fräulein Lipp had been with the car herself then.

She, at least, *did* know about ferrying cars by sea. However, that only made the whole thing more mysterious.

And then I remembered something. Harper had spoken of the possibility of a *return* journey, of my being wanted to drive the car back from Istanbul to Athens. Supposing *that* was the real point of the whole thing. I drive from Greece into Turkey. Everything is perfectly open and above board. Both Greek and Turkish customs would see and remember car and chauffeur. Some days later, the same car and chauffeur return. 'How was Istanbul, friend? Is your stomach still with you? Anything to declare? No fat-tailed sheep hidden in the back? Pass, friend, pass.' And then the car goes back to the garage in the Piraeus, for the man in the blue suit to recover the packages of heroin concealed along the inner recesses of the chassis members, under the wheel arches of the body, and inside the cowling beside the automatic transmission. Unless, that is, there is a Macedonian son-of-a-bitch on the Greek side who's out to win himself a medal. In that event, what you get is the strange case of the respectable Swiss lady's disreputable chauffeur who gets caught smuggling heroin, and Yours Truly is up the creek.

All I could do was play it by ear.

I got the Lincoln back on the road again and drove on. I reached Salonika soon after six that evening. Just to be on the safe side, I pulled into a big garage and gave the boy a couple of drachmas to put the car up on the hydraulic lift. I said I was looking for a rattle. There were no signs of new welding. I was not surprised. By then I had pretty well made up my mind that it would be the return journey that mattered.

I found a small comfortable hotel, treated myself to a good dinner and a bottle of wine at Harper's expense, and went to bed early. I made an early start the following morning, too. It is an eight-hour run from Salonika across Thrace to the Turkish frontier near Edirne (Adrianople as it used to be called), and if you arrive late you sometimes find that the road-traffic customs post has closed for the night.

I arrived at about four-thirty and went through the Greek control without difficulty. At Karaagac, on the Turkish side, I had to wait while they cleared some farm trucks ahead of me. After about twenty minutes, however, I was able to drive up to the barrier. When I went into the customs post with the *carnet* and my other papers, the place was practically empty.

Naturally, I was more concerned about the car than with myself, so I simply left my passport and currency declaration with the security man, and went straight over to the customs desk to hand in the *carnet*.

Everything seemed to be going all right. A customs inspector went out to the car with me, looked in my bag and merely glanced in the car. He was bored and looking forward to his supper.

'*Tourisme?*' he asked.

'Yes.'

We went back inside and he proceeded to stamp and validate the *carnet* for the car's entry, and tear out his part of the counterfoil. He was just folding the *carnet* and handing it back when I felt a sharp tap on my shoulder.

It was the security man. He had my passport in his hand.

I went to take it, but he shook his head and began waving it under my nose and saying something in Turkish.

I speak Egyptian Arabic and there are many Arabic words in Turkish; but the Turks pronounce them in a funny way and use a lot of Persian and old Turkish words mixed up with them. I shrugged helplessly. Then he said it in French and I understood.

My passport was three months out of date.

I knew at once how it had happened. Earlier in the year I had had some differences with the Egyptian consular people (or 'United Arab Republic' as they preferred to call themselves) and had allowed the whole question of my passport to slide. In fact, I had made up my mind to tell the Egyptians what they could do with their passport, and approach the British with a view to reclaiming my United Kingdom citizenship; to which, I want to make it clear, I am perfectly entitled. The thing was that, being so busy, I had just not bothered to fill in all the necessary forms. My Greek *permis de séjour* was in order, and that was all I normally needed in the way of papers. Frankly, I find all this paper regimentation we have to go through nowadays extremely boring. Naturally, with all the anxiety I had had over Harper, I had not thought to look at the date on my passport. If I had known that it was out of date, obviously I would have taken more trouble with the security man, kept him in conversation while he was doing the stamping or something like that. I have never had any bother like that before.

As it was, the whole thing became utterly disastrous; certainly through no fault of mine. The security man refused to stamp the passport. He said that I had to drive back to Salonika and have the passport renewed by the Egyptian vice-consul there before I could be admitted.

That would have been impossible as it happened; but I did not even have to try to explain why. The customs inspector chimed in at that point, waving the *carnet* and shouting that the car *had* been admitted and was now legally in Turkey. As *I* had *not* been admitted and was *not*, therefore, legally in Turkey, how was I, *legally*, to take the car out again? What did it matter if the passport was out of date? It was only a matter of three months. Why did he not just stamp the passport, admit me and forget about it?

At least that was what I think he said. They had lapsed into Turkish now and were bawling at one another as if I did not exist. If I could have got the security man alone, I would have tried to bribe him; but with the other one there it was too dangerous. Finally, they both went off to see some superior officer and left me standing there, without *carnet* or passport, but with, I admit it frankly, a bad case of the jitters. Really, my only hope at that point was that they would do what the customs inspector wanted and overlook the date on the passport.

With any luck, that might have happened. I say 'with any luck', although things would still have been awkward even if they had let me through. I would have had somehow to buy an Egyptian consular stamp in Istanbul and forge the renewal in the passport—not easy. Or I would have had to have gone to the British Consulate-General, reported a lost British passport and tried to winkle a temporary travel document out of them before they had had time to check up—not easy either. But at least those would have been the sort of difficulties a man in my anomalous position would understand and could cope with. The difficulties that, in fact, I did have to face were quite outside anything I had ever before experienced.

I stood there in the customs shed for about ten minutes, watched by an armed guard on the door who looked as if he would have liked nothing better than an excuse for shooting me. I pretended not to notice him; but his presence did not improve matters. In fact, I was beginning to get an attack of my indigestion.

After a while, the security man came back and beckoned to me. I went with him, along a passage with a small barrack-room off it, to a door at the end.

'What now?' I asked in French.

'You must see the Commandant of the post.'

He knocked at the door and ushered me in.

Inside was a small bare office with some hard chairs and a green baize trestle table in the centre. The customs inspector stood beside the table. Seated at it was a man of about my own age with a lined, sallow face. He wore some sort of officer's uniform. I think he belonged to the military security police. He had the *carnet* and my passport on the table in front of him.

He looked up at me disagreeably. 'This is your passport?' He spoke good French.

'Yes, sir. And I can only say that I regret extremely that I did not notice that it was not renewed.'

'You have caused a lot of trouble.'

'I realize that, sir. I must explain, however, that it was only on Monday evening that I was asked to make this journey. I left early yesterday morning. I was in a hurry. I did not think to check my papers.'

He looked down at the passport. 'It says here that your occupation is that of journalist. You told the customs inspector that you were a chauffeur.'

So he had an inquiring mind; my heart sank.

'I am acting as a chauffeur, sir. I was, I *am* a journalist, but one must live and things are not always easy in that profession.'

'So now you are a chauffeur, and the passport is incorrect in yet another particular, eh?' It was a very unfair way of putting it, but I thought it as well to let him have his moment.

'One's fortunes change, sir. In Athens I have my own car, which I drive for hire.'

He peered, frowning, at the *carnet*. 'This car here is the property of Elizabeth Lipp. Is she your employer?'

'Temporarily, sir.'

'Where is she?'

'In Istanbul, I believe, sir.'

'You do not know?'

'Her agent engaged me, sir—to drive her car to Istanbul where she is going as a tourist. She prefers to make the journey to Istanbul by sea.'

There was an unpleasant pause. He looked through the *carnet* again and then up at me abruptly.

'What nationality is this woman?'

'I don't know, sir.'

'What age? What sort of woman?'

'I have never seen her, sir. Her agent arranged everything.'

'And she is going from Athens to Istanbul by sea, which takes twenty-four hours, but she sends her car fourteen hundred kilometres and three days by road. If she wants the car in Istanbul why didn't she take the car on the boat with her? It is simple enough and costs practically nothing.'

I was only too well aware of it. I shrugged. 'I was paid to drive, sir, and well paid. It was not for me to question the lady's plans.'

He considered me for a moment, then drew a sheet of paper towards him and scribbled a few words. He handed the result to the customs inspector, who read, nodded and went out quickly.

The Commandant seemed to relax. 'You say you know nothing about the woman who owns the car,' he said. 'Tell me about her agent. Is it a travel bureau?'

'No, sir, a man, an American, a friend of Fräulein Lipp's father he said.'

'What's his name? Where is he?'

I told him everything I knew about Harper, and the nature of my relationship to him. I did not mention the disagreement over the traveller's cheques. That could have been of no interest to him.

He listened in silence, nodding occasionally. By the time I had finished, his manner had changed considerably. His expression had become almost amiable.

'Have you driven this way before?' he asked.

'Several times, sir.'

'With tourists?'

'Yes, sir.'

'Ever without tourists?'

'No, sir. They like to visit Olympus, Salonika and Alexandropolis on their way to Istanbul.'

'Then did you not think this proposal of Mr Harper's strange?'

I permitted myself to smile. *'Monsieur le Commandant,'* I said, 'I thought it so strange that there could be only two possible reasons for it. The first was that Mr Harper was so much concerned to impress the daughter of a valuable business associate with his *savoir faire* that he neglected to ask anyone's advice before he made his arrangements.'

'And the second?'

'That he knew that uncrated cars carried in Denizyollari ships to Istanbul must be accompanied by the owner as a passenger, and that he did not wish to be present when the car was inspected by customs for fear that something might be discovered in the car that should not be there.'

'I see.' He smiled slightly. 'But *you* had no such fear.'

We were getting cosier by the minute. *'Monsieur le Commandant,'* I said, 'I may be a trifle careless about having my passport renewed, but I am not a fool. The moment I left Athens yesterday, I stopped and searched the car thoroughly, underneath as well as on top, the wheels, everywhere.'

There was a knock on the door and the customs inspector came back. He put a sheet of paper down in front of the Commandant. The Commandant read it and his face suddenly tightened. He looked up again at me.

'You say you searched everywhere in the car?'

'Yes, sir. Everywhere.'

'Did you search inside the doors?'

'Well, no, sir. They are sealed. I would have damaged…'

He said something quickly in Turkish. Suddenly, the security man locked an arm round my neck and ran his free hand over my pockets. Then he shoved me down violently on to a chair.

I stared at the Commandant dumbly.

'Inside the doors there are—' he referred to the paper in his hand—'twelve tear-gas grenades, twelve concussion grenades, twelve smoke grenades, six gas respirators, six Parabellum pistols, and one hundred and twenty rounds of nine-millimetre pistol ammunition.' He put the paper down and stood up. 'You are under arrest.'

CHAPTER THREE

THE POST HAD NO FACILITIES FOR HOUSING PRISONERS, AND I was put in the lavatory under guard while the Commandant reported my arrest to headquarters and awaited orders. The lavatory was only a few yards from his office, and during the next twenty minutes the telephone there rang four times. I could hear the rumble of his voice when he answered. The tone of it became more respectful with each call.

I was uncertain whether I should allow myself to be encouraged by this or not. Police behaviour is always difficult to anticipate, even when you know a country well. Sometimes Higher Authority is more responsive to a reasonable explanation of the misunderstanding, and more disposed to accept a dignified expression of regret for inconvenience caused, than some self-important or sadistic minor official who is out to make the most of the occasion. On the other hand, the Higher Authority has more power to abuse, and, if it comes to the simple matter of a bribe, bigger ideas about his nuisance value. I must admit, though, that what I was mainly concerned about at that point was the kind of physical treatment I would receive. Of course, every police authority, high or low, considers its behaviour 'correct' on all occasions; but in my experience (although I have only really been arrested ten or twelve times in my whole life) the word 'correct' can mean almost anything from hot meals brought in from a near-by restaurant and plenty of cigarettes, to tight-handcuffing in the cell and a knee in the groin if you dare to complain. My previous encounters with the Turkish police had been uncomfortable only in the sense that they had been inconvenient and humiliating; but then the matters in dispute had been of a more or less technical nature. I had to face the fact that 'being in possession of arms, explosives and other offensive weapons, attempting to smuggle them into the Turkish Republic, carrying concealed fire-arms and illegal entry without valid identification papers' were rather more serious charges. My complete and absolute innocence of them would take time to establish, and a lot of quite unpleasant things could happen in the interim.

The possibility that my innocence might *not* be established was something that, realist though I am, I was not just then prepared to contemplate.

After the fourth telephone call, the Commandant came out of his office, gave some order to the security man, who had been waiting in the passage, and then came into the lavatory.

'You are being sent at once to the garrison jail in Edirne,' he said.

'And the car I was driving, sir?'

He hesitated. 'I have no orders about that yet. No doubt it will be wanted as evidence.'

Direct communication with Higher Authority seemed to have sapped a little of his earlier self-confidence. I decided to have one more shot at bluffing my way out. 'I must remind you, sir,' I said loudly, 'that I have already protested formally to you against my detention here. I repeat that protest. The car and its contents are within your legal jurisdiction. I am not. I was refused entry because my papers were not in order. Therefore, legally, I was not in Turkey and should have been at once returned to the Greek side of the border. In Greece, I have a *permis de séjour* which *is* in order. I think that when your superiors learn these facts, you will find that you have a lot to answer for.'

It was quite well said. Unfortunately, it seemed to amuse him.

'So you are a lawyer, as well as a journalist, a chauffeur and an arms-smuggler.'

'I am simply warning you.'

His smile faded. 'Then let me give you a word of warning, too. In Edirne you will not be dealing with the ordinary police authorities. It is considered that there may be political aspects to your case and it has been placed under the jurisdiction of the Second Section, the Ikinci Büro.'

'Political aspects? What political aspects?' I tried, not very successfully, to sound angry instead of alarmed.

'That is not for me to say. I merely warn you. The Director Second Section is General Haki. It will be his men who will interrogate you. You will certainly end by co-operating with them. You would be well advised to begin by doing so. Their patience, I hear, is quite limited. That is all.'

He went. A moment or two later the security man came in.

I was driven to the garrison jail in a covered jeep with my right wrist handcuffed to a grab-rail, and an escort of two soldiers. The jail was an old stone building on the outskirts of the town. It had a walled courtyard, and there were expanded metal screens as well as bars over the windows.

One of the soldiers, an N.C.O., reported to the guard on the inner gate, and after a few moments two men in a different sort of uniform came out through a smaller side door. One of them had a paper which he handed to the N.C.O. I gathered that it was a receipt for me. The N.C.O. immediately unlocked the handcuffs and waved me out of the jeep. The new escort-in-charge prodded me towards the side door.

'*Girmek, girmek!*' he said sharply.

All jails seem to smell of disinfectants, urine, sweat and leather. This was no exception. I went up some wooden stairs to a steel gate which was opened from the inside by a man with a long chain of keys. Beyond it and to the right was a sort of reception-room with a man at a desk and two cubicles at the back. The guard shoved me up to the desk and rapped out an order. I said in French that I didn't understand. The man at the desk said: *'Vide les poches.'*

I did as I was told. They had taken all my papers and keys from me at the frontier post. All I had left in my pockets was my money, my watch, a packet of cigarettes and matches. The desk man gave me back the watch and the cigarettes, and put the money and the matches into an envelope. A man in a grubby white coat now arrived and went into one of the cubicles. He was carrying a thin yellow file folder. After a moment or two he called out an order and I was sent in to him.

The cubicle contained a small table and a chair and a covered bucket. In one corner there was a wash basin, and on the wall a white metal cabinet. The white-coated man was at the table preparing an inking plate of the kind used for fingerprinting. He glanced up at me and said in French: 'Take your clothes off.'

People who run jails are all the same. When I was naked, he searched the inside of the clothes and the shoes. Next, he looked in my mouth and ears with a flashlight. Then he took a rubber glove and a jar of petroleum jelly from the wall cabinet and searched my rectum. I have always deeply resented that indignity. Finally, he took my fingerprints. He was very businesslike about it all; he even gave me a piece of toilet paper to wipe the ink off my hands before he told me to dress and go into the next cubicle. In there, was a camera, set up with photofloods and a fixed focus bar. When I had been photographed, I was taken along some corridors to a green wooden door with the word ISTIFHAM lettered on it in white paint. *Istifham* is a Turkish word I know; it means 'interrogation'.

There was only one small screened and barred window in the room; the sun was beginning to set and it was already quite dark in there. As I went in, one of the guards followed me and switched on the light. His friend shut and locked the door from the outside. The guard who was to stay with me sat down on a bench against the wall and yawned noisily.

The room was about eighteen feet square. Off one corner there was a washroom with no door on it. Apart from the bench, the furniture consisted of a solid-looking table bolted to the floor and half a dozen chairs. On the wall was a telephone and a framed lithograph of Kemal Ataturk. The floor was covered with worn brown linoleum.

I got out my cigarettes and offered one to the guard. He shook his head and looked contemptuous as if I had offered him an inadequate bribe. I shrugged and, putting the cigarette in my own mouth, made signs that I wanted a light. He shook his head again. I put the cigarette away and sat down at the table. I had to assume that at any moment now a representative of the Second Section would arrive and start questioning me. What I needed, very badly, was something to tell him.

It is always the same with interrogation. I remember my father trying to explain it to Mum one night just before he was killed. It's no good for a soldier who is up on a charge before his C.O. just telling the truth; he has to have something more, something fancy to go with it. If he got back to barracks half an hour after lights-out just because he'd had too much beer and missed the last bus, who cares about him? He's simply a careless bloody fool—seven days confined to barracks, next case. But if, when he's asked if he has anything to say, he can tell the tale so that the C.O. gets a bit of fun out of

hearing it, things are different. He may be only admonished. My
father said that there was a corporal in his old regiment who was so
good at making up yarns for the orderly room that he used to sell
them for half a crown apiece. They were known as 'well-sirs'. My
father bought a well-sir once when he was 'crimed' for overstaying
an evening pass. It went like this:

'*Well, sir, I was proceeding back along Cantonment Road towards the
barracks in good time for lights-out and in a soldierly manner. Then, sir,
just as I was passing the shopping arcade by Ordnance Avenue, I heard a
woman scream.*' Pause. '*Well, sir, I stopped to listen and heard her scream
again. There were also some confused cries. The sound was coming from one
of the shops in the arcade, so I went to investigate.*' Pause again, then go
on slowly. '*Well, sir, what I found was one of these Wogs—beg pardon,
sir, a native—molesting a white woman in a doorway. I could see she was
a lady, sir.*' Let that sink in a bit. '*Well, sir, the moment this lady saw me
she appealed to me for help. She said she'd been on her way home to her
mother's house, which was over on the other side of Artillery Park, when
this native had attempted to—well, interfere with her. I told him to clear
out. In reply, sir, he became abusive, calling me some very dirty names in
his own lingo and using insulting language about the Regiment.*' Take a
deep breath. '*Well, sir, for the lady's sake I managed to hold on to my
temper. As a matter of fact, sir, I think the man must have been drunk or
under the influence of drugs. He had sense enough to keep his distance,
but the moment I escorted the lady out of the arcade I realized that he was
following us. Just waiting for a chance to molest her again, sir. She knew it,
too. I've never seen a lady more frightened, sir. When she appealed to me
to escort her to her mother's house, sir, I realized that it would make me
late. But if I'd just gone on my way and something terrible had happened
to her, I'd have never forgiven myself, sir.*' Stiffen up and look without
blinking at the wall space over the C.O.'s head. '*No excuse to offer,*

sir, I'll take my medicine.' C.O. can't think of anything to say except, 'Don't let it happen again.' Charge dismissed.

The only trouble is that in the Army, unless you are always making a damned nuisance of yourself, they would sooner give you the benefit of the doubt than not, because it's easier for them that way. Besides, they know that even if you *have* made the whole thing up, at least they've had you sweating over it. The police are much more difficult. They don't *want* you to have the benefit of any doubt. They want to start checking and double-checking your story, and getting witnesses and evidence, so that there *is* no doubt. 'What was the lady's name? Describe her. Exactly where was the house to which you escorted her? Was her mother in fact there? Did you see her? It takes twenty-two minutes to walk from the shopping arcade to the other side of Artillery Park, and a further thirty minutes to walk from there to the barracks. That makes fifty-two minutes. But you were two hours late getting in. Where did you spend the other hour and eight minutes? We have a witness who says that he saw you...' And so on. You can't buy well-sirs good enough for the police for half a crown. Intelligence people are even worse. Nine times out of ten they don't even have to worry about building up a case against you to go into court. *They* are the court—judge, jury and prosecutor, all in one.

I did not know anything about this Second Section which the Commandant had mentioned; but it was not hard to guess what it was. The Turks have always been great borrowers of French words and phrases. The Ikinci Büro sounded to me like the Turkish counterpart of the Deuxième Bureau. I wasn't far wrong.

I think that if I were asked to single out one specific group of men, one type, one category, as being the most suspicious, unbelieving, unreasonable, petty, inhuman, sadistic, double-crossing set of bastards in any language, I would say without any hesitation 'the people who run counter-espionage departments'. With them, it is no use having just one story; and especially not a true story; they automatically disbelieve that. What you must have is a series of stories, so that when they knock the first one down you can bring out the second, and then, when they scrub that out, come up with a third. That way they think they are making progress and keep their hands off you, while you gradually find out the story they really want you to tell.

My position at Edirne was hopeless from the start. If I had known what was hidden in the car *before* the post Commandant had started questioning me, I wouldn't have told him about Harper. I would have pretended to be stupid, or just refused to say anything. Then, later, when I had finally broken down and 'told all', they would have believed at least some of what I had said. As it was, I had told a story that happened to be true, but sounded as if I thought they were half-witted. You can imagine how I felt as I waited. With no room at all for manœuvre, I knew that I must be in for a bad time.

The sun went down and the window turned black. It was very quiet. I could hear no sounds at all from other parts of the jail. Presumably, things were arranged so that there they could hear no sounds made in the interrogation room—screams etc. When I had been there two hours, there were footsteps in the corridor outside, the door was unlocked and a new guard came in with a tin bowl of mutton soup and a hunk of bread. He put these on the table in front of me, then nodded to his friend, who went out and relocked the door. The new man took his place on the bench.

There was no spoon. I dipped a piece of bread in the soup and tasted it. It was lukewarm and full of congealed fat. Even without my indigestion I could not have eaten it. Now, the smell alone made me want to throw up.

I looked at the guard. '*Su?*' I asked.

He motioned to the washroom. Evidently, if I wanted water I would have to drink from the tap. I did not relish the idea. Indigestion was bad enough; I did not want dysentery, too. I made myself eat some of the bread and then took out my cigarettes again in the hope that the new man might be ready to give me a match. He shook his head. I pointed to a plastic ash-tray on the table to remind him that smoking was not necessarily prohibited. He still shook his head.

A little before nine, a twin-engined plane flew over the jail and then circled as if on a landing pattern. The sound seemed to mean something to the guard. He looked at his watch and then absently ran his hand down the front of his tunic as if to make sure that the buttons were all done up.

More to break the interminable silence in the room than because I wanted to know, I asked: 'Is there a big airport at Edirne?'

I spoke in French, but it meant nothing to him. I made signs which he misunderstood.

'*Askeri ucak,*' he said briefly.

An Army plane. That concluded that conversation; but I noticed that he kept glancing at his watch now. Probably, I thought, it was time for his relief and he was becoming impatient.

Twenty minutes later there was the distant sound of a car door slamming. The guard heard it, too, and promptly stood up. I stared at him and he glowered back.

'*Hazirol!*' he snapped, and then exasperatedly, '*Debout! Debout!*'

I stood up. I could hear approaching footsteps and voices now. Then the door was unlocked and flung open.

For a moment nothing more happened, except that someone in the corridor, whom I could not see, went on speaking. He had a harsh peremptory voice which seemed to be giving orders that another voice kept acknowledging deferentially—'*Evet, evet efendim, derhal.*' Then the orders ceased and the man who had been giving them came into the room.

He was about thirty-five I would think, perhaps younger, tall and quite slim. There were high cheekbones, grey eyes and short brown hair. He was handsome, I suppose, in a thin-lipped sort of way. He was wearing a dark civilian suit that looked as if it had been cut by a good Roman tailor, and a dark-grey silk tie. He looked as if he had just come from a diplomatic corps cocktail party; and for all I know he may have done so. On his right wrist there was a gold identity bracelet. The hand below it was holding a large manila envelope.

He examined me bleakly for a moment, then nodded. 'I am Major Tufan, Deputy-Director Second Section.'

'Good evening, Major.'

He glanced at the guard, who was staring at him round-eyed, and suddenly snapped out an order: '*Defol!*'

The guard nearly fell over himself getting out of the room.

As soon as the door closed the Major pulled a chair up to the table and sat down. Then he waved me back to my seat by the bread.

'Sit down, Simpson. I believe that you speak French easily, but not Turkish.'

'Yes, Major.'

'Then we will speak in French instead of English. That will be easier for me.'

I answered in French. 'As you wish, sir.'

He took cigarettes and matches from his pocket and tossed them on the table in front of me. 'You may smoke.'

'Thank you.'

I was glad of the concession, though not in the least reassured by it. When a policeman gives you a cigarette it is usually the first move in one of those 'let's-see-if-we-can't-talk-sensibly-as-man-to-man' games in which he provides the rope and you hang yourself. I lit a cigarette and waited for the next move.

He seemed in no hurry to make it. He had opened the envelope and taken from it a file of papers which he was searching through and rearranging, as if he had just dropped the whole lot and was trying to get it back into the right order.

There was a knock at the door. He took no notice. After a moment or two the door opened and a guard came in with a bottle of *raki* and two glasses. Tufan motioned to him to put them on the table, and then noticed the soup.

'Do you want any more of that?' he asked.

'No thank you, sir.'

He said something to the guard, who took the soup and bread away and locked the door again.

Tufan rested the file on his knees and poured himself a glass of *raki*. 'The flight from Istanbul was anything but smooth,' he said; 'we are still using piston-engined planes on these short runs.' He swallowed the drink as if he were washing down a pill, and pushed the bottle an inch or two in my direction. 'You'd better have a drink, Simpson. It may make you feel better.'

'And also make me more talkative, sir?' I thought the light touch might show that I was not afraid.

He looked up and his grey eyes met mine. 'I hope not,' he said coldly; 'I have no time to waste.' He shut the file with a snap and put it on the table in front of him.

'Now then,' he went on, 'let us examine your position. First, the offences with which you are charged render you liable upon conviction to terms of imprisonment of at least twenty years. Depending on the degree of your involvement in the political aspects of this affair, we might even consider pressing for a death sentence.'

'But I am not involved at all, Major, I assure you. I am a victim of circumstances—an innocent victim.' Of course he could have been bluffing about the death sentence, but I could not be sure. There was that phrase 'political aspects' again. I had read that they had been hanging members of the former government for political crimes. I wished now that I had taken the drink when he had offered it. Now my hands were shaking, and I knew that, if I reached for the bottle and glass, he would see that they were.

Apparently, however, he did not have to see them; he knew what he was doing to me, and wanted me to know that he knew. Quite casually, he picked up the bottle, poured me half a glass of *raki* and pushed it across to me.

'We will talk about the extent of your involvement in a minute,' he said. 'First, let us consider the matter of your passport.'

'It is out of date. I admit that. But it was a mere oversight. If the post Commandant had behaved correctly I would have been sent back to the Greek post.'

He shrugged impatiently. 'Let us be clear about this. You had already committed serious criminal offences on Turkish soil. Would you expect to escape the consequences because your papers were not in order? You know better. You also know that your passport was not invalid through any oversight. The Egyptian Government had refused to renew it. In fact they revoked your citizenship two years ago on the grounds that you made false statements on your naturalization papers.' He glanced in the file. 'You stated that you had never been convicted of a criminal offence and that you had never served a prison sentence. Both statements were lies.'

This was such an unfair distortion of the facts that I could only assume that he had got it from the Egyptians. I said: 'I have been fighting that decision.'

'And also using a passport to which you were not entitled and had failed to surrender.'

'My case was still *sub judice.* Anyway, I have already applied for restoration of my British citizenship, to which I am entitled as the son of a serving British officer. In fact, I *am* British.'

'The British don't take that view. After what happened you can scarcely blame them.'

'Under the provisions of the British Nationality Act of nineteen-forty-eight I remain British unless I have specifically renounced that nationality. I have never formally renounced it.'

'That is unimportant. We are talking about your case here and the extent of your involvement. The point I wish to make is that our action in your case is not going to be governed in any way by the fact that you are a foreigner. No consul is going to intercede on your behalf. You have none. You are stateless. The only person who can help you is my Director.' He paused. 'But he will have to be persuaded. You understand me?'

'I have no money.'

It seemed a perfectly sensible reply to me, but for some reason it appeared to irritate him. His eyes narrowed and for a moment I thought he was going to throw the glass he was holding in my face. Then he sighed. 'You are over fifty,' he said, 'yet you have learned nothing. You still see other men in your own absurd image. Do you really believe that I could be bought, or that, if I could be, a man like you could ever do the buying?'

It was on the tip of my tongue to retort that that would depend on the price he was asking, but if he wanted to take this high-and-mighty attitude, there was no sense in arguing. Obviously, I had touched him in a sensitive area.

He lit a cigarette as if he were consciously putting aside his irritation. I took the opportunity to drink some of the *raki*.

'Very well.' He was all business again. 'You understand your position, which is that you have no position. We come now to the story you told to the post Commandant before your arrest.'

'Every word I told the Commandant was the truth.'

He opened the file. 'On the face of it that seems highly unlikely. Let us see. You stated that you were asked by this American, Harper, to drive a car belonging to a Fräulein Lipp from Athens to Istanbul. You were to be paid one hundred dollars. You agreed. Am I right?'

'Quite right.'

'You agreed, even though the passport in your possession was not in order?'

'I did not realize it was out-of-date. It has been months since I used it. The whole thing was arranged within a few hours. I scarcely had time to pack a bag. People are using out-of-date passports all the time. Ask anyone at any international airline. They will tell you. That is why they always check passengers' passports when they weigh their baggage. They do not want difficulties at the other end. I had nobody to check. The Greek control scarcely looked at the passport. I was leaving the country. They were not interested.'

I knew I was on safe ground here, and I spoke with feeling.

He thought for a moment then nodded. 'It is possible, and, of course, you had good reason not to think too much about the date on your passport. The Egyptians were not going to renew it anyway. That explanation is acceptable, I think. We will go on.' He referred again to the file. 'You told the Commandant that you suspected this man Harper of being a narcotics smuggler.'

'I did.'

'To the extent of searching the car after you left Athens.'

'Yes.'

'Yet you still agreed to make the journey.'

'I was being paid one hundred dollars.'

'That was the only reason?'

'Yes.'

He shook his head. 'It really will not do.'

'I am telling you the truth.'

He took a clip of papers from the file. 'Your history does not inspire confidence.'

'Give a dog a bad name.'

'You seem to have earned one. Our dossier on you begins in 'fifty-seven. You were arrested on various charges and fined on a minor count. The rest were abandoned by the police for lack of evidence.'

'They should never have been brought in the first place.'

He ignored this. 'We did, however, ask Interpol if they knew anything about you. It seemed they knew a lot. Apparently you were once in the restaurant business.'

'My mother owned a restaurant in Cairo. Is that an offence?'

'Fraud is an offence. Your mother was *part* owner of a restaurant. When she died, you sold it to a buyer who believed that you now owned all of it. In fact, there were two other shareholders. The buyer charged you with fraud but withdrew his complaint when the police allowed you to regularize the transaction.'

'I didn't know of the existence of these other shareholders. My mother had never told me that she had sold the shares.' This was perfectly true. Mum was entirely responsible for the trouble I got into over that.

'In nineteen thirty-one you bought a partnership in a small publishing business in Cairo. Outwardly it concerned itself with distributing foreign magazines and periodicals. Its real business was the production of pornography for the Spanish and English-speaking markets. And that became your real business.'

'That is absolutely untrue.'

'The information was supplied through Interpol in 'fifty-four by Scotland Yard. It was given in response to an inquiry by the New York police. Scotland Yard must have known about you for a long time.'

I knew it would do no good for me to become angry. 'I have edited and sometimes written for a number of magazines of a literary nature over the years,' I said quietly. 'Sometimes they may have been a little daring in their approach and have been banned by various censoring authorities. But I would remind you that books like *Ulysses* and *Lady Chatterley's Lover,* which were once described by those same authorities as pornographic or obscene, are now accepted as literary works of art and published quite openly.'

He looked at his papers again. 'In January 'fifty-five you were arrested in London. In your possession were samples of the various obscene and pornographic periodicals which you had been attempting to sell in bulk. Among them was a book called *Gents Only* and a monthly magazine called *Enchantment.* All were produced by your Egyptian company. You were charged under the British law governing such publications, and also with smuggling them. At your trial you said nothing about their being literary works of art. You pleaded guilty and were sentenced to twelve months' imprisonment.'

'That was a travesty of justice.'

'Then why did you plead guilty?'

'Because my lawyer advised me to.' In fact, the C.I.D. inspector had tricked me into it. He had as good as promised me that if I pleaded guilty I would get off with a fine.

He stared at me thoughtfully for a moment then shut the file. 'You must be a very stupid man, Simpson. You say to me, "I am telling you the truth," and yet when I try to test that statement all I hear from you is whining and protestation. I am not interested in how you explain away the past, or in any illusions about yourself that you may wish to preserve. If you cannot even tell the truth when there is nothing to be gained by lying, then I can believe nothing you tell me. You were caught by the British, smuggling pornography and trying to peddle it. Why not admit it? Then, when you tell me that you did not know that you were smuggling arms and ammunition this afternoon, I might at least think, "This man is a petty criminal, but it is remotely possible that for once he is being truthful." As it is, I can only assume that you are lying and that I must get the truth from you in some other way.'

I admit that 'some other way' gave me a jolt. After all, five minutes earlier he had been pouring me a glass of *raki*. He meant to put the fear of God into me, of course, and make me panic. Unfortunately, and only because I was tired, upset and suffering from indigestion, he succeeded.

'I am telling you the truth, sir.' I could hear my own voice cracking and quavering but could do nothing to control it. 'I swear to God I am telling you the truth. My only wish is to tell you all I can, to bring everything out of the darkness into the light of day.'

He stared at me curiously; and then, as I realized what I had said, I felt myself reddening. It was awful. I had used those absurd words Harper had made me write in that confession about the cheques.

A sour smile touched his lips for an instant. 'Ah yes,' he said. 'I was forgetting that you have been a journalist. We will try once more then. Just remember that I do not want speeches in mitigation, only plain statements.'

'Of course.' I was too confused to think straight now.

'Why did you go to London in 'fifty-five? You must have known that Scotland Yard knew all about you.'

'How could I know? I hadn't been in England for years.'

'Where were you during the war?'

'In Cairo doing war work.'

'What work?'

'I was an interpreter.'

'Why did you go to London?'

I cleared my throat and took a sip of *raki*.

'Answer me!'

'I was going to answer, sir.' There was nothing else for it. 'The British distributor of our publications suddenly ceased making payments and we could get no replies from him to our letters. I went to England to investigate and found his offices closed. I assumed that he had gone out of business and began to look for another distributor. The man I eventually discussed the possibility with turned out to be a Scotland Yard detective. We used to send our shipments to Liverpool in cotton bales. It seems that the customs had discovered this and informed the police. Our distributor had been arrested and sent to prison. The police had kept it out of the papers somehow. I just walked into a trap.'

'Better, much better,' he said. He looked almost amused. 'Naturally, though, you felt bitter towards the British authorities.'

I should have remembered something he had let drop earlier, but I was still confused. I tried to head him off.

'I was bitter at the time, of course, sir. I did not think I had had a fair trial. But afterwards I realized that the police had their job to do—' I thought that would appeal to him—'and that they weren't responsible for making the laws. So I tried to be a model prisoner. I think I was. Anyway I received the maximum remission for good behaviour. I certainly couldn't complain of the treatment I had in Maidstone. In fact, the Governor shook hands with me when I left and wished me well.'

'And then you returned to Egypt?'

'As soon as my probationary period was up, yes. I went back to Cairo, sir.'

'Where you proceeded to denounce a British business man named Colby Evans to the Egyptian authorities as a British secret agent.'

It was like a slap in the face, but I managed to keep my head this time. 'Not immediately, sir. That was later, during the Suez crisis.'

'Why did you do it?'

I didn't know what to say. How could I explain to a man like that that I had to pay back the caning they had given me? I said nothing.

'Was it because you needed to prove somehow to the Egyptian authorities that you were anti-British, or because you didn't like the man, or because you were sincerely anti-British?'

It was all three, I suppose; I am not really sure. I answered almost without thinking.

'My mother was Egyptian. My wife was killed by a British bomb in the attack they made on us. Why shouldn't I feel sincerely anti-British?'

It was probably the best answer I had given so far; it sounded true, even though it wasn't quite.

'Did you really believe this man was an agent?'

'Yes, sir.'

'And then you applied for Egyptian citizenship.'

'Yes, sir.'

'You stayed in Egypt until 'fifty-eight. Was that when they finally decided that Evans had *not* been a British agent after all and released him?'

'He was convicted at his trial. His release was an act of clemency.'

'But the Egyptians did start to investigate you at that time.' It was a statement.

'I suppose so.'

'I see.' He refilled my glass. 'I think we are beginning to understand one another, Simpson. You now realize that it is neither my business nor my inclination to make moral judgements. I, on the other hand, am beginning to see how your mind works in the areas we are discussing—what holds the pieces together. So now let us go back to your story about Mr Harper and Fräulein Lipp.' He glanced again at the file. 'You see, for a man of your experience it is quite incredible. You suspect that Harper may be using you for some illegal purpose which will be highly profitable to him, yet you do as he asks for a mere hundred dollars.'

'It was the return journey I was thinking of, sir. I thought that when he realized that I had guessed what he was up to, he would have to pay me to take the risk.'

He sat back, smiling. 'But you had accepted the hundred dollars before that possibility had occurred to you. You would not have searched the car outside Athens otherwise. You see the difficulty?'

I did. What I didn't see was the way out of it.

He lit another cigarette. 'Come now, Simpson, you were emerging very sensibly from the darkness a few minutes ago. Why not continue? Either your whole story is a lie, or you have left something of importance out. Which is it? I am going to find out anyway. It will be easier for both of us if you just tell me now.'

I know when I am beaten. I drank some more *raki*. 'All right. I had no more choice with him than I have with you. He was black-mailing me.'

'How?'

'Have you got an extradition treaty with Greece?'

'Never mind about that. I am not the police.'

So I had to tell him about the traveller's cheques after all.

When I had finished, he nodded. 'I see,' was all he said. After a moment, he got up and went to the door. It opened the instant he knocked on it. He began to give orders.

I was quite sure that he had finished with me and was telling the guards to take me away to a cell, so I swallowed the rest of the *raki* in my glass and put the matches in my pocket on the off-chance that I might get away with them.

I was wrong about the cell. When he had finished speaking, he shut the door and came back.

'I have sent for some eatable food,' he said.

He did not stop at the table, but went across to the telephone. I lighted a cigarette and returned the matches to the table. I don't think he noticed. He was asking for an Istanbul number and making a lot of important-sounding noises about it. Then he hung up and came back to the table.

'Now tell me everything you remember about this man Harper,' he said.

I started to tell him the whole story from the beginning, but he wanted details now.

'You say that he spoke like a German who has lived in America for some years. When did you reach that conclusion? After you heard him speak German to the man at the garage?'

'No. Hearing him speak German only confirmed the impression I had had.'

'If you were to hear me speak German fluently could you tell whether it was my mother tongue or not?'

'No.'

'How did he pronounce the English word "later", for example?'

I tried to tell him.

'You know, the German "I" is more frontal than that,' he said; 'but in Turkish, before certain vowels, the "I" is like the English consonant you were pronouncing. If you were told that this man had a Turkish background, would you disbelieve it?'

'Not if I were told it was true perhaps. But is Harper a Turkish name?'

'Is it a German one?'

'It could be an anglicization of Hipper.'

'It could also be an anglicization of Harbak.' He shrugged. 'It could also be an alias. It most probably is. All I am trying to discover is if the man could be Turkish.'

'Because of the political aspects you mentioned?'

'Obviously. Tear-gas grenades, concussion grenades, smoke grenades, six pistols, six times twenty rounds of ammunition. Six determined men, equipped with that material, making a surprise attack on some important person or group of persons could accomplish a great deal. There are still many supporters of the former régime. They do not like the Army's firm hands.'

I refrained from telling him that I wasn't so very fond of those firm hands myself.

'But, of course,' he went on; 'we keep our eyes on them. If they wished to attempt anything they would need help from outside. You say he had Swiss francs and West German marks as well as dollars?'

'Yes.'

'Naturally it is possible that what we have here is only one small corner of a much larger plan. If so, there is a lot of money behind it. This man Harper went to a great deal of trouble and expense to get that material through. Perhaps…'

The telephone rang and he broke off to answer it. His call to Istanbul had come through. I understood about one word in ten of his side of the conversation. He was reporting to his boss; that much was easily gathered. My name was mentioned several times. After that he mostly listened, just putting in an occasional *evet* to show that he was getting the point. I could hear the faint quacking of the voice at the other end of the line. Finally, it stopped. Tufan asked a question and received a brief reply. That was all. Tufan made a respectful sound, then hung up and looked across at me.

'Bad news for you, Simpson,' he said. 'The Director does not feel disposed to help you in any way. He regards the charges against you as too serious.'

'I'm sorry.' There seemed nothing more to say. I downed another *raki* to try to settle my stomach.

'He considers that you have not been sufficiently helpful to us. I was unable to persuade him.'

'I've told you everything I know.'

'It is not enough. What we need to know is more about this man Harper, who his associates and contacts are, who this Fräulein Lipp is, where the arms and ammunition are going, how they are to be used. If you could supply that information or help to supply it, of course, your case might be reconsidered.'

'The only way I could possibly get information like that would be to drive on to Istanbul tomorrow as if nothing had happened, go to the Park Hotel and wait for somebody to contact me as arranged. Is that what you're telling me I have to do?'

He sat down facing me. 'It is what we might tell you to do, if we thought that we could trust you. My Director is doubtful. Naturally, he is thinking of your past record.'

'What has that to do with it?'

'Isn't it obvious? Supposing you warn these people that the car was searched. Perhaps they would reward you.'

'Reward me?' I laughed loudly; I think I must have been getting a bit tight. 'Reward me for telling them that they are under surveillance? Are you serious? You were talking about a group of men determined enough to risk their lives. At the moment, the only contact I can identify is Harper. He may or may not be in Istanbul. Supposing he's not. Someone has to contact me to get at the car. What do I do? Whisper "Fly, all is discovered" into his ear, and expect him to tip me before he leaves? Or do I wait until I've made a few more contacts before I tell them the good news, so that they can pass the hat round? Don't be ridiculous! They'd know at once that they wouldn't get far, because you'd pick me up again and make me talk. Reward? I'd be lucky if they let me stay alive.'

He smiled. 'The Director wondered if you would have the sense to see that.'

But I was too annoyed by what I thought was his stupidity to grasp the implication of what he had said. I went on in English. I didn't care any more whether he understood me or not. I said: 'In any case, what have *you* got to lose? If I don't turn up in Istanbul tomorrow, they'll know that something's gone wrong, and all you'll have is a couple of names that don't mean anything to you, and a second-hand Lincoln. You'll have me, too, of course, but you already know all I know about this, and you're going to look damn silly standing up in court trying to prove that I was going to carry out a one-man *coup d'état*. Your bloody Director may be one of these fine, upstanding, crap-packed bastards who thinks that everybody who doesn't smell to high heaven of sweetness and roses isn't worth a second thought, but if his brain isn't where his arse ought to be he must know he's got to trust me. He has no bloody alternative.'

Tufan nodded calmly and moved the *raki* bottle just out of my reach. 'Those were more or less the Director's own words,' he said.

CHAPTER FOUR

I WOKE UP THE NEXT MORNING WITH A HANGOVER; AND NOT just because of the *raki*. Nervous strain always has that effect on me. It was a wonder that I had been able to sleep at all.

The 'eatable food' that Tufan had ordered had turned out to be yoghourt (which I detest) and some sort of sheep's milk cheese. I had just eaten some more bread while Tufan made telephone calls.

The Lincoln had been left out at the Karaagac customs post, which was closed for the night. He had had to get the Commandant out of bed to open the place up, and arrange for an army driver to take the car to the garrison repair shop. The grenades and arms, and my bag, had been removed to the local Army H.Q. for examination. That meant that more people, including the customs inspector who had searched the car, had then had to be rounded up so that the stuff could be put back inside the doors again exactly as it had been found.

Even with all the authority he had, it had taken an hour just to organize the work. Then, the question of a hotel room for me had come up. I was so exhausted by then that I would not have minded sleeping in a cell. I had told him so; but, of course, it had not been my comfort he had been thinking about. I had had to listen to a lecture. Supposing Harper asked me where I had spent the night; supposing this, supposing that. An agent sometimes had to take risks, but he should never take unnecessary ones. To be caught out through carelessness over trifles was unforgivable; and so on. That had been the first time he had referred to me as an 'agent'. It had given me an uncomfortable feeling.

He had told me to meet him outside a new apartment building near the hotel at nine o'clock. He was already there when I arrived. His clothes were still quite neat, but he hadn't shaved and his eyes were puffy. He looked as if he had been up all night. Without even saying 'good morning' he motioned me to follow him and led the way down a ramp to a small garage in the basement of the building.

The Lincoln was there and looking very clean.

'I had it washed,' he said. 'It had too many fingerprints on it. It'll be dusty again by the time you get to Istanbul. You had better look at the doors.'

I had warned him to be careful about the interior door panels. They were leather and had been quite clean when I had taken the car over in Athens. If some clumsy lout of an army fitter had made scratches or marks when replacing them, Harper would be bound to notice.

I could see nothing wrong, however. If I had not been told, I would not have known that the panels had ever been taken off.

'It's all inside there, just as it was before?' I asked.

'The customs inspector says so. All the objects were taped out of the way of the window glasses against the metal. Photographs were taken before they were removed.'

He had a set of prints in his pocket and he showed them to me. They didn't convey much. They looked like pictures of hibernating bats.

'Have you any idea where the stuff was bought?' I asked.

'A good question. The pistols and ammunition are German, of course. The grenades, all kinds, are French. That doesn't help us much. We do know that the packing was done in Greece.'

'How?'

'It was padded with newspapers to stop any rattling. There are bits of Athens papers dated a week ago.' He took a sealed envelope from the front seat of the car and opened it up. 'These are the things that were taken from you at the frontier post,' he said. 'You had better put them back in your pockets now and I will keep the envelope. I have a special tourist visa stamped in the passport validating it as a travel document within Turkey for one month. That is in case the hotel clerk should notice the expiry date or if you are stopped by the traffic police for any reason. If Harper or anyone else should happen to see it, you simply say that the security control made no difficulties when you promised to get the passport renewed in Istanbul. The *carnet* is in order, of course, and there are your other personal papers.' He handed them to me, then tore the envelope in four and put the pieces in his pocket.

'Now,' he went on, 'as to your orders. You know the information we want. First, the names and addresses of all contacts, their descriptions, what they say and do. Secondly, you will attempt, by keeping your ears and eyes open, to discover where and how these arms are to be used. In that connection you will take particular note of any place names mentioned, no matter in what context. Buildings or particular areas, too. Do you understand that?'

'I understand. How do I report?'

'I am coming to that. First, from the moment you leave here you will be under surveillance. The persons allocated to this duty will be changed frequently, but if you should happen to recognize any of them you will pretend not to. Only in an emergency or in a case of extreme urgency will you approach them. In that event they will help you if you say my name. You will report normally by telephone, but not from a telephone that goes through a private switchboard. Certainly not from the telephone in a hotel room. Use café telephones. Unless, for physical or security reasons, it is impossible, you will report at ten every night, or at eight the following morning if you have missed the ten o'clock call.' He took a box of matches from his pocket. 'The number is written here underneath the matches. As soon as you are certain that you will not forget it, throw the box away. If you want to communicate other than at the daily report times, a duty officer will pass your call or give you another number at which I can be reached. Is that all clear?'

'Yes.' I took the matches and looked at the number.

'Just one more thing,' he said. 'The Director is not an amiable or kindly man. You will keep faith with us because it would not be in your interests to do otherwise. He knows that, of course. But, for him, stupidity or clumsiness in carrying out orders are just as unacceptable as bad faith and have the same consequences. I would strongly advise you to be successful. That is all, I think, unless you have any questions.'

'No. No questions.'

With a nod, he turned away and walked up the ramp to the street. I put my bag in the back of the car again. Ten minutes later I was clear of Edirne and on the Istanbul road.

After a few miles I identified the surveillance car as a sand-coloured Peugeot two or three hundred yards behind me. It kept that distance, more or less, even when trucks or other cars got between us, or going through towns. It never closed up enough for me to see the driver clearly. When I stopped at Corlu for lunch he did not overtake me. I did not see the Peugeot while I was there.

The restaurant was a café with a few shaky tables under a small vine-covered terrace outside. I had a glass or two of *raki* and some stuffed peppers. My stomach began to feel a bit better. I sat there for over an hour. I would have liked to have stayed longer. There

were moments like that at school, too; when one bad time had
ended and the next had not yet begun. There can be days of it also,
the days when one is on remand awaiting trial—not innocent, not
guilty, not responsible, out of the game. I often wish that I could
have an operation—not a painful or serious one, of course—just so
as to be convalescent for a while after it.

The Peugeot picked me up again three minutes after I left Corlu. I
stopped again only once, for petrol. I reached Istanbul just after four.

I put the Lincoln in a garage just off Taxim Square and walked
to the hotel, carrying my bag.

The Park Oteli is built against the side of a hill overlooking the
Bosphorus. It is the only hotel that I know of which has the foyer at
the top, so that the lift takes you down to your room instead of up.
My room was quite a long way down and on a corner overlooking a
street with a café in it. The café had a gramophone and an inexhaust-
ible supply of Turkish *caz* records. Almost level with the window
and about fifty yards away was the top of a minaret belonging to
a mosque lower down the hill. It had loudspeakers in it to amplify
the voice of the *muezzin* and his call to prayer was deafening. When
Harper had made the reservation, he had obviously asked for the
cheapest room in the hotel.

I changed into a clean shirt and sat down to wait.

At six o'clock the telephone rang.

'Monsieur Simpson?' It was a man's voice with a condescending
lilt to it and an unidentifiable accent. He wasn't an Englishman or
an American.

'This is Simpson,' I answered.

'Miss Lipp's car is all right? You have had no accidents or trouble
on the journey from Athens?'

'No. The car is fine.'

'Good. Miss Lipp has a pressing engagement. This is what you are to do. You know the Hilton Hotel?'

'Yes.'

'Drive the car to the Hilton at once and put it in the car-park opposite the entrance to the hotel and behind the Kervansaray night-club. Leave the *carnet* and insurance papers in the glove compartment and the ignition key beside the driver's seat on the floor. Is it understood?'

'It is understood, yes. But who is that speaking?'

'A friend of Miss Lipp. The car should be there in ten minutes.' He rang off abruptly as if my question had been impertinent.

I sat there wondering what I ought to do. I was certainly not going to do as he had told me. The only hope I had of my making any sort of contact with the people Tufan was interested in was through the car. If I just let it go like that I would be helpless. Even without Tufan's orders to carry out I would have refused. Harper had said that I would be paid and get my letter back when the job was done. He, or someone on his behalf, would have to fulfil those conditions before I surrendered control of the car. He must have known that, too. After what had happened in Athens he could scarcely have expected me to trust to his good nature. And what had happened to all that talk of driving for Miss Lipp while she was in Turkey?

I hid the *carnet* under some shelf-lining paper on top of the wardrobe and went out. It took me about ten minutes to walk to the Hilton.

I approached the car-park briskly, swinging my keys in my hand as if I were going to pick up a car already there. I guessed that either the man who had telephoned, or someone acting on his instructions, would be waiting for the Lincoln to arrive, all ready to drive it away the instant I had gone. In Istanbul it is unwise to leave even the poorest car unlocked and unattended for very long.

I spotted him almost immediately. He was standing at the outer end of the Hilton driveway smoking a cigarette and staring into the middle distance, as if he were trying to decide whether to go straight home to his wife or visit his girl-friend first. Remembering that I would have to give Tufan his description, I took very careful note of him. He was about forty-five and thick-set with a barrel chest and a mop of crinkly grey hair above a brown puffy face. The eyes were brown, too. He was wearing a thin light-grey suit, yellow socks and plaited leather sandals. Height about five-ten, I thought.

I walked through the car-park to make sure that there were no other possibilities there, then came out the other side and walked back along the street for another glimpse of him.

He was looking at his watch. The car should have been there by then if I were following instructions.

I walked straight back to the Park Hotel. As I unlocked the door to my room I could hear the telephone inside ringing.

It was the same voice again, but peremptory now.

'Simpson? I understand that the car is not yet delivered. What are you doing?'

'Who is that speaking?'

'The friend of Miss Lipp. Answer my question, please. Where is the car?'

'The car is quite safe and will remain so.'

'What are you talking about?'

'The *carnet* is in the hotel strong-room and the car is garaged. It will remain that way until I hand it over to Mr Harper or someone holding credentials from Mr Harper.'

'The car is the property of Miss Lipp.'

'The *carnet* is in the name of Miss Lipp,' I answered; 'but the car was placed in my care by Mr Harper. I am responsible for it. I don't know Miss Lipp except by name. I don't know you *even* by name. You see the difficulty?'

'Wait.'

I heard him start to say something to someone with him: '*Il dit que...*' And then he clamped a hand over the telephone.

I waited. After a few moments he spoke again. 'I will come to your hotel. Remain there.' Without waiting for my agreement, he hung up.

I went upstairs to the foyer and told the desk clerk that I would be out on the terrace if I were wanted. The terrace was crowded, but I eventually managed to find a table and order a drink. I was quite prepared to make the contact; but I had not liked the sound of the man on the telephone, and preferred to encounter him in a public place rather than in the privacy of my room.

I had left my name with the head waiter, and after about twenty minutes I saw him pointing me out to a tall, cadaverous man with a narrow, bald head and large projecting ears. The man came over. He was wearing a cream and brown striped sports shirt and tan linen slacks. He had a long, petulant upper lip and a mouth that drooped at the corners.

'Simpson?'

'Yes.'

He sat down facing me. Brown eyes, one gold tooth left side lower jaw, gold-and-onyx signet ring on little finger of left hand; I made mental notes.

'Who are you?' I asked.

'My name is Fischer.'

'Will you have a drink, Mr Fischer?'

'No. I wish to clear this misunderstanding relative to Miss Lipp's car.'

'There is no misunderstanding in my mind, Mr Fischer,' I answered. 'My orders from Mr Harper were quite explicit.'

'Your orders were to await orders at the hotel,' he snapped. 'You have not complied with them.'

I looked respectfully apologetic. 'I am not doubting that you have a perfect right to give those orders, Mr Fischer, but I assumed, naturally, that Mr Harper would be here, or, if not here in person, that he would have given a written authorization. That is a very valuable car and I…'

'Yes, yes,' he broke in impatiently. 'I understand. The point is that Mr Harper has been delayed until tomorrow afternoon and Miss Lipp wishes her car at once.'

'I'm sorry.'

He leaned across the table towards me and I caught a whiff of after-shave lotion. 'Mr Harper would not be pleased that you put Miss Lipp to the trouble of coming to Istanbul herself to claim her car,' he said menacingly.

'I thought Miss Lipp *was* in Istanbul.'

'She is at the villa,' he said shortly. 'Now we will have no more of this nonsense, please. You and I will go and get the car immediately.'

'If you have Mr Harper's written authority, of course.'

'I have Mr Harper's authority.'

'May I see it, sir?'

'That is not necessary.'

'I'm afraid that is for me to decide.'

He sat back, breathing deeply. 'I will give you one more chance,' he said after a pause. 'Either you hand over the car immediately or steps will be taken to *compel* you to do so.'

As he said the word 'compel', his right hand came out and deliberately flicked the drink in front of me into my lap.

At that moment something happened to me. I had been through an awful twenty-four hours, of course; but I don't think it was only that. I suddenly felt as if my whole life had been spent trying to defend myself against people compelling me to do this or that, and always succeeding because they had all the power on their side; and then, just as suddenly, I realized that for once the power was mine; for once I wasn't on my own.

I picked up the glass, set it back on the table and dabbed at my trousers with my handkerchief. He watched me intently, like a boxer waiting for the other man to get to his feet after a knock-down, ready to move in for the kill.

I called the waiter over. 'If this gentleman wished to make a report about a missing car to the police, where should he go?'

'There is a police post in Taxim Square, sir.'

'Thank you. I spilled my drink. Wipe the table and bring me another, please.'

As the waiter got busy with his cloth, I looked across at Fischer. 'We could go there together,' I said. 'Or, if you would prefer it, I could go alone and explain the situation. Of course, I expect the police would want to get in touch with you. Where should I tell them to find you?'

The waiter had finished wiping the table and was moving away. Fischer was staring at me uncertainly.

'What are you talking about?' he said. 'Who said anything about the police?'

'You were talking of compelling me to hand over the car to you. Only the police could make me do that.' I paused. 'Unless, that is, you had some other sort of compulsion in mind. In that case, perhaps I should go to the police anyway.'

He did not know what to say to that. He just stared. It was all I could do not to smile. It was quite obvious that he knew perfectly well what was hidden in the car, and that the very last thing he wanted was the police taking an interest in it. Now he had to make sure that I didn't go to them.

'There is no need for that,' he said finally.

'I'm not so sure.' The waiter brought me the drink and I motioned to Fischer. 'This gentleman will pay.'

Fischer hesitated, then threw some money on the table and stood up. He was doing his best to regain control of the situation by trying to look insulted.

'Very well,' he said stiffly; 'we shall have to wait for Mr Harper's arrival. It is very inconvenient and I shall report your insubordinate behaviour to him. He will not employ you again.'

And then, of course, I had to go too far. 'When he knows how careless you can be, maybe he won't have much use for you either.'

It was a silly thing to say, because it implied that I knew that the situation was not what it appeared on the surface, and I wasn't supposed to know.

His eyes narrowed. 'What did Harper tell you about me?'

'Until tonight I didn't even know you existed. What should he have told me?'

Without answering he turned and went.

I finished my drink slowly and planned my movements for the evening. It would be best, I thought, to dine in the hotel. Apart from the fact that the cost of the meal would go on the bill, which Harper could be paying, I wasn't too keen on going out just then. Fischer had seemed to accept the situation; but there was just a chance that he might change his mind and decide to get rough after all. Tufan's men would be covering me, presumably, but I didn't know what their orders were. If someone were to beat me up it wouldn't be much consolation to know that they were standing by, taking notes. It was certainly better to stay in. The only problem was the ten o'clock telephone report. I had already noticed that the public telephones in the foyer were handled by an operator who put the calls through the hotel switchboard, so I would have to risk going out later. Unless, that is, I missed the ten o'clock call and left it until the morning at eight. The only trouble was that I would then have to explain to Tufan why I had done so, and I did not want to have to explain that I was afraid of anything that Fischer might do. My trousers were still damp where he had upset the drink over me, and I was still remembering how good it had felt to make him climb down and do what *I* wanted. I could not expect Tufan to realize how successfully I had handled Fischer if I had to start by admitting that I had been too nervous to leave the hotel afterwards.

All I could do was to minimize the risk. The nearest café I knew of was the one on the side street below my room. With so many lighted hotel windows above, the street would not be too dark for safety. The telephone would probably be on the bar, but with any luck the noise of the music would compensate for the lack of privacy. Anyway, it would have to do.

By the time I had finished dinner I was feeling so tired that I could hardly keep my eyes open. I went back to the terrace and drank brandy until it was time for the call.

As I walked from the hotel entrance to the road I had to get out of the way of a taxi and was able to glance over my shoulder casually as if to make sure that it was safe to walk on. There was a man in a chauffeur's cap about twenty yards behind me.

Because of the contours of the hill and the way the street twisted and turned, it took me longer than I had expected to get to the café.

The man in the chauffeur's cap stayed behind me. I listened carefully to his footsteps. If he had started to close in, I would have made a dash for the café; but he kept his distance, so I assumed that he was one of Tufan's men. All the same it was not a very pleasant walk.

The telephone was on the wall behind the bar. There was no coin-box and you had to ask the proprietor to get the number so that he knew what to charge you. He couldn't speak anything but Turkish, so I wrote the number down and made signs. The noise of the music wasn't as bad inside the place as it sounded from my room, but it was loud enough.

Tufan answered immediately and characteristically.

'You are late.'

'I'm sorry. You told me not to call through the hotel switchboard. I am in a café.'

'You went to the Hilton Hotel just after six. Why? Make your report.'

I told him what happened. I had to repeat the descriptions of the man at the Hilton car-park and of Fischer so that he could write them down. My report on the meeting with Fischer seemed to amuse him at first. I don't know why. I had not expected any thanks, but I felt that I had earned at least a grunt of approval for my quick thinking. Instead, he made me repeat the conversation and then began harping on Fischer's reference to a villa outside Istanbul and asking a lot of questions for which I had no answers. It was very irritating; although, of course, I didn't say so. I just asked if he had any additional orders for me.

'No, but I have some information. Harper and the Lipp woman have reservations on an Olympic Airways plane from Athens tomorrow afternoon. It arrives at four. The earliest you will hear from him probably will be an hour after that.'

'Supposing he gives me the same orders as Fischer—to hand over the car with its papers—what do I do?'

'Ask for your wages and the letter you wrote.'

'Supposing he gives them to me?'

'Then you must give up the car, but forget to bring the *carnet* and the insurance papers. Or remind him of his promise that you could work for Miss Lipp. Be persistent. Use your intelligence. Imagine that he is an ordinary tourist whom you are trying to cheat. Now, if there is nothing more, you can go to bed. Report to me again tomorrow night.'

'One moment, sir. There is something.' I had had an idea.

'What is it?'

'There is something that you could do, sir. If, before I speak to Harper, I could have a licence as an official guide with tomorrow's date on it, it might help.'

'How?'

'It would show that in the expectation of driving Miss Lipp on her tour, I had gone to the trouble and expense of obtaining the licence. It would look as if I had taken him seriously. If he or she really wanted a driver for the car it might make a difference.'

He did not answer immediately. Then he said: 'Good, very good.'

'Thank you, sir.'

'You see, Simpson, when you apply your intelligence to carrying out orders instead of seeing only the difficulties, you become effective.' It was just like The Bristle in one of his good moods. 'You remember, of course,' he went on, 'that as a foreigner you could not hold a guide's licence. Do you think Harper might know that?'

'I'm almost sure he doesn't. If he does, I can say that I bribed someone to get it. He would believe me.'

'I would believe you myself, Simpson.' He chuckled fatuously, enchanted by his own joke. 'Very well, you shall have it by noon, delivered to the hotel.'

'You will need a photograph of me for it.'

'We have one. Don't tell me you have forgotten so soon. And a word of caution. You know only a few words of Turkish. Don't attract attention to yourself so that you are asked to show the licence. It might cause trouble with museum guards. You understand?'

'I understand.'

He hung up. I paid the proprietor for the call and left.

Outside, the man in the chauffeur's cap was waiting up the street. He walked ahead of me back to the hotel. I suppose he knew why I had been to the café.

There was a guide to Istanbul on sale at the concierge's desk. I bought one with the idea of brushing up on my knowledge of the Places of Interest and how to get to them. On my way down to my room I had to laugh to myself. 'Never volunteer for anything,' my father had said. Well, I hadn't exactly volunteered for what I was doing now, but it seemed to me that I was suddenly getting bloody conscientious about it.

I spent most of the following morning in bed. Just before noon I got dressed and went up to the foyer to see if Tufan had remembered about the guide's licence. He had; it was in a sealed Ministry of Tourism envelope in my mail-box.

For a few minutes I felt quite good about that. It showed, I thought, that Tufan kept his promises and that I could rely on him to back me. Then I realized that there was another way of looking at it. I had asked for a licence and I had promptly received one; Tufan expected results and wasn't giving me the smallest excuse for not getting them.

I had made up my mind not to have any drinks that day so as to keep a clear head for Harper; but now I changed my mind. You can't have a clear head when there's a sword hanging over it. I was careful though and only had three or four *rakis*. I felt much better for them, and after lunch I went down to my room to take a nap.

I must have needed it badly because I was still asleep when the phone rang at five. I almost fell off the bed in my haste to pick it up, and the start that it gave me made my head ache.

'Arthur?' It was Harper's voice.

'Yes.'

'You know who this is?'

'Yes.'

'Car okay?'

'Yes.'

'Then what have you been stalling for?'

'I haven't been stalling.'

'Fischer says you refused to deliver the car.'

'You told me to wait for *your* instructions, so I waited. You didn't tell me to hand the car to a perfect stranger without any proof of his authority…'

'All right, all right, skip it! Where is the car?'

'In a garage near here.'

'Do you know where Sariyer is?'

'Yes.'

'Get the car right away and hit the Sariyer road. When you get to Yeniköy look at your mileage reading, then drive on towards Sariyer for exactly four more miles. On your right you'll come to a small pier with some boats tied up alongside it. On the left of the road opposite the pier you'll see a driveway entrance belonging to a villa. The name of the villa is Sardunya. Have you got that?'

'Yes.'

'You should be here in about forty minutes. Right?'

'I will leave now.'

Sariyer is a small fishing port at the other end of the Bosphorus where it widens out to the Black Sea, and the road to it from Istanbul runs along the European shore. I wondered if I should try to contact Tufan before I left and report the address I had been given, then decided against it. Almost certainly, he had had Harper followed from the airport, and in any case I would be followed to the villa. There would be no point in reporting.

I went to the garage, paid the bill and got the car. The early evening traffic was heavy and it took me twenty minutes to get out of the city. It was a quarter to six when I reached Yeniköy. The same Peugeot which had followed me down from Edirne was following me again. I slowed for a moment to check the mileage and then pushed on.

The villas of the Bosphorus vary from small waterfront holiday places, with window-boxes and little boat-houses, to things like palaces. Quite a lot of these *were* palaces once; and before the capital was moved from Istanbul to Ankara the diplomatic corps used to have summer embassy buildings out along the Bosphorus, where there are cool Black Sea breezes even when the city is sweltering. The Kösk Sardunya looked as if it had started out in some such way.

The entrance to the drive was flanked by huge stone pillars with wrought-iron gates. The drive itself was several hundred yards long and wound up the hillside through an avenue of big trees which also served to screen the place from the road below. Finally, it left the trees and swept into the gravel courtyard in front of the villa.

It was one of those white stucco wedding-cake buildings of the kind you see in the older parts of Nice and Monte Carlo. Some

French or Italian architect must have been imported around the turn of the century to do the job. It had everything—a terrace with pillars and balustrades, balconies, marble steps up to the front portico, a fountain in the courtyard, statuary, a wonderful view out over the Bosphorus—and it was huge. It was also run down. The stucco was peeling in places and some of the cornice mouldings had crumbled or broken away. The fountain basin had no water in it. The courtyard was fringed with weeds.

As I drove in, I saw Fischer get up from a chair on the terrace and go through a french window into the house. So I just pulled up at the foot of the marble steps and waited. After a moment or two, Harper appeared under the portico and I got out of the car. He came down the steps.

'What took you so long?'

'They had to make out a bill at the garage, and then there was the evening traffic.'

'Well…' He broke off as he noticed me looking past him and over his shoulder.

A woman was coming down the steps.

He smiled slightly. 'Ah yes. I was forgetting. You haven't met your employer. Honey, this is Arthur Simpson. Arthur, this is Miss Lipp.'

CHAPTER FIVE

SOME MEN CAN MAKE A GOOD GUESS AT A WOMAN'S AGE JUST by looking at her face and figure. I never can. I think that this may be because, in spite of Mum, I fundamentally respect women. Yes, it must be that. If she is very attractive, but obviously not a young girl, I always think of twenty-eight. If she has let herself go a bit, but is obviously not elderly, I think of forty-five. For some reason I never think of any ages in between those—or outside them, for that matter—except my own, that is.

Miss Lipp made me think of twenty-eight. In fact she was thirty-six; but I only found that out later. She looked twenty-eight to me. She was tall with short brownish-blonde hair, and the kind of figure that you have to notice, no matter what dress covers it. She also had the sort of eyes, insolent, sleepy and amused, and the full good-humoured mouth which tell you that she knows you can't help watching the way her body moves, and that she doesn't give a damn whether you do so or not; watching is not going to get you anywhere anyway. She wasn't wearing a dress that first time; just white slacks and sandals, and a loose white shirt. Her complexion was golden brown and the only make-up she was wearing was lipstick. Obviously, she had just bathed and changed.

She nodded to me. 'Hullo. No trouble with the car?' She had the same combination of accents as Harper.

'No, madam.'

'That's good.' She did not seem surprised.

Fischer was coming down the steps behind her. Harper glanced at him.

'Okay, Hans, you'd better run Arthur into Sariyer.' To me he said: 'You can take the ferry-boat back to town. Are the *carnet* and Green Card in the glove compartment?'

'Of course not. They are in the hotel safe.'

'I told you to put them in the glove compartment,' said Fischer angrily.

I kept my eyes on Harper. '*You* didn't tell me,' I said; 'and you didn't tell me to take orders from your servant.'

Fischer swore angrily in German, and Miss Lipp burst out laughing.

'But isn't he a servant?' I asked blandly; 'he behaved like one, though not a very good one, perhaps.'

Harper raised a repressive hand. 'Okay, Arthur, you can cut that out. Mr Fischer is a guest here and he only meant to be helpful. I'll arrange to have the documents picked up from you tomorrow before you leave. You'll be paid off when you hand them over.'

My stomach heaved. 'But I understood, sir, that I was to act as Miss Lipp's driver while she is in Turkey.'

'That's okay, Arthur. I'll hire someone locally.'

'I can drive the car,' said Fischer impatiently.

Harper and Miss Lipp both turned on him. Harper said something sharply in German and she added in English: 'Besides you don't know the roads.'

'And I do know the roads, madam.' I was trying hard to make my inner panic come out sounding like respectful indignation. 'Only today I went to the trouble and expense of obtaining an official guide's licence so that I could do the job without inconvenience to you. I was a guide in Istanbul before.' I turned to Harper and thrust the licence under his nose. 'Look, sir!'

He frowned at it and me incredulously. 'You mean you really *want* the job?' he demanded. 'I thought all you wanted was this.' He took my letter out of his pocket.

'Certainly, I want that, sir.' It was all I could do to stop myself reaching out for it. 'But you are also paying me a hundred dollars for three or four days' work.' I did my best to produce a grin. 'As I told you in Athens, sir, for that money I do not have to be persuaded to work.'

He glanced at her and she answered, with a shrug, in German. I understood the last three words: '… man English speaks.'

His eyes came to me again. 'You know, Arthur,' he said thoughtfully, 'you've changed. You could be off the hook if you wanted, but now you don't want to be off. Why?'

This was just answerable. I looked at the letter in his hand. 'You didn't send that. I was afraid all the time that you'd sent it anyway, out of spite.'

'Even though it would have cost me three hundred dollars?'

'It wouldn't have cost you anything. The cheques would have been returned to you eventually.'

'That's true.' He nodded. 'Not bad, Arthur. Now tell me what you meant when you told Mr Fischer that he'd been careless. What did you think he'd been careless about?'

They were all three waiting for my answer to that. The men's suspicion of me was in the air and Miss Lipp had smelt it as well. What was more, she didn't look in the least puzzled by what Harper was saying. Whatever the game was, they were all in it.

I did the best I could. 'Why? Because of the way he'd behaved, of course. Because he *had* been careless. Oh, he knew your name all right and he knew enough to get in touch with me, but I knew he couldn't be acting on your orders.'

'How did you know?'

I pointed to the letter. 'Because of that. You told me it was your insurance. You'd know I wouldn't turn the car over to a complete stranger without getting my letter back. He didn't even mention it.'

Harper looked at Fischer. 'You see?'

'I was only trying to save time,' said Fischer angrily. 'I have said so. This does not explain why he used that word.'

'No, it doesn't,' I said. The only way was to bull it through. 'But this does. When he started threatening me I offered to go with him to the police and settle the matter. I've never seen anyone back down so fast in my life.'

'That is a lie!' Fischer shouted; but he wasn't so sure of himself now.

I looked at Harper. 'Anyone who pulls that sort of bluff without knowing what to do when it's called is careless to my way of thinking. If Mr Fischer had been a dishonest servant instead of your helpful guest, you'd have said I'd been pretty careless to let him get away with a fourteen-thousand-dollar car. I'd be lucky if that was all you said.'

There was a brief silence, then Harper nodded. 'Well, Arthur, I guess Mr Fischer won't mind accepting your apology. Let's say it was a misunderstanding.'

Fischer shrugged.

Just what Harper thought that I was making of the situation I cannot imagine. Even if I hadn't known what was hidden in the car, I would have realized by now that there was something really fishy going on. Miss Lipp, in Turkey for a little ten-day tourist trip with a Lincoln and a villa the size of the Taj Mahal, was sufficiently improbable. The shenanigans over the delivery of the car had been positively grotesque.

However, it was soon apparent that nothing I might think or suspect was going to give Harper any sleepless nights.

'All right, Arthur,' he said, 'you've gotten yourself a deal. A hundred a week. You still have that fifty dollars I gave you?'

'Yes, sir.'

'Will that take care of the bill at the Park?'

'I think so.'

'Right. Here's the hundred you have coming for the trip down. Go back to town now. In the morning check out of the hotel. Then, take a ferry-boat back to Sariyer pier so that you get there around eleven. Someone will meet you. We'll find a room for you here.'

'Thank you, sir, but I can find a room in a hotel.'

'There isn't a hotel nearer than Sariyer, and that's too far away. You'd have to use the car to get to and fro, and it'd always be there when we wanted it here. Besides, we've got plenty of rooms.'

'Very well, sir. May I have my letter?'

He put it back in his pocket. 'Sure. When you're paid off at the end of the job. That was the deal, remember?'

'I remember,' I said grimly.

Of course, he thought that by still holding the letter over me he was making sure that I toed the line, and that, if I happened to see or hear anything that I shouldn't, I would be too scared to do anything but keep my mouth shut about it. The fact that he wasn't being as clever as he thought was no consolation to me. I wanted to get back to Athens and Nicki, but I wanted that letter first.

'You will drive,' said Fischer.

I said 'Good-night, madam,' to Miss Lipp, but she didn't seem to hear. She was already walking back up the steps with Harper.

Fischer got into the back seat. I thought at first that he merely intended, in a petty way, to show me who was boss; but, as I drove back down to the road, I saw him looking over the door panels. He was obviously still suspicious. I thanked my stars that the packing had been carefully done. It was almost comforting to see the sand-coloured Peugeot in the driving mirror.

He didn't say anything to me on the way. In Sariyer, I stopped at the pier approach and turned the car for him. Then I got out and opened the door as if he were royalty. I'd hoped it would make him feel a bit silly, but it didn't seem to. Without a word he got in behind the wheel, gave me a black look and tore off back along the coast road like a maniac.

The Peugeot had stopped and turned about a hundred yards back, and a man was scrambling out of its front passenger seat. He slammed the door and the Peugeot shot away after the Lincoln. There was a ferry-boat already at the pier, and I did not wait to see if the man who had got out followed me. I suppose he did.

I was back at the Kabatas ferry pier soon after eight and shared a *dolmus* cab going up to Taxim Square. Then I walked down to the hotel and had a drink or two.

I needed them. I had managed to do what Tufan wanted, up to a point. I was in touch with Harper and would for the moment remain so. On the other hand, by agreeing to stay at the villa I had put myself virtually *out* of touch with Tufan; at least as far as regular contact was concerned. There was no way of knowing what life at the villa was going to be like, nor what would be expected of me there. It might be easy for me to get out to a safe telephone, or it might be quite difficult. If I were seen telephoning, Harper would immediately get suspicious. Who did I know in Istanbul? What was the number? Call it again—and so on. Yet I didn't see how I could have refused to stay there. If I had argued the point any further, Harper might have changed his mind about keeping me on. Tufan couldn't have it both ways; and I made up my mind to tell him so if he started moaning at me.

I had some dinner and went down to the café beside the hotel. A man with a porter's harness on his back followed me this time.

Tufan did not moan at me as a matter of fact; but when I had finished my report he was silent for so long that I thought he'd hung up. I said: 'Hullo.'

'I was thinking,' he said; 'it will be necessary for us to meet tonight. Are you in the café in the street by the hotel?'

'Yes.'

'Wait five minutes, then go up to the hotel and walk along the street past it for about a hundred yards. You will see a small brown car parked there.'

'The Peugeot that's been following me?'

'Yes. Open the door and get in beside the driver. He will know where to take you. Is that clear?'

'Yes.'

I paid for the telephone call and bought a drink. When the five minutes were up I left.

As I approached the Peugeot, the driver leaned across and pushed open the door for me to get in. Then he drove off past the hotel and down the hill towards the Necati Bey Avenue.

He was a young, plump, dark man. The car smelt of cigarettes, hair-oil and stale food. In his job, I suppose, he had to eat most of his meals sitting in the car. There was a V.H.F. two-way taxi radio fitted under the dash and every now and again Turkish voices would squawk through the loudspeaker. He appeared not to be listening to them. After a minute or so he began to talk to me in French.

'Did you like driving the Lincoln?' he asked.

'Yes, it's a good car.'

'But too big and long. I saw the trouble you had in the narrow streets this afternoon.'

'It's very fast, though. Were you able to keep up with him when he drove back to the villa?'

'Oh, he stopped about a kilometre up the road and began looking at the doors. Did they rattle?'

'Not that I noticed. Did he stop long?'

'A minute or two. After that he did not go so fast. But this little…'

He broke off and picked up a microphone, as a fresh lot of squawks came over the radio.

'*Evet, efendi, evet,*' he answered, then put the microphone back. 'But this little machine can show those big ones a thing or two. On a narrow hill with corners I can leave them standing.'

He had turned on to the Avenue and we were running parallel to the shore.

'Where are we going?' I asked.

'I am not permitted to answer questions.'

We were passing the state entrance to the Dolmabahçe Palace now.

It was built in the last century when the Sultans gave up wearing robes and turbans and took to black frock-coats and the fez. From the sea it looks like a lakeside grand hotel imported from Switzerland; but from the road, because of the very high stone wall enclosing the grounds, it looks like a prison. There is about half a mile of this wall running along the right-hand side of the road, and just to look up at it gave me an uncomfortable feeling. It reminded me of the yard at Maidstone.

Then I saw a light high up on the wall ahead, and the driver began to slow down.

'What are we stopping here for?' I asked.

He did not answer.

The light came from a reflector flood and the beam of it shone down vertically on to an armed sentry. Behind him was a pair of huge iron-bound wooden gates. One of them was half-open.

The car stopped just short of the gates and the driver opened his door.

'We get out,' he said.

I joined him on the roadway and he led the way up to the gates. He said something to the sentry, who motioned us on. We went through the gap between the gates and turned left. There was a light burning in what I assumed was the guardroom. He led the way up a low flight of steps to the door. Inside was a bare room with a table and chair. A young lieutenant—I suppose he was orderly officer of the day—sat on the table talking to the sergeant of the guard, who was standing. As we came in, the officer stood up, too, and said something to the driver.

He turned to me. 'You have a guide's licence,' he said. 'You are to show it to this officer.'

I did so. He handed it back to me, picked up a flashlight and said in French: 'Follow me, please.'

The driver stayed behind with the sergeant of the guard. I followed the lieutenant down the steps again and across some uneven cobblestones to a narrow roadway running along the side of a building which seemed to be a barracks. The windows showed lights and I could hear the sound of voices and a radio playing *caz*. There were light posts at intervals, and, although the surface of the road was broken in places, it was just possible to see where one was walking. Then we went through a high archway out of the barracks area into some sort of garden. Here it was very dark. There was some moonlight and I could see parts of the white bulk of the palace looming to the left of us, but trees shadowed the ground. The lieutenant switched on his flashlight and told me to be careful where I walked. It was necessary advice. Restoration work seemed to be in progress. There were loose flagstones and masonry rubble everywhere. Finally, however, we came to a solidly paved walk. Ahead was a doorway and, beside it, a lighted window.

The lieutenant opened the door and went in. The light came from a janitor's room just inside, and, as the lieutenant entered, a man in a drab blue uniform came out. He had some keys in his hand. The lieutenant said something to him. The janitor answered briefly, and then, with a curious glance at me, led the way across a hall and up a staircase, switching on lights as he went. At the landing he turned off down a long corridor with a lot of closed doors along one side and grilled, uncurtained windows on the other. There was carpet on the floor with a narrow drugget running down the centre to save wear.

From the proportions of the staircase and the height of the ceilings it was obvious that we were in a large building; but there was nothing noticeably palatial about that part of it. We might have been in a provincial town hall. The walls were covered with dingy oil paintings. There seemed to be hundreds of them, mostly landscapes with cattle or battle scenes, and all with the same yellowy-brown varnish colour. I don't know anything about paintings. I suppose they must have been valuable or they would not have been in a palace; but I found them depressing, like the smell of moth-balls.

There was a pair of heavy metal doors at the end of that corridor, and beyond it more corridors and more paintings.

'We are in what used to be the palace harem now,' the lieutenant said impressively. 'The steel doors guarded it. Each woman had her

own suite of rooms. Now certain important government departments have their offices here.'

I was about to say, 'Ah, taken over by the eunuchs, you mean', but
thought better of it. He did not look as if he cared for jokes. Besides,
I had had a long day and was feeling tired. We went on through
another lot of steel doors. I was resigned to more corridors, when
the janitor stopped and unlocked the door of one of the rooms. The
lieutenant turned on the lights and motioned me in.

It was not much larger than my room at the Park, but probably the height of the ceiling and the heavy red and gold curtains
over the window made it seem smaller. The walls were hung with
patterned red silk and several large paintings. There was a parquet
floor and a white marble fireplace. A dozen gilt armchairs stood
around the walls, as if the room had just been cleared for dancing.
The desk and chairs standing in the centre looked like a party of
badly-dressed gate-crashers.

'You may sit down and you may smoke,' the lieutenant said;
'but please be careful if you smoke to put out your cigarettes in
the fireplace.'

The janitor left, shutting the door behind him. The lieutenant
sat down at the desk and began to use the telephone.

The paintings in the room were, with one exception, of the kind
I had seen in the corridors, only bigger. On one wall was a Dutch
fishing-boat in a storm; facing it, alongside a most un-Turkish group
of nymphs bathing in a woodland stream, was a Russian cavalry
charge. The painting over the fireplace, however, was undoubtedly
Turkish. It showed a bearded man in a frock-coat and fez facing
three other bearded men who were looking at him as if he had
B.O. or had said something disgusting. Two of the group wore
glittering uniforms.

When the lieutenant had finished telephoning, I asked him what the painting was about.

'That is the leaders of the nation demanding the abdication of Sultan Abdul Hamid the Second.'

'Isn't that rather a strange picture to have in a Sultan's palace?'

'Not in this palace. A greater man than any of the Sultans died here, greater even than Suleiman.' He gave me a hard, challenging look, daring me to deny it.

I agreed hastily. He went into a long rambling account of the iniquities of the Bayar-Menderes government and of the reasons why it had been necessary for the Army to clean out that rats' nest and form the Committee of National Union. Over the need to shoot down without mercy all who were trying to wreck the Committee's work, especially those members of the Democratic Party who had escaped justice at the Army's hands, he became so vehement that he was still haranguing me when Major Tufan walked into the room.

I felt almost sorry for the lieutenant. He snapped to attention, mumbling apologies like a litany. Tufan had been impressive enough in civilian clothes; in uniform and with a pistol on his belt he looked as if he were on his way to take charge of a firing squad—and looking forward keenly to the job. He listened to the lieutenant for about five seconds, then dismissed him with a flick of a hand.

As the door closed on the lieutenant, Tufan appeared to notice me. 'Do you know that President Kemal Ataturk died in this palace?' he asked.

'I gathered so from the lieutenant.'

'It was in nineteen-thirty-eight. The Director was much with him before the end and the President talked freely. One thing he said the Director has always remembered. "If I can live another fifteen years I can make Turkey a democracy. If I die sooner, it will take three generations." That young officer probably represents the type of difficulty he had in mind.' He put the briefcase on the desk and sat down. 'Now, as to your difficulties. We have both had time to think. What do you propose?'

'Until I know what it's going to be like at the villa, I don't see how I can propose anything.'

'As you are their chauffeur it will obviously be necessary for you to attend to the fuelling of the car. There is a garage outside Sariyer that you could go to. It has a telephone.'

'I had thought of that, but it may not be reliable. It depends on how much the car is used. For example, if I only drive into Istanbul and back, I can't pretend to need petrol immediately. That car takes over a hundred litres. If I were always going to the garage at a fixed time to fill up, no matter what mileage I had driven, they would become suspicious.'

'We can dispense with the fixed time. I have arranged for a twenty-four-hour watch. And even if you foresee future difficulties, you should be able to make one single call to report on them. After that, if necessary, we will use a different method. It will entail more risk for you, but that cannot be avoided. You will have to write your reports. Then you will put the report inside an empty cigarette packet. The person following you at the time—I have arranged to have the car changed every day—will then pick the reports up.'

'You mean you expect me to throw them out of the window and hope they won't notice?'

'Of course not. You will drop them whenever you find a suitable moment when you have stopped and are outside the car.'

I thought it over; that part of it might not be so bad. I would just have to make sure that I had plenty of cigarette packets. What I did not like was having to write out the reports. I said so.

'There is a slight risk, I agree,' he said; 'but you will have to take it. Remember, they will only search you if you have given them reason to suspect you. You must be careful not to.'

'I still have to write the reports.'

'You can do that in the toilet. I do not imagine you will be observed there. Now, as to our communicating information and orders to you.' He opened his briefcase and took out a small portable transistor radio of the type I had seen German tourists carrying. 'You will carry this in your bag. If it should be seen, or you should be heard using it, you will say that it was given to you by a German client. Normally it receives only standard broadcast frequencies, but this one has been modified. I will show you.' He slipped it out of the carrying case, took the back off and pointed to a small switch just by the battery compartment. 'If you operate that switch it will receive V.H.F. transmissions on a fixed frequency from up to half a mile away. The transmissions will be made to you from a surveillance car. It is a system we have tried out, and, providing there are no large obstacles such as buildings between the two points, it works. Your listening times will be seven in the morning and eleven at night. Is that clear? For security it will be better if you use the earphone attachment.'

'I see. You say it has been modified. Does that mean that it won't receive ordinary broadcasts? Because, if so, I couldn't explain it…'

'It will work normally unless you move this switch.' He replaced the back. 'Now then, I have some information for you. Both Harper and Miss Lipp are travelling on Swiss passports. We had no time at the airport to discover, without arousing suspicion, if the passports were genuine or not. The relevant particulars are as follows: Robert Karl Harper, aged thirty-eight, described as an engineer, place of birth Berne, and Elizabeth Maria Lipp, aged thirty-six, described as a student, place of birth Schaffhausen.'

'A student?'

'Anyone can be described as a student. It is meaningless. Now,
as to the Kösk Sardunya.' He referred to a paper in the briefcase. 'It
is the property of the widow of a former minister in the government of President Inönü. She is nearly eighty now and has for some
years lived quietly with her daughter in Izmir. She has from time
to time tried to sell Sardunya, but nobody has wished to buy at the
price she asks. For the past two years, she has leased it furnished to
a N.A.T.O. naval mission which had business in the zone. The mission's work ended at the beginning of the year. Her agent here in
Istanbul was unable to find another tenant until three months ago.
Then he received an inquiry from an Austrian named Fischer—yes,
exactly—who was staying at the Hilton Hotel. Fischer's other names
are Hans Andreas, and he gave an address in Vienna. He wanted a
furnished villa for two months, not a particular villa, but one in that
neighbourhood and near to the shore. He was willing to pay well
for a short lease, and gave a deposit in Swiss francs. On the lease,
which is in his name, his occupation is given as manufacturer. He
arrived three weeks ago when the lease began and has not registered
with the police. We have not yet traced the record of his entry, so
we do not have all passport particulars about him.'

'What is he a manufacturer of?'

'We do not know. We have sent an inquiry to Interpol, but I
expect a negative reply. We received negative replies on both Harper
and Lipp. That increases the probability that they are politicals.'

'Or that they are using aliases.'

'Perhaps. Now, the other personnel at the villa. There are a
husband and wife who live over what was the stabling. Their name
is Hamul and they are old servants who have been there for some
years as caretakers and who do cleaning work. Then there is the

cook. Through the owner's agent, Fischer requested a cook with experience of Italian cooking. The agent found a Turkish Cypriot named Geven who had worked in Italy. The police here have had trouble with him. He is a good cook, but he gets drunk and attacks people. He served a short prison sentence for wounding a waiter. It is believed that the agent did not know this when he recommended the man to Fischer.'

'Is there anything against the couple?'

'No. They are honest enough.' He put his papers away. 'That is all we know so far, but, as you see, the shape of a conspiracy begins to unfold. One person goes ahead to establish a base of operations, a second person arranges for the purchase of weapons, a third arrives with the means of transporting them and a prepared cover story. Probably the real leaders have not yet arrived. When they do, it will be your duty to report the fact. Meanwhile, your orders are, specifically, first to ascertain whether the weapons have been removed from the car or not, and secondly, if they have been removed, where they are cached. The first will be easy, the second may be difficult.'

'If not impossible.'

He shrugged. 'Well, you must run no risks at this stage. Thirdly, you will continue to listen for any mention of names—names of persons or places—and report movements. Finally, you will listen particularly for any political content in their conversation. The smallest hint may be of importance in that connection. That is all, I think. Have you any questions?'

'Dozens,' I said; 'only I don't know what they are at the moment.'

I could see he hadn't liked that at once. It was a bit cheeky, I suppose; but I was really tired of him.

He pursed his lips at me. 'The Director is very pleased with you so far, Simpson,' he said. 'He even spoke of the possibility of helping you in some way beyond the withdrawal of the charges against you, perhaps in connection with your papers, if your co-operation brought about a successful disposal of this matter. It is your chance. Why don't you take it?'

This boy could do better. He should be encouraged to adopt a more positive attitude towards his schoolwork. Athletics: *Fair.* Punctuality: *Fair.* Conduct: *Has left much to be desired this term.* Signed: *G. D. Brush M.A. (Oxon.)* Headmaster.

I did my best. 'What do you mean by "political context"?' I asked. 'Do you mean, are they in favour of democratic ideals? Or against a military dictatorship?—that's what some people call your government, isn't it? Do they talk about capitalist oppression or Soviet domination or the welfare of mankind? Things like that? Because, if so, I can tell you now that the only section of mankind that Harper is interested in is the bit represented by himself.'

'That could be said of a great many political conspirators. Obviously, what we are concerned with is their attitudes to the political situation here, where the Army acts at present as a trustee for the Republic.' He said that stiffly; he hadn't liked the bit about military dictatorship either. 'As I have said, Harper may be merely a hired operative, but we cannot say yet. Remember, there are six pistols and ammunition for six.'

'That's another thing I don't understand, sir. I know that there are all those grenades, too—but *pistols*? Is that enough for a *coup d'état*? If they were machine-guns now...'

'My dear Simpson, the head of a secret political organization in Belgrade once handed out four pistols to four rather stupid students. In the event only one was used, but it was used to assassinate the Archduke Ferdinand of Austria and it started a European war. Pistols can be carried in the pocket. Machine-guns cannot.'

'You think these people are out to assassinate somebody?'

'That is for you to help us discover. Have you any more questions?'

'Is there any information yet about this business machine company, Tekelek? Harper seemed to be using it as a cover.'

'We are still awaiting word from Switzerland. If it is of interest I will let you know.'

He handed me the portable radio, then, as I got up to go, went to the door and gave an order to the lieutenant waiting outside about taking me back to the gate. I had started to move when he had an afterthought and stopped me.

'One more thing,' he said: 'I do not wish you to take foolish risks, but I do wish you to feel confidence in yourself if you are obliged to take necessary ones. Some men have more confidence in themselves if they are armed.'

I couldn't help glancing at the polished pistol-holster on his belt. He smiled thinly. 'This pistol is part of an officer's uniform. You may borrow it if you wish. You could put it in your bag with the radio.'

I shook my head. 'No, thank you. It wouldn't make me feel better. Worse, more likely. I'd be wondering how to explain it away if anyone happened to see it.'

'You are probably wise. Very well, that is all.'

Of course, I hadn't the slightest intention of taking any sort of risk if I could help it. All I intended to do was to go through the motions of co-operating so as to keep Tufan happy, and somehow get my letter back from Harper before Tufan's people pulled him in. Of course, I was quite certain that he was going to be pulled in. He *had* to be!

Tufan stayed behind, telephoning. As I went back along the corridors with the lieutenant, I saw him glancing at me, wondering if it were better to make polite conversation with someone who seemed on such good terms with the powerful Major Tufan, or to say nothing and keep his nose clean. In the end, all he said was a courteous good-night.

The Peugeot was still outside. The driver glanced at the radio I was carrying. I wondered if he knew about the modification, but he made no comment on it. We drove back to the hotel in silence. I thanked him and he nodded amiably, patting the wheel of his car. 'Better on the narrow roads,' he said.

The terrace was closed. I went to the bar for a drink. I had to get the taste of the Dolmabahçe out of my mouth.

'Conspiracy,' Tufan had said. Well, that much I was prepared to concede. The whole Harper-Lipp-Fischer set-up was obviously a cover for something; but all this cloak and dagger stuff about *coups d'état* and assassination plots I really couldn't swallow. Even sitting in the palace with a painting about a Sultan being deposed staring down from the wall, it had bothered me. Sitting in a hotel bar with a glass of brandy—well, frankly I didn't believe a bloody word of it. The point was that I knew the people concerned—or, anyway, I had met them—and Tufan didn't know and hadn't met any of them. 'Political context', for Heaven's sake! Suddenly, Major Tufan appeared in my mind's eye not as a man in charge of a firing squad, but as a military old maid always looking for secret agents and assassins under her bed—a typical counter-espionage man in fact.

For a moment or two I almost enjoyed myself. Then I remembered the doors of the car and the arms and the respirators and the grenades, and went back to zero.

If it hadn't been for those things, I thought, I could have made two good guesses about the Harper set-up, and one of them would certainly have been right. My first guess would have been narcotics. Turkey is an opium-producing country. If you had the necessary technical personnel—Fischer, the 'manufacturer', Lipp, the 'student'—all you would need would be a quiet, secluded place like the Kösk Sardunya in which to set up a small processing plant to make heroin, and an organizer—Harper, of course—to handle distribution and sales.

My second guess would have been some *de luxe* variation of the old badger game. It begins in the romantic villa on the Bosphorus graced by the beautiful, blue-blooded Princess Lipp, whose family once owned vast estates in Rumania, her faithful servitor Andreas (Fischer), and a multi-millionaire sucker enslaved by the lady's beauty. Then, just as the millionaire is preparing to dip his wick, in comes the mad, bad, dangerous husband Prince (Harper) Lipp, who threatens to spread the whole story (with pictures, no doubt) over the front pages of every newspaper from Istanbul to Los Angeles, *unless...* The millionaire can't wait to pay up and get out. Curtain.

On the whole, though, I would have made narcotics the first choice. Not that I didn't see Harper as a con man, or in the role of blackmailer (I knew all too well that he could play that), but the cost and extent of the preparatory work suggested that big profits were expected. Unless the supply of gullible millionaires had suddenly increased in the Istanbul area, it seemed more likely that the expectation was based on the promise of a successful narcotics operation.

It seemed to me so obviously the right answer that I began to think again about the grenades and pistols. Supposing they did fit into the narcotics picture after all, but in a subsidiary sort of way. Supposing they had no direct relationship to Harper, but had been carried for someone *outside* the villa group—someone Turkish with political intentions of the kind in which Tufan was interested. The narcotics picture had to include a supplier of illicit raw opium. Almost certainly that supplier would be Turkish. Why shouldn't the price for his illicit opium have included a small shipment of illicit arms? No reason at all. Or the delivery of the arms might merely have been one of those little gestures of goodwill with which businessmen sometimes like to sweeten their contractual relationships. 'I'm bringing a car in anyway. Why not let me take care of that other little matter for you? Just give me a letter to your man in Athens.'

There was only one thing that I could see that was not quite right about it—the time factor. The villa had been taken on a short lease. The car had been imported on a tourist *carnet*. I didn't know how long it took to set up a laboratory and process enough heroin to make a killing in the dope market; but, on the face of it, two months seemed a bit short. I decided in the end that, for safety, they might well want to avoid remaining for too long in any one place and intended to keep the laboratory on the move.

I think I knew, secretly, that it wasn't a highly convincing explanation; but, at that moment, it was the best that I could think of, and until a better one occurred to me I was prepared to be uncritical. I liked my arms-for-opium theory. At least it held out a promise of release. When Tufan realized that, as far as the arms were concerned, Harper was only an intermediary, his interest must shift from the villa group to someone somewhere else. My usefulness would be at an end. Harper would accept my resignation with a shrug, return my letter and pay me off. Tufan's delighted Director would help me over my papers. A few hours later I would be back in Athens, safe and sound.

I remembered that I hadn't yet written to Nicki. Before I went to bed, I bought a postcard from the concierge and wrote a few lines. *'Still on Lincoln job. Money good. Should last a few more days. Home mid-week latest. Be good. Love, Papa.'*

I didn't put the villa address, because that would have made her curious. I didn't want to have to answer a lot of questions when I got back. Even when I've had a good time, I don't like having to talk about it. Good or bad, what's over's done with. Anyway, there was no point really in giving an address. I knew she wouldn't write back to me.

The following morning I went out early, bought a dozen packets of cigarettes and then looked for a shop which sold tools. If I were to make sure that the stuff had been removed from the car doors I would have to look inside at least one of them. The only trouble was that the screws which fastened the leather panels had Phillips heads. If I tried to use an ordinary screwdriver on them, there would be a risk of making marks or possibly scratching the leather.

I could not find a tool shop, so, in the end, I went to the garage off Taxim Square, where they knew me, and persuaded the mechanic there to sell me a Phillips. Then I went back to the hotel, paid my bill and took a taxi to the ferry pier. There was no sign of the Peugeot following.

A ferry-boat came in almost immediately and I knew that I was going to be early at Sariyer. In fact, I was twenty minutes early, so I was all the more surprised to see the Lincoln coming along the road as the boat edged into the pier.

Miss Lipp was driving.

CHAPTER SIX

A S I CAME OFF THE PIER, SHE GOT OUT OF THE CAR. SHE WAS wearing a light yellow cotton dress that did even less to obscure the shape of her body than the slacks and shirt I had seen her in the day before. She had the keys of the car in her hand, and, as I came up, she handed them to me with a friendly smile.

'Good morning, Arthur.'

'Good morning, madam. It's good of you to meet me.'

'I want to do some sight-seeing. Why don't you put your bag in the trunk for now, then we won't have to stop off at the villa?'

'Whatever you say, madam.' I put my bag down and went to hold the rear door open for her, but she was already walking round to the front passenger seat, so I had to scuttle round to get to that door ahead of her.

When she was installed, I hurriedly put my bag in the luggage compartment and got into the driving seat. I was sweating slightly, not only because it was a warm day, but also because I was flustered. I had expected Fischer to meet me with the car; I had expected to go straight to the villa, to be told where I would sleep, to be given a moment to orient myself, a chance to think and time to plan. Instead, I was on my own with Miss Lipp, sitting where she had been sitting until a few moments ago, and smelling the scent she used. My hand shook a little as I put the ignition key in, and I felt I had to say something to cover my nerves.

'Isn't Mr Harper joining you, madam?'

'He had some business to attend to.' She was lighting a cigarette. 'And by the way, Arthur,' she went on, 'don't call me madam. If you have to call me something, the name's Lipp. Now, tell me what you have on the tour menu.'

'Is this your first time in Turkey, Miss Lipp?'

'First in a long time. All I remember from before is mosques. I don't think I want to see any more mosques.'

'But you would like to begin with Istanbul?'

'Oh yes.'

'Did you see the Seraglio?'

'Is that the old palace where the Sultans' harem used to be?'

'That's it.' I smiled inwardly. When I had been a guide in Istanbul before, it had been the same. Every woman tourist was always interested in the harem. Miss Lipp, I thought to myself, was no different.

'All right,' she said, 'let's go see the Seraglio.'

I was regaining my composure now. 'If I may make a suggestion.'

'Go ahead.'

'The Seraglio is organized as a museum now. If we go straight there we shall arrive before it opens. I suggest that I drive you first to the famous Pierre Loti café, which is high up on a hill just outside the city. There you could have a light lunch in pleasant surroundings and I could take you to the Seraglio afterwards.'

'What time would we get there?'

'We can be there soon after one o'clock.'

'Okay, but I don't want to be later.'

That struck me as rather odd, but I paid no attention. You do get the occasional tourist who wants to do everything by the clock. She just had not impressed me as being of that type.

I started up and drove back along the coast road. I looked for the Peugeot, but it wasn't there that day. Instead, there was a grey Opel with three men in it. When we got to the old castle at Rumelihisari, I stopped and told her about the blockade of Constantinople by

Sultan Mehmet Fatih in 1453, and how he had stretched a great chain boom across the Bosphorus there to cut off the city. I didn't tell her that it was possible to go up to the main keep of the castle because I didn't want to exhaust myself climbing up all those paths and stairs; but she didn't seem very interested anyway, so, in the end, I cut the patter short and pushed on. After a while, it became pretty obvious that she wasn't really much interested in anything in the way of ordinary sight-seeing. At least, that was how it seemed at the time. I don't think she was bored, but when I pointed places out to her she only nodded. She asked no questions.

It was different at the café. She made me sit with her at a table outside under a tree and order *raki* for us both; then she began asking questions by the dozen, not about Pierre Loti, the Turkophile Frenchman, but about the Seraglio.

I did my best to explain. To most people, the word 'palace' means a single very big building planned to house a monarch. Of course, there are usually a few smaller buildings around it, but the big building is the Palace. Although the word 'seraglio' really means 'palace', it isn't at all like one. It is an oval-shaped walled area over two miles in circumference, standing on top of the hill above Seraglio Point at the entrance to the Bosphorus; and it is a city within a city. Originally, or at least from the time of Suleiman the Magnificent until the mid-nineteenth century, the whole central government, ministers and high civil servants, as well as the Sultan of the time, lived and worked in it. There were household troops and a cadet school as well as the Sultan's harem inside the walls. The population was generally over five thousand, and there was always new building going on. One reason for this was a custom of the Ottomans. When a new Sultan came to the throne, he naturally inherited all the wealth and property accumulated by his father; but he could not take the personalized property for his own personal use without losing face. Consequently, all the old regalia had to be stored away and new pieces made, a new summer palace had to be built and, of course, new private apartments inside the Seraglio, and a new mosque. As I say, this went on well into the nineteenth century. So the Seraglio today is a vast rabbit-warren of reception rooms, private apartments, pavilions, mosques, libraries, gateways, armouries, barracks and so on, interspersed by a few open courtyards and gardens. There are no big buildings in the 'palace' sense. The two biggest single structures happen to be the kitchens and the stables.

Although the guide-books try to explain all this, most tourists don't seem to understand it. They think 'seraglio' means 'harem' anyway and all they are interested in apart from that is the 'Golden Road', the passage that the chosen girls went along to get from the harem to the Sultan's bed. The harem area isn't open to the public as a matter of fact, but I always used to take the tourists I had through the Mustafa Pasha pavilion at the back and tell them that that was part of the harem. They never knew the difference, and it was something they could tell their friends.

Miss Lipp soon got the idea, though. I found that she knew something about Turkish history; for instance, who the Janissaries had been. For someone who, only an hour or so earlier, had been asking if the Seraglio was the old palace, that was a little surprising. At the time, I suppose, I was too busy trying to answer her other questions to pay much attention. I had shown her the guide-book plan and she was going through all the buildings marked on it.

'The White Eunuchs' quarters along here, are they open?'

'Only these rooms near the Gate of Felicity in the middle.'

'The Baths of Selim the Second—can we see them?'

'That is part of the museum now. There is a collection of glass and silverware there, I think.'

'What about the Hall of the Pantry?'

'I think that building has the administration offices in it now.'

Some of the questions I couldn't answer at all, even vaguely, but she still kept on. Finally, she broke off, swallowed her second *raki* at a gulp and looked across at me.

'Are you hungry, Arthur?'

'Hungry? No, Miss Lipp, not particularly.'

'Why don't we go to the palace right now, then?'

'Certainly, if you wish.'

'Okay. You take care of the check here. We'll settle later.'

I saw the eyes of one or two men sitting in the café follow her as she went back to the car, and I noticed them glancing at me as I paid for the drinks. Obviously they were wondering what the relationship was—father, uncle or what? It was oddly embarrassing. The trouble was, of course, that I didn't know what to make of Miss Lipp and couldn't decide what sort of attitude to adopt towards her. To add to the confusion, a remark Harper had made at the Club in Athens, about Nicki's legs being too short, kept coming into my mind. Miss Lipp's legs were particularly long, and, for some reason, that was irritating as well as exciting; exciting because I couldn't help wondering what difference long legs would make in bed; irritating because I knew damn well that I wasn't going to be given the chance to find out.

I drove her to the Seraglio and parked in what used to be the Courtyard of the Janissaries, just outside the Ortakapi Gate by the Executioner's block. As it was so early, there were only two or three other cars besides the Lincoln. I was glad of that, because I was able to get off my piece about the gate without being overheard by official guides with other parties. The last thing I wanted at that moment was to have my guide's licence asked for and challenged.

The Ortakapi Gate is a good introduction to the 'feel' of the Seraglio. 'It was here at this gate that the Sultans used to stand to watch the weekly executions. The Sultan stood just there. You see the block where the beheading was done. Now, see that little fountain built in the wall there? That was for the Executioner to wash the blood off himself when he had finished. He was also the Chief Gardener. By the way, this was known as the Gate of Salvation. Rather ironic, don't you think? Of course, only high palace dignitaries who had offended the Sultan were beheaded here. When princes of the royal house were executed—for instance, when a new Sultan had all his younger brothers killed off to prevent arguments about the succession—their blood could not be shed, so they were strangled with a silk cord. Women who had offended were treated in a different way. They were tied up in weighted sacks and dropped into the Bosphorus. Shall we go inside now?'

Until Miss Lipp, I had never known it to fail.

She gave me a blank stare. 'Is any of that true, Arthur?'

'Every word of it.' It *is* true, too.

'How do you know?'

'Those are historic facts, Miss Lipp.' I had another go. 'In fact, one of the Sultans got bored with his whole harem and had them all dumped into the Bosphorus. There was a shipwreck off Seraglio Point soon after, and a diver was sent down. What he saw there almost scared him to death. There were all those weighted sacks standing in a row on the bottom and swaying to and fro with the current.'

'Which Sultan?'

Naturally, I thought it was safe to guess. 'It was Murad the Second.'

'It was Sultan Ibrahim,' she said. 'No offence, Arthur, but I think we'd better hire a guide.'

'Whatever you say, Miss Lipp.'

I tried to look as if I thought it a good idea, but I was really quite angry. If she had asked me right out whether I was an historical expert on the Seraglio, I would have told her, quite frankly, that I was not. It was the underhand way in which she had set out to trap me that I didn't like.

We went through the gate, and I paid for our admissions and selected an English-speaking guide. He was solemn and pedantic, of course, and told her all the things I had already explained all over again; but she did not seem to mind. From the way she bombarded him with questions you would have thought she was going to write a book about the place. Of course, that flattered him. He had a grin like an ape.

Personally, I find the Seraglio rather depressing. In Greece, the old buildings, even when they are in ruins and nothing much has been done in the way of restoration, always seem to have a clean, washed look about them. The Seraglio is stained, greasy and dilapidated. Even the trees and shrubs in the main courtyards are neglected, and the so-called Tulip Garden is nothing but a scrubby patch of dirt.

As far as Miss Lipp was concerned, though, the place might have been Versailles. She went everywhere, through the kitchens, through the museum rooms, the exhibition of saddles, this kiosk, that pavilion, laughing at the guide's standard jokes and scuffing her shoes on the broken paving stones. If I had known what was going on in her mind, of course, I would have felt differently; but as it was,

I became bored. After a bit, I gave up following them everywhere and just took the short cuts.

I was looking forward to a sit-down by the Gate of the Fountain while they 'did' the textiles exhibition, when she called me over.

'Arthur, how long will it take us to get to the airport from here?'

I was so surprised that I must have looked at her a bit blankly. 'The airport?'

She put on a slight heaven-give-me-patience look. 'Yes, Arthur, the airport. Where the planes arrive. How long from here?'

The guide, who hadn't been asked, said: 'Forty minutes, *madame.*'

'Better allow forty-five, Miss Lipp,' I said, ignoring him.

She looked at her watch. 'The plane gets in at four,' she said. 'I tell you what, Arthur. You go get yourself a sandwich or something. I'll meet you where you parked the car in an hour. Right?'

'As you wish, Miss Lipp. Are we meeting someone at the airport?'

'If that's all right with you.' Her tone was curt.

'I only meant that if I knew the line and flight number I could check if the plane is going to be on time.'

'So you could, Arthur. I didn't think of that. It's Air France from Geneva.'

I was in the sunshine of her smile again, the bitch.

There was a restaurant of sorts near the Blue Mosque, and when I had ordered some food I telephoned Tufan.

He listened to my report without comment until I had finished. 'Very well,' he said then, 'I will see that the passports of the Geneva passengers are particularly noted. Is that all?'

'No.' I started to tell him my theory about the drug operation and its necessary link with a raw opium supplier, but almost at once he began interrupting.

'Have you new facts to support this?'

'It fits the information we have.'

'Any imbecile could think of ways of interpreting the information we have. It is the information we do not have that I am interested in. Your business is to get it, and that is all you should be thinking about.'

'Nevertheless...'

'You are wasting time. Report by telephone, or as otherwise arranged, and remember your listening times. Now, if that is all, I have arrangements to make.'

The military mind at work! Whether he was right or wrong (and, as it happens, he was both right *and* wrong) made no difference. It was the arrogance of the man I couldn't stand.

I ate a disgusting meal of lukewarm mutton stew and went back to the car. I was angry with myself, too.

I have to admit it; what had really exasperated me was not so much Tufan's anxiety-bred offensiveness as my own realization that the train of thought which had seemed so logical and reasonable the previous night was not looking as logical and reasonable in the morning. My conception of the 'student' Miss Lipp as a laboratory technician was troublesome enough; but speaking again with Tufan had reminded me that the villa, which I had so blithely endowed with a clandestine heroin-manufacturing plant, also housed an elderly married couple and a cook. So that, in addition to the time factor improbability, I now had to accept another: either the plant was to be so small that the servants would not notice it, or Harper counted on buying their discretion.

Then, in sheer desperation, I did something rather silly. I felt that I had to know if the grenades and pistols were still in the car. If they had been taken out, at least one bit of my theory was still just tenable. I could assume that they had been delivered or were in process of delivery to the persons who wanted them.

I had about twenty minutes to spare before Miss Lipp came out of the Seraglio; but in case she was early I drove the car to the other end of the courtyard under some trees opposite the church of St Irene. Then I got the Phillips screwdriver out of my bag and went to work on the door by the driver's seat.

I wasn't worried about anyone seeing me. After all, I was only carrying out Tufan's orders. The men in the Opel wouldn't interfere; and, if some cab-driver became inquisitive, I could always pretend that I was having trouble with a door lock. All that mattered was the time, because I had to do it carefully to avoid making marks.

I loosened all the screws carefully first, and then began to remove them. It seemed to take an age. And then a horrible thing happened. Just as I was taking out the last screw but one, I happened to glance up and saw Miss Lipp with the guide walking across the courtyard from the alleyway leading to the Archaeological Museum.

I knew at once that she had seen the car because she was walking straight towards it. She was about two hundred yards away, and on the opposite side of the car to the door I had been working on, but I knew that I couldn't get even one of the screws back in time. Besides, I was not in the place she had told me to be. There was only one thing I could do: stuff the screws and screwdriver into my pocket, start the car, drive around the courtyard to meet her and hope to God the two loose screws would hold the panel in place when I opened the door to get out.

I had one piece of luck. The guide practically fell over himself opening her door for her, so I didn't have to open the one on my side. I was able to get my apology in at the same time.

'I'm sorry, Miss Lipp. I thought you might be visiting the Saint Irene Church and I wanted to save you the walk back.'

That got by all right because she couldn't thank the guide and answer me at the same time. The guide was an unexpected help, too, as he immediately asked her if she would like to see the church, 'pure Byzantine, built in the reign of Justinian, and of great historical interest'.

'I'll leave that for another time,' she said.

'But you will be here tomorrow, *madame*, when the Treasury Museum is on view?'

'Well, maybe.'

'Otherwise, it must be Thursday, *madame*. That part and the pictures are on view only two days in the week, when all the other rooms are closed.' He was obviously panting for her to come again. I wondered how much she had tipped him.

'I'll try and make it tomorrow. Thank you again.' She gave him the smile. To me, she said: 'Let's go.'

I drove off. As soon as we got on to the cobbles the panel started to vibrate. I immediately pressed my knee against it and the vibration stopped; but I was really scared now. I didn't think that she would notice that the screws were out; but Fischer or Harper certainly would, and there was this unknown we were going to meet. I knew that I had somehow to replace the screws while the car was at the airport.

'Is the plane on time?' she asked.

A donkey cart came rattling out of a side street at that moment, and I made a big thing of braking and swerving out of its way. I didn't have to pretend that the cart had shaken me up. I was shaken up all right. My call to Tufan and the argument with him had made me forget completely about calling the airline. I did the best I could.

'They didn't know of any delay,' I said; 'but the plane was making an intermediate stop. Would you like me to check again?'

'No, it's not worth it now.'

'Did you enjoy the Seraglio, Miss Lipp?' I thought if I kept talking it might quieten my stomach down a bit.

'It was interesting.'

'The Treasury is worth seeing, too. Everything the Sultans used was covered with jewels. Of course, a great many of the things were gifts from kings and emperors who wanted to impress the Sultans with their greatness. Even Queen Victoria sent things.'

'I know.' She chuckled. 'Clocks and cut glass.'

'But some of the things are really incredible, Miss Lipp. There are coffee cups sculptured out of solid amethyst, and, you know, the largest emerald in the world is there on the canopy of one of the thrones. They even did mosaic work with rubies and emeralds instead of marble.' I went on to tell her about the gem-encrusted baldrics. I gave her the full treatment. In my experience every normal woman likes talking about jewels. But she didn't seem much interested.

'Well,' she said, 'they can't be worth much.'

'All those hundreds and thousands of jewels, Miss Lipp!' My leg was getting stiff trying to stop the panel vibrating. I wriggled surreptitiously into a new position.

She shrugged. 'The guide told me that the reason they have to close some rooms on the days they open up the others is because they're understaffed. The reason they're understaffed is because the government hasn't the money to spend. That's why the place is so shabby, too. Pretty well all of the money they have for restoration goes into the older, the Byzantine buildings. Besides, if all those stones were real gems they'd be in a strong-room, not a museum. You know, Arthur, quite a lot of these old baubles turn out in the end to be just obsidian and garnet.'

'Oh these are real gems, Miss Lipp.'

'What's the biggest emerald in the world look like, Arthur?'

'Well it's pear-shaped, and about the size of a pear, too.'

'Smooth or cut?'

'Smooth.'

'Couldn't it be green tourmaline?'

'Well, I suppose I don't know really, Miss Lipp. I'm not an expert.'

'Do you care *which* it is?'

I was getting bored with this. 'Not much, Miss Lipp,' I answered. 'It just makes a more interesting story if it's an emerald.'

She smiled. 'It makes a more amusing story if it's not. Have you ever been to the mysterious East?'

'No, Miss Lipp.'

'But you've seen pictures. Do you know what makes those tall pagodas glitter so beautifully in the moonlight?'

'No, Miss Lipp.'

'They're covered with little pieces of broken bottle glass. And the famous emerald Buddha in Bangkok isn't emerald at all; it's carved from a block of ordinary green jasper.'

'Little known facts,' I thought. 'Why don't you send it in to the *Reader's Digest*?' I didn't say it, though.

She took a cigarette from the gold case in her bag and I fumbled in my pocket for matches; but she had a gold lighter, too, and didn't notice the matches I held out to her. 'Have you always done this sort of work?' she asked suddenly.

'Driving? No, Miss Lipp. Most of my life I have been a journalist. That was in Egypt. When the Nasser crowd took over, things became impossible. It was a matter of starting again.' Simple, straight-forward—a man who has suffered the slings and arrows of outrageous fortune but wasn't looking for anyone's shoulder to weep on.

'I was thinking about the traveller's cheques,' she said. 'Is that what you meant by "starting again"?'

'I'm sorry Mr Harper had to tell you about that.' It was no surprise, of course, that Harper had told her; but with so many other things on my mind—driving, keeping the door panel from rattling, cramp in my leg and wondering how the hell I was going to replace the screws—all I could think of was that obvious reply.

'Did you think he wouldn't tell me?' she went on.

'I didn't think about it either way, Miss Lipp.'

'But since he did tell me and since you're driving this car, that must mean that I don't mind too much about things like that, mustn't it?'

For one idiotic moment I wondered if she were making some sort of pass at me; but it was a brief moment.

'I suppose so,' I answered.

'And that Mr Harper doesn't mind either?'

'Yes.'

'And that, in fact, we're all very sensible, tolerant persons?'

I couldn't help glancing at her. She was watching me in her amused, considering way, but there was nothing sleepy about her eyes now. They were steadily intent.

And then I got the message. I was being sounded, either to discover what I had made of the set-up and if they had left any shirt-tails showing, or to find out if I could be trusted in some particular way. I knew that how I answered would be very important indeed to me; but I didn't know what to say. It was no use pretending to be stupid any more, or trying to avoid the issue. A test was being applied. If I failed it, I was out—out with Harper, out with Tufan and his Director, out with the Turkish customs and, in all probability, out with the Greek police as well.

I felt my face getting red and knew that she would notice. That decided me. People get red when they feel guilty or nervous; but they also get red when they are angry. In order not to seem nervous or guilty, all I could do was to seem angry.

'Including Mr Fischer?' I asked.

'What about Mr Fischer?'

'Is he sensible, too, Miss Lipp?'

'Does that matter?'

I glanced at her again. 'If my personal safety—safety from some sort of bad luck, let us say—depended on Fischer's being sensible, I'd be quite worried.'

'Because he upset a drink over you?'

'Ah, he told you that, did he? No, that was only stupid. I'd be worried because he was careless, because he gave himself away.'

'Only himself?' There was quite an edge to her voice now. I knew that I had gone far enough.

'What else is there to give away, Miss Lipp?' *I am wary but not treacherous, Miss Lipp. I watch my own interests, Miss Lipp, but I know how to be discreet, too, no matter how phony the set-up looks.*

'What indeed?' she said shortly.

She said no more. The test was over. I did not know whether I had passed or not; but there was nothing more that I could do, and I was glad of the relief. I hoped she would not notice that I was sweating.

We arrived at the airport ten minutes before the plane was due. She got out and went into the arrivals section, leaving me to find a place to park. I quickly did the two loose screws up before I went to join her.

She was at the Air France counter.

'Fifteen minutes to wait,' she said.

'And at least another fifteen before they get through customs,' I reminded her. 'Miss Lipp, you have had no lunch. The café here is quite clean. Why not wait there and have some cakes and tea? I will keep a check on the plane and arrange for a porter to be ready. When the passengers are in customs I will let you know.'

She hesitated, then, to my relief, nodded. 'All right, you do that.'

'May I ask who it is that we are meeting?'

'Mr Miller.'

'I will take care of everything.'

I showed her where the café was, hung around long enough to make sure that she was going to stay there, and then hurried back to the car.

I was sweating so much by this time that my fingers kept slipping on the screwdriver. In fact, I did what I had been trying hard to avoid doing and scratched the leather; but it couldn't be helped. I rubbed some spit on the place and hoped for the best. The Opel was parked about a dozen yards away and I could see the men in it watching me. They probably thought I'd gone mad.

When the last screw was in place, I put the screwdriver back in my bag and went inside again to the Air France counter. The plane was just landing. I found a porter, gave him five lira and told him about Mr Miller. Then I went to the men's room and tried to stop myself sweating by running cold water over my wrists. It helped a little. I cleaned myself up and went back to the café.

'The passengers are beginning to come through now, Miss Lipp.'

She picked up her bag. 'Take care of the check, will you, Arthur?'

It took me a minute or two to get the waiter's attention, so I missed the meeting between Miss Lipp and Mr Miller. They were already on their way out to the car when I saw them. The porter was carrying two pieces of luggage, one suitcase and one smaller bag. I went ahead and got the luggage compartment open.

Mr Miller was about sixty with a long neck and nose, lined grey cheeks and a bald head with brown blotches on the skin. The backs of his hands had blotches, too. He was very thin and his light tussore suit flapped as he walked as if it had been made for someone with more flesh to cover. He had rimless glasses, pale lips, a toothy smile and that fixed stare ahead which says: 'You'll have to get out of my way, I'm afraid, because I haven't the time to get out of yours.'

As they came up to the car Miss Lipp said: 'This is Arthur Simpson who's driving for us, Leo.'

Before I could even say 'good afternoon' he had handed me the raincoat he had been carrying over his arm. 'Good, good,' he said and climbed into the back seat. She smiled slightly as she got in after him, though not at me, to herself.

The coat smelt of lavender water. I put it with the luggage, tipped the porter again and got into the driving seat.

'To the villa, Miss Lipp?'

'Yes, Arthur.'

'Wait a minute.' It was Miller. 'Where is my coat?'

'With your luggage, sir.'

'It will get dirty in there. It should be on a seat in here.'

'Yes, sir.'

I got out again and retrieved the coat.

'What a fuss you make, Leo,' I heard her say. 'The car's quite clean.'

'The baggage in there is not clean. It has been in the belly of a plane with other baggage. It has been on the floor and table of the customs place. It has been handled by the man who searched it, handled again by the porter. Nothing is clean.' His accent had no American inflections, and he couldn't pronounce his 'th's'. I thought he might be French.

I draped the coat over the back of the seat in front of him. 'Will that be all right, sir?'

'Yes, of course,' he said impatiently.

That type is always the same. *They* make the difficulties and then behave as if *you're* the one who's being the nuisance.

'Let's go, Arthur,' said Miss Lipp. Her tone was noncommittal. I couldn't tell whether she found him tiresome or not. I watched them in the driving mirror.

As soon as we were clear of the airport, he settled back and looked her over in a fatherly way.

'Well, my dear, you're looking healthy. How are Karl and Giulio?'

'Karl's fine. Giulio we haven't seen yet. He's with the boat. Karl was thinking of going over there tomorrow.'

'Have you anything planned for them?'

'We thought you might like to do a little sight-seeing. That is unless you're tired.'

'You are more considerate than a daughter, my dear.' The teeth leered at her and the pale eyes behind the rimless glasses flickered towards my back.

I had already realized that this was a conversation conducted solely for my benefit, but now I saw her face stiffen. She knew that I was listening hard and was afraid that he was overdoing it.

'You must persuade Arthur to show you around the Seraglio Palace,' she said. 'He is quite an authority on it. Isn't that right, Arthur?'

That was as good as telling me that the old fool would believe any cock-and-bull story I cared to tell him. On the other hand it must be telling him something, too; perhaps warning him that the driver wasn't such a fool as he looked. I had to be careful.

'I would be happy to show Mr Miller what there is to see,' I said.

'Well, we must certainly think about that,' he replied; 'certainly, we must think about it.'

He glanced at her to see if he had said the right thing. A sentence of my father's came into my mind: 'One moment they're all full of piss and wind and the next moment…' At that point he would make a raspberry sound with his tongue. Vulgar, of course, but there was never any doubt about the kind of man he meant.

Mr Miller kept quiet after that. Once or twice she pointed out places of interest, in the manner of a hostess with a newly arrived guest; but the only thing he asked about was the tap water at the villa. Was it safe to drink or was there bottled water available? There was bottled water, she told him. He nodded, as if that had confirmed his worst fears, and said that he had brought plenty of Entero Vioforme for intestinal prophylaxis.

We reached the villa a little after five. Miss Lipp told me to sound the horn as I went up the drive.

The reception committee consisted of Harper and Fischer. Hovering in the background, ready to carry luggage, was an old man wearing an apron whom I took to be Hamul, the resident caretaker.

Tufan had said that Fischer was the lessee of the villa, but there was no doubt who was the real host there. All Fischer received from the incoming guest was a nod of recognition. Harper got a smile and an 'Ah, my dear Karl'. They shook hands with business-like cordiality, and then Harper, Miller and Miss Lipp went straight into the house. To Fischer were left the menial tasks of telling Hamul where Miller's bags were to go, and of showing me where to put the car and where I was to sleep.

At the back of the villa there was a walled stable yard. Part of the stabling had been converted into a garage with room for two cars. It was empty except for a Lambretta motor-scooter.

'The Lambretta belongs to the cook,' Fischer said; 'see that he does not steal gasoline from the car.'

I followed him across the yard to the rear entrance of the house.

Inside, I had a brief glimpse of the polished wood flooring of a passage beyond the small tiled hallway, before he led the way up a narrow staircase to the top floor. All too obviously we were in the old servants' quarters. There were six small attic cubicles with bare wood floors, bare wood partition walls and a single skylight in the roof for all of them. The sanitary arrangements consisted of an earthenware sink with a water tap in the wall at the head of the stairs. It was stiflingly hot under the low roof and there were dust and cobwebs everywhere. Two of the cubicles showed signs of having been swept out recently. Each contained an iron bedstead with a mattress and grey blankets. In one there was a battered composition leather suitcase. Fischer showed me the other.

'You will sleep here,' he said. 'The chef has the next bed. You will eat your meals with him in the kitchen.'

'Where is the toilet?'

'There is a *pissoir* across the yard in the stables.'

'And the bathroom?'

He waved his hand towards the sink. He was watching my face and enjoying himself just a bit too obviously. I guessed that this had been his own wonderful idea of a punishment for the crime of calling him a servant, and that Harper probably did not know of it. In any case, I had to protest. Without some privacy, especially at night, I could neither use the radio nor write reports.

I had put my bag down on the floor to rest my arm. Now I picked it up and started to walk back the way we had come.

'Where are you going?'

'To tell Mr Harper that I'm not sleeping here.'

'Why not? If it is good enough for the chef it is good enough for you, a driver.'

'It will not be good enough for Miss Lipp if I smell because I am unable to take a bath.'

'What did you expect—the royal apartment?'

'I can still find a hotel room in Sariyer. Or you can get another driver.'

I felt fairly safe in saying that. If he were to call my bluff I could always back down; but I thought it more likely that I had already called his. The very fact that he was arguing with me suggested weakness.

He glared at me for a moment, then walked to the stairs.

'Put the car away,' he said. 'It will be decided later what is to be done with you.'

I followed him down the stairs. At the foot of them, he turned off left into the house. I went out to the yard, left my bag in the garage and walked back to the car. When I had put it away, I went into the house and set about finding the kitchen. It wasn't difficult. The passage which I had glimpsed from the back entrance ran along the whole length of the house, with a servants' stairway leading to the bedroom floor, and, on the right, a series of doors which presumably gave the servants access to the various reception rooms in front. There was a smell of garlic-laden cooking. I followed the smell.

The kitchen was a big stone-floored room on the left of the passage. It had an old charcoal range along the rear wall with three battered flues over it, and a heavy pinewood table with benches in the middle. The table was cluttered with cooking debris and bottles, and scarred from years of use as a chopping block. Empty butcher's hooks hung from the beams. There was a barrel on a trestle, and beside it a sinister-looking zinc ice-box. A doorway to one side gave on to what appeared to be the scullery. A short man in a dirty blue denim smock stood by the range, stirring an iron pot. This was Geven, the cook. As I came in he looked up and stared.

He was a dark, moon-faced, middle-aged man with an upturned nose and large nostrils. The mouth was wide and full with a lower lip that quivered much of the time as if he were on the verge of tears. The thick, narrow chest merged into a high paunch. He had a three-day growth of beard, which was hardly surprising in view of the fact that he had nowhere to shave.

I remembered that he was a Cypriot and spoke to him in English. 'Good evening. I am the chauffeur, Simpson. Mr Geven?'

'Geven, yes.' He stopped stirring and we shook hands. His hands were filthy and it occurred to me that Mr Miller was probably going to need his Entero Vioforme. 'A drink, eh?' he said.

'Thanks.'

He pulled a glass out of a bowl of dirty water by the sink, shook it once and poured some *konyak* from an already opened bottle on the table. He also refilled his own half-empty glass, which was conveniently to hand.

'Here's cheers!' he said and swallowed thirstily. A sentence of Tufan's came into my mind—'He gets drunk and attacks people.' I had not thought to ask what sort of people he usually attacked, the person with whom he was drinking or some casual bystander.

'Are you British?' he asked.

'Yes.'

'How you know I speak English?'

An awkward question. 'I didn't know, but I don't speak Turkish.'

He nodded, apparently satisfied. 'You worked for these people before?'

'A little. I drove the car from Athens. Normally, I work there with my own car.'

'Driving tourists?'

'Yes.'

'Are these people tourists?' His tone was heavily ironical.

'I don't know. They say so.'

'Ah!' He winked knowingly and went back to his stirring again. 'Are you by the week?'

'Paid, you mean? Yes.'

'You had some money from them?'

'For the trip from Athens.'

'Who paid? The Fischer man?'

'The Harper man. You don't think they really are tourists?'

He made a face and rocked his head from side to side as if the question were too silly to need an answer.

'What are they, then?'

He shrugged. 'Spies, Russia spies. Everyone know—Hamul and his wife, the fishermen down below, everyone. You want something to eat?'

'That smells good.'

'It *is* good. It is for us. Hamul's wife cooks for him in their room before they come to wait table in the dining-room. Then I cook for the spies. Maybe, if I feel like it, I give them what is left after we eat, but the best is for us. Get two dishes, from the shelf there.'

It was a chicken and vegetable soup and was the first thing I had eaten with any pleasure for two days. Of course, I knew that I would have trouble with the garlic later; but, with my stomach knotted up by nerves the way it was, I would have had trouble with anything.

Geven did not eat much. He went on drinking brandy; but he smiled approvingly when I took a second helping of the soup.

'Always I like the British,' he said. 'Even when you are backing the Greeks in Cyprus against us, I like the British. It is good you are here. A man does not like drinking alone. We can take a bottle upstairs with us every night.' He smiled wetly at the prospect.

I returned the smile. It was not the moment, I felt, to tell him that I hoped not to be sharing the servants' quarters with him.

And then Fischer had to come in.

He looked at the brandy bottle disapprovingly, and then at me. 'I will show you your room,' he said.

Geven held up an unsteadily protesting hand. '*Efendi*, let him finish his dinner. I will show him where to sleep.'

It was Fischer's opportunity. 'Ah no, chef,' he said; 'he thinks himself too good to sleep with you.' He nodded to me. 'Come.'

Geven's lower lip quivered so violently that I was sure he was about to burst into tears; but his hand went to the bottle as if he were about to throw it at me. It was possible, I thought, that he might be going to do both things.

I whispered hurriedly: 'Harper's orders, nothing to do with me,' and got out of the room as quickly as I could.

Fischer was already at the staircase in the passage.

'You will use these stairs,' he said; 'not those in the front of the house.'

The room to which he now showed me was at the side of the house on the bedroom floor. He pointed to the door of it.

'There is the room,' he said, and then pointed to another door along the corridor; 'and there is a bathroom. The car will be wanted in the morning at eleven.' With that he left, turning off the lights in the corridor as he went.

When he had gone, I turned the lights on again. The corridor had cream lincrusta dadoes with flowered wallpaper above. I had a look at the bathroom. It was a most peculiar shape and had obviously been installed, as an afterthought, in a disused storage closet. There was no window. The plumbing fixtures were German, *circa* 1905. Only the cold water taps worked.

The bedroom wasn't too bad. It had a pair of french windows, a brass bedstead, a chest of drawers and a big wardrobe. There was also a deal table with an ancient hand-operated sewing-machine on it. At the time when women guests in big houses always brought their ladies' maids with them to stay, the room had probably been given to one of the visiting maids.

There was a mattress on the bed, but no sheets or blankets. I knew it would be unwise to complain again. Before I got my bag from the garage, I went back up to the servants' quarters and took the blankets from the cubicle which Fischer had allocated to me. Then I returned to the room. The car radio transmission wasn't due until eleven; I had time to kill. I began by searching the room.

I always like looking inside other people's drawers and cupboards. You can find strange things. I remember once, when I was at Coram's, my aunt had pleurisy and the district nurse said that I would have to be boarded out for a month. Some people with an old house off the Lewisham High Road took me in. The house had thick laurel bushes all round it and big chestnut trees that made it very dark. I hated going past the laurel bushes at night, because at that time I believed (in the way a boy does) that a madman with a German bayonet was always lying in wait ready to pounce on me from behind and murder me. But inside the house it was all right. There was a smell of Lifebuoy soap and furniture polish. The people had had a son who had been killed on the Somme, and they gave me his room. I found all sorts of things in the cupboard. There was a stamp collection, for instance. I had never collected stamps, but a lot of chaps at school did and I took one or two of the stamps and sold them. After all, he was dead, so he didn't need them. The thing I liked most though was his collection of minerals. It was in a flat wooden case divided up into squares with a different piece of mineral in each one and labels saying what they were—graphite, galena, mica, quartz, iron pyrites, chalcocite, fluorite, wolfram and so on. There were exactly sixty-four squares and exactly sixty-four pieces of mineral, so at first I couldn't see how to keep any of them for myself because the empty square would have shown that something was missing. I did take one or two of them to school to show the chemistry master and try to get in his good books; but he only got suspicious and asked me where I had found them. I had to tell him that an uncle had lent them to me before he would let me have them back. After that, I just kept them in the box and looked at them; until I went back to my aunt's, that is, when I took the iron pyrites because it looked as if it had gold in it. I left a small piece of coal in the square instead. I don't think they ever noticed. I kept that piece of iron pyrites for years. 'Fools' gold', some people call it.

All I found in the room at Sardunya was an old Russian calendar made of cardboard in the shape of an ikon. There was a dark brown picture of Christ on it. I don't read Russian, so I couldn't make out the date. It wasn't worth taking.

I had the windows wide open. It was so quiet up there that I could hear the diesels of a ship chugging upstream against the Black Sea current towards the boom across the narrows above Sariyer. Until about eight-thirty there was a faint murmur of voices from the terrace in front. Then they went in to dinner. Some time after nine, I became restless. After all, nobody had told me to stay in my room. I decided to go for a stroll.

Just to be on the safe side, in case anyone took it into his head to go through my things, I hid the radio on top of the wardrobe. Then I went down, out through the rear door and skirted the front courtyard to the drive.

It was so dark there under the trees that I couldn't really see where I was going, and after I had gone a hundred yards or so I turned back. Miss Lipp, Harper, Miller and Fischer were coming out on to the terrace again when I reached the courtyard, and Hamul was lighting candles on the tables.

Along the side of the courtyard it was quite dark, and the weeds made it easy to move quietly over the gravel. At the entrance to the stable yard I stopped by the wall to see if I could hear anything they said.

I must have waited there for twenty minutes or more before I heard anything but an indistinct mumble. Then one of the men laughed loudly—Miller it was—and I heard him saying seven words as if they were the climax of a joke.

'Let the dogs be fed and clothed!' he cackled, and then repeated it. 'Let the dogs be fed and clothed!'

The others laughed with him, and then the mumbling began again. I went on in and up to my room.

I made the bed as comfortable as I could with the blankets, and then shaved to save myself the trouble of doing so in the morning.

Just before eleven, I took the radio out of its case, opened the back and turned the small switch. All I got was a hissing sound. I waited. I did not trouble to use the earphone, because I did not see any reason to then. I had not even shut the windows.

On the stroke of eleven, the set made a harsh clacking noise. A moment later, a voice crackled through the tiny loudspeaker at such a high volume level that I could feel the whole set vibrating in my hands. I tried to turn the thing down, but, with the V.H.F. on, the control seemed to have no effect. All I could do was stuff the set under the blankets. Even there it seemed like a public address system. I scrambled to the windows and shut them. The loudspeaker began repeating its message:

'Attention period report. Attention period report. New arrival is Leopold Axel Miller. Belgian passport gives following data: age sixty-three, described as importer, place of birth Antwerp. Data now also received concerning Tekelek S.A., a Swiss corporation registered in Berne. Nominal capital fifty thousand Swiss francs. Directors are K. W. Hoffman, R. E. Kohner, G. D. Bernadi and L. A. Mathis, all of whom are believed to have personal numbered and secret accounts at Banque Crédit Suisse, Zürich. Business of Tekelek said to be sale of electronic accounting machines manufactured in West Germany. Urgent you report progress. Attention period report...'

I fumbled under the blankets, turned the V.H.F. switch off and replaced the back on the set. Then I tuned in a Turkish station in case anyone had heard the noise and came to investigate.

Nobody did.

'Urgent you report progress.'

I had a cigarette packet with two cigarettes left in it. I lit one, put the other in my pocket and went to the bathroom for a piece of toilet paper.

When I returned I locked the door and sat down to write my progress report. It was quite short.

Cook, caretaker and local fishermen all believe suspects to be Russian spies.

I folded the toilet paper, put it inside the cigarette packet, crumpled the packet and put the result in my pocket ready for disposal in the morning.

I felt I had done my duty for that day.

CHAPTER SEVEN

I WOKE UP VERY EARLY IN THE MORNING AND WITH THAT NASTY sick feeling that I used to have when it was a school day and I hadn't done my homework properly the night before.

I got the cigarette packet out of my pocket and had another look at my toilet paper report. It really was not good enough. Unless I could think of something else to say, Tufan would think that I was trying to be funny. I went and had an extremely uncomfortable cold bath, collected some more sheets of toilet paper and started again.

Period report heard. Attempts to check door contents frustrated. Will try again today, I wrote.

I thought about the 'today'. Fischer had ordered the car for eleven o'clock. With that instruction to rely upon, it would be perfectly natural for me to go and fill up the car with petrol without asking anyone's permission; and, as long as I didn't keep them waiting, I could take my time about it. If, when I got back, they objected to my having taken the car out by myself or wanted to know why I had been so long, I could say that I had been to buy razor-blades or something, and be the injured innocent.

It was six-forty-five by then and in a few minutes I would have to get ready for the seven o'clock radio contact. Two other things occurred to me that I might add to my report.

Will telephone you from garage after inspection if time and circumstances allow, or will add to this report. During conversation Lipp—Miller yesterday name 'Giulio' was mentioned in connection with a boat. No other details.

Then I added the bit about the Russian spies. It didn't look quite so bald and stupid now.

I hid the report under the lining paper of one of the drawers, shut the french windows tight and got the radio ready with the earphone attachment plugged in. Promptly at seven the car began transmitting.

'Attention period report. Attention period report. Advice received from Swiss source that no passports have been legally issued to Harper and Lipp. In view Miller contact and Tekelek papers with Harper, possibility must be considered that correct names of Harper and Lipp are Hoffman and Kohner or vice versa. Miller may be Mathis. Imperative you report progress.'

As the voice began repeating I switched off. When I had packed the set away, I got the report out and added five words.

Hoffman, Kohner and Mathis names noted.

At least, I ought to get an 'E' for Effort. I put the new report in the cigarette packet, burnt my earlier effort and started to get dressed. As I did so, I heard the Lambretta start up and then go whining off down the drive. About twenty minutes later, I heard the sound of it returning. I looked out of the window and saw it disappearing into the stable yard with a bundle of partially-wrapped loaves strapped to the rear seat.

Geven was back in the kitchen when I went down. He gave me a sullen look and did not answer when I said 'good morning'. He was probably hung over as well as disgusted with me; but he looked such a mess anyway that it was hard to tell.

There was a pot of coffee on the range and I looked from it to him inquiringly. He shrugged, so I got a cup and helped myself. He was slicing the bread by hacking at it with a heavy chopping knife. From the neat way the slices fell I knew that the chopping knife was as sharp as a razor. As I had no desire to lose any fingers, I waited until he had put it aside before taking a piece of bread.

The coffee did not taste much like coffee, but the bread was good. I considered attempting to heal the breach by offering him the use of my bathroom; but I only had one towel and the thought of what it would look like by the time he had finished with it kept me silent. Instead, I offered him a cigarette.

He took it and motioned to a basket of apricots on the table. I don't like apricots, but it seemed as well to accept the offer. Soon he began to mutter about the breakfasts which had to be served, each on a separate tray to the four 'lords and ladies' above. I offered to lay the trays and, although he waved away the offer, friendly relations seemed to be re-established. After a while, Mr and Mrs Hamul arrived and were introduced. Mrs Hamul was a small, stout, sad-looking old woman with the black dress and head-scarf of the conservative Turkish matron. As neither she nor her husband spoke a word of anything but Turkish, the formalities were brief. I lingered there, though, and had another piece of bread. The best time to leave without attracting attention, I had decided, would be while Harper and the rest were having their breakfasts.

As soon as the trays started going up, I told Geven that I had to buy petrol and asked if there was anything I could get for him while I was in town. At once he wanted to come with me. I got out of that by saying that I had to go immediately in order to be back at the time for which the car had been ordered. I left him, sulking, picked up the Phillips screwdriver from my room and went to the garage.

The Lincoln was a quiet car, and I knew that all they would probably hear of my going would be the sound of the tyres on the gravel of the courtyard; but I was so afraid of Harper or Fischer suddenly appearing on one of the bedroom balconies and yelling at me to stop that in my haste to reach the drive I almost hit the basin of the fountain. As I went on down the drive I broke into a sweat and my legs felt weak and peculiar. I wanted to stop and be sick. That may sound very stupid, but when you are like I am, the bad things that *nearly* happen are just as hard, in a way, as the bad things that do actually happen. They are certainly no easier to forget. I always envied those characters in *Alice* who only felt pain before they were hurt. I seem to feel things before, during and after as well; nothing ever goes completely away. I have often thought of killing myself, so that I wouldn't have to think or feel or remember any more, so that I could rest; but then I have always started worrying in case this after-life they preach about really exists. It might turn out to be even bloodier than the old one.

The Peugeot was back on duty again. I drove towards Sariyer for about half a mile, and then turned left on to one of the roads leading up to the forest. It was Sunday morning and families from Istanbul would soon be arriving at the municipal picnic grounds to spend the day; but at that early hour the car-parking areas were still fairly empty, and I had no difficulty in finding a secluded place under the trees.

I decided to try the same door again. I had scratched the leather on it once already; but if I were very careful it need not be scratched again. In any case, as long as I drove the car, scratches would be less noticeable on that door than on the others. The earlier attempt had taught me something, too. If I removed all the screws on the hinge side of the door first and only loosened the others, I thought it might be possible to ease the panel back enough to see inside the door without taking the whole panel and electric window mechanism completely away.

It took me twenty minutes to find out that I was right about the panel, and a further five seconds to learn that I had been completely wrong about the stuff having been removed. There it still was, just as I had seen it in the photographs Tufan had shown me at Edirne. In this particular door there were twelve small, paper-wrapped cylinders—probably grenades.

I screwed the panel back into place, and then sat there for a while thinking. The Peugeot was parked about a hundred yards away—I could see it in the mirror—and I very nearly got out and walked back to tell the driver what I had found. I wanted badly to talk to someone. Then I pulled myself together. There was no point in talking to someone who wouldn't, or couldn't, usefully talk back. The sensible thing would be to obey orders.

I took my report out of the cigarette packet and added to it.

9.20 a.m. inspected interior front door driver's side. Material still in place as per photo. In view of time absent from villa and inability to add to this report, will not telephone from garage now.

I replaced the toilet paper in the packet, tossed it out of the window and drove back on to the road. I waited just long enough to see a man from the Peugeot pick up the report, then I drove into Sariyer and filled the tank. I arrived back at the villa just before ten.

I half expected to find an angry Fischer pacing the courtyard and demanding to know where the hell I'd been. There was nobody. I drove the car into the stable yard, emptied the ash-trays, brushed the floor carpeting and ran a duster over the body. The Phillips screwdriver in my pocket worried me. Now that I knew that the stuff was still in the car, it seemed an incriminating thing to have. I certainly did not want to put it back in my room. It might be needed again, so I could not throw it away. In the end, I hid it inside the cover of an old tyre hanging on the wall of the garage. Then I went and tidied myself up. Shortly before eleven o'clock I drove the car round to the marble steps in the front courtyard.

After about ten minutes Harper came out. He was wearing a blue sports shirt with blue slacks, and he had a map in his hand. He nodded in response to my greeting.

'Are we all right for gas, Arthur?'

'I filled it this morning, sir.'

'Oh, you did?' He looked agreeably surprised. 'Well, do you know a place called Pendik?'

'I've heard the name. On the other side somewhere, isn't it? There's supposed to be a good restaurant there, I think.'

'That's the place. On the Sea of Marmara.' He spread the map out and pointed to the place. From Uskudar, on the Asian side of the Bosphorus, it was twenty-odd miles south along the coast. 'How long will it take us to get there?'

'If we have luck with the car ferry, about an hour and a half from here, sir.'

'And if we don't have luck?'

'Perhaps ten or twenty minutes more.'

'All right. Here's what we do. First, we go into town and drop Miss Lipp and Mr Miller off at the Hilton Hotel. Then you drive Mr Fischer and me to Pendik. We'll be there a couple of hours. On the way back we stop off at the Hilton to pick the others up. Clear?'

'Yes, sir.'

'Who paid for the gas?'

'I did, sir. I still have some of the Turkish money you gave me. I have the garage receipt here.'

He waved it aside. 'Do you have any money left?'

'Only a few lira now.'

He gave me two fifty-lira notes. 'That's for expenses. You picked up a couple of checks for Miss Lipp, too. Take the money out of that.'

'Very well, sir.'

'And, Arthur—stop needling Mr Fischer, will you?'

'I rather thought that he intended to needle me, sir.'

'You got the room and bathroom you asked for, didn't you?'

'Yes, sir.'

'Well, then, cut it out.'

I started to point out that since I had been shown to the room the previous night I had not even set eyes on Fischer, much less 'needled' him, but he was already walking back to the house.

They all came out five minutes later. Miss Lipp was in white linen; Miller, draped with camera and lens attachment case, looked very much the tourist; Fischer, in *maillot,* white jeans and sandals, looked like an elderly beach-boy from Antibes.

Harper sat in front with me. The others got into the back. Nobody talked on the way into Istanbul. Even at the time, I didn't feel that it was my presence there that kept them silent. They all had the self-contained air of persons on the way to an important business conference who have already explored every conceivable aspect of the negotiations that lie ahead, and can only wait now to learn what the other side's attitude is going to be. Yet two of them seemed headed for a sight-seeing tour, and the others for a seaside lunch. It was all rather odd. However, the Peugeot was following and, presumably, those in it would be able to cope with the situation when the party split up. There was nothing more I could do.

Miss Lipp and Miller got out at the door of the Hilton. A tourist bus blocked the driveway long enough for me to see that they went inside the hotel, and that a man from the Peugeot went in after them. The narcotics operation suddenly made sense again.

The raw opium supplier would be waiting in his room with samples which Miller, the skilled chemist, would proceed to test and evaluate. Later, if the samples proved satisfactory, and *only* if they did, Harper would consummate the deal. In the meantime, a good lunch seemed to be in order.

We had to wait a few minutes for the car ferry to Uskudar. From the ferry pier it is easy to see across the water the military barracks which became Florence Nightingale's hospital during the Crimean War. Just for the sake of something to say, I pointed it out to Harper.

'What about it?' he said rudely.

'Nothing, sir. It's just that that was Florence Nightingale's hospital. Scutari the place was called then.'

'Look, Arthur, we know you have a guide's licence, but don't take it too seriously, huh?'

Fischer laughed.

'I thought you might be interested, sir.'

'All we're interested in is getting to Pendik. Where's this goddam ferry you talked about?'

I didn't trouble to answer that. The ferry-boat was just coming in at the pier, and he was merely being offensive—for Fischer's benefit, I suspected. I wondered what they would have said if I had told them what the sand-coloured Peugeot just behind us in the line of cars was there for, and whose orders its driver was obeying. The thought kept me amused for quite a while.

From Uskudar I took the Ankara road, which is wide and fast, and drove for about eighteen miles before I came to the secondary road which led off on the right to Pendik. We arrived there just before one o'clock.

It proved to be a small fishing port in the shelter of a headland. There were several yachts anchored in the harbour. Two wooden piers jutted out from the road, which ran parallel to the foreshore; one had a restaurant built on it, the other served the smaller boats and dinghies as a landing stage. The place swarmed with children.

I was edging my way along the narrow road towards the restaurant when Harper told me to stop.

We were level with the landing stage and a man was approaching the road along it. He was wearing a yachting cap now, but I recognized him. It was the man who had been waiting at the Hilton car-park on the night I had arrived in Istanbul.

He had obviously recognized the car and raised his hand in greeting as Harper and Fischer got out.

'Park the car and get yourself something to eat,' Harper said to me. 'Meet us back here in an hour.'

'Very good, sir.'

The man in the yachting cap had reached the road and I heard Harper's greeting as the three met.

'Hi, Giulio. *Sta bene?*'

And then they were walking back along the landing stage. In the driving mirror, I could see a man from the Peugeot sauntering down to the quayside to see what happened next.

At the end of the landing stage they climbed into an outboard dinghy. Giulio started it up and they shot away towards a group of yachts anchored about two hundred yards out. They went alongside a sixty-foot cabin cruiser with a squat funnel. The hull was black, the upper works white, and the funnel had a single band of yellow round it. A Turkish flag drooped from the staff at the stern. There was a small gangway down, and a deck hand with a boat-hook to hold the dinghy as the three went on board. It was too far away for me to see the name on the hull.

I parked the car and went into the restaurant. The place was fairly full, but I managed to get a table near a window from which I could keep an eye on the cruiser. I asked the head waiter about her and learned her name, *Bulut,* and the fact that she was on charter to a wealthy Italian gentleman, Signor Giulio, who could eat two whole lobsters at a sitting.

I did not pursue my inquiries; Tufan's men would doubtless get what information was to be had from the local police. At least I knew now what Giulio looked like, and where the boat which Miss Lipp had mentioned to Miller had been based. I could also guess that Giulio was no more the true charterer of the *Bulut* than was Fischer the true lessee of the Kösk Sardunya. Wealthy Italian gentlemen with yachts do not lurk in the Istanbul Hilton car-park waiting to drive away cars stuffed with contraband arms; they employ underlings to do such things.

Just as my grilled swordfish cutlet arrived, I saw that the *Bulut* was moving. A minute or two later, her bow anchor came out of the water and there was a swirl of white at her stern. The dinghy had been left moored to a buoy. The only people on the deck of the cabin cruiser were the two hands at the winches. She headed out across the bay towards an offshore island just visible in the distant haze. I wondered whether the Peugeot men would commandeer a motor-boat and follow; but no other boat of any kind left the harbour. After about an hour, the *Bulut* returned and anchored in the same place as before. I paid my bill and went to the car.

Giulio brought Harper and Fischer back to the landing stage in the dinghy, but did not land with them. There was an exchange of farewells that I could see but not hear, and then they walked ashore to the car. Harper was carrying a flat cardboard box about two feet long by six inches wide. It was roughly tied with string.

'Okay, Arthur,' he said as he got into the car. 'Back to the Hilton.'

'Very good, sir.'

As I drove off he glanced back at the piers.

'Where did you lunch?' he asked. 'That restaurant there?'

'Yes, sir.'

'Good food?'

'Excellent, sir.'

He grinned over his shoulder at Fischer. 'Trust Giulio!'

'Our man Geven can cook well,' said Fischer defensively. 'And I intend to prove it to you.'

'He's a lush,' Harper said shortly.

'He cooked a *castradina* before you arrived which would have made you think you were in the Quadri.' Fischer was getting worked up now and leaning forward over the back of the front seat. His breath smelt of garlic and wine.

I could not resist the opportunity. 'If you don't mind my saying so, sir,' I said to Harper, 'I think Mr Fischer is right. Geven is an excellent cook. The chicken soup he gave me last night was perfect.'

'What soup?' Fischer demanded. 'We did not get soup.'

'He was upset,' I said. 'You remember, Mr Fischer, that you told him that he was not good enough to have a bathroom. He was upset. I think he threw away the soup he had made.'

'I told him no such a thing!' Fischer was becoming shrill.

'Wait a minute,' said Harper. 'The cook doesn't have a *bathroom*?'

'He has the whole of the servants' rooms for himself,' Fischer said.

'But no bathroom?'

'There is no bathroom there.'

'What are you trying to do, Hans—poison us?'

Fischer flung himself against the back seat with a force that made the car lurch. 'I am tired,' he declared loudly, 'of trying to arrange every matter as it should be arranged and then to receive nothing but criticism. I will not so to be accused, thus…' His English broke down completely and he went into German.

Harper answered him briefly in the same language. I don't know what he said, but it shut Fischer up. Harper lit a cigarette. After a moment or two he said: 'You're a stupid crook, aren't you, Arthur?'

'Sir?'

'If you were a smart one, all you'd be thinking about would be how much dough you could screw out of this deal without getting your fingers caught in the till. But not you. That miserable little ego of yours has to have its kicks, too, doesn't it?'

'I don't understand, sir.'

'Yes, you do. I don't like stupid people around me. They make me nervous. I warned you once before. I'm not warning you again. Next time you see a chance of getting cute, you forget it, quick; because if you don't that ego's liable to get damaged permanently.'

It seemed wiser to say nothing.

'You're not still saying that you don't understand, Arthur?' He flicked my knee viciously with the back of his hand. The pain startled me and I swerved. He flicked me again. 'Watch where you're going. What's the matter? Can't you talk while you're driving, or has the cat got your tongue?'

'I understand, sir.'

'That's better. Now you apologize like a little Egyptian gentleman to Mr Fischer.'

'I'm very sorry, sir.'

Fischer, appeased, signified his forgiveness with a short laugh.

The ferry from Uskudar was crowded with returning Sunday motorists and it took half an hour to get on a boat. Miss Lipp and Miller were waiting at the hotel entrance when I pulled up.

Miller gave a wolfish grin and, as usual, leapt into the car ahead of Miss Lipp.

'You took your time,' he said to no one in particular.

'The ferry was crowded,' Harper replied. 'Did you have a good afternoon?'

It was Miss Lipp who answered him. 'Let the dogs be fed and clothed,' she said. It was the same sentence that I had heard Miller cackling over the previous night, and I wondered idly what it could mean.

Harper nodded to her. 'Let's get back to the villa, Arthur,' he said.

None of them uttered a word on the drive back. I sensed a feeling of tension between them, and wondered who was waiting to report to whom. As they got out of the car, Harper picked the cardboard box up off the floor and turned to me.

'That's it for today, Arthur.'

'What time tomorrow, sir?'

'I'll let you know.'

'The car is very dusty, sir, and there is no proper hose here. I would like to get it washed at a garage.'

'You do that.' He could not have cared less what I did.

I drove into Sariyer and found a garage where they would wash the car. I left it there and went to a café. I had a drink before I telephoned Tufan.

The written report of the morning had been supplemented by reports from the surveillance squad and he had more to tell me than I had to tell him. Giulio's other name was Corzo, and his Swiss passport gave his occupation as 'industrial designer'. His age was forty-five and his place of birth Lugano. The cabin cruiser had been chartered a week earlier, for one month, through a yacht-broker in Antalya. The crew of three were local men of good reputation. As for Miss Lipp and Miller, they had lunched in the Hilton grill-room, then hired a car. They had spent forty-five minutes sight-seeing and returned to the Hilton, where Miss Lipp had visited the hairdresser. She had had a shampoo and set. Miller had passed the time reading French newspapers on the terrace.

'Then it must have been the meeting with Giulio they wanted to hear about,' I said.

'What do you mean?'

I told him of the feeling I had had on the way back that they had been impatient for a chance to talk privately.

'Then why are you not at the villa? Go back there immediately.'

'If they wish to have private talk, there is nothing I can do to overhear it. Their part of the house on the ground floor is separate. I have not even seen those rooms.'

'Are there no windows?'

'Giving on to their private terrace, yes. I could have no excuse for being even near it, let alone on it.'

'Then do without an excuse.'

'You told me to take no risks.'

'No *unnecessary* risks. An important discussion justifies risk.'

'I don't *know* that it is important. I just had a feeling. I don't know that it's a discussion either. Harper may just have wanted to pass on a piece of private information he had received from Giulio to the others. The whole thing could have been over in a minute.'

'The meeting at Pendik was obviously important. We must know why. So far all you have learned is gossip from a fool of a cook. What do these people with arms and ammunition hidden in their car and false passports discuss when they are alone? What do they say? It is for you to find out.'

'I can tell you one thing they say—"Let the dogs be fed and clothed." I overheard it first last night. It seemed to be some sort of private joke.'

He was silent for a moment and I waited for another angry outburst. None came. Instead he said thoughtfully: 'That is quite an interesting joke.'

'What does it mean?'

'When one of the old Sultans was preparing to receive a certain class of persons, he would always keep them waiting a long time, perhaps a whole day. Then, when he thought that they had been sufficiently humbled, he would give that order—"Let the dogs be fed and clothed." After that, they would be admitted to the chamber of the Grand Vizier, given food and robed in caftans.'

'What class of persons?'

'The ambassadors of foreign powers.' He paused. Obviously, he was still thinking about it. Then he dismissed me curtly. 'You have your orders. Report as arranged.'

I went and got the car. The man at the garage who had the key to the petrol pump had gone home, and there was only the old man who had washed the car waiting for me. I wasn't too pleased about that, as it meant that I would have to fill the tank in the morning. Opportunities for making telephone reports to Tufan did not seem particularly desirable at that moment.

When I got back to the villa it was almost dark and the lights were on in the terrace rooms. I put the car away and went to the kitchen.

Geven was in a jovial mood. Fischer had moved him to a bedroom near mine and told him to share my bathroom. Whether this was due to spite on Fischer's part or a shortage of bathrooms, I couldn't tell. Geven, through some obscure reasoning process of his own, had decided that the whole thing had been my idea. In a way, I suppose, he was right; but there was nothing to be done about it. I took a tumbler of brandy from him and beamed like an idiot as if I had earned every drop. He had cooked a spaghetti *Bolognese* for the kitchen. The spies were having canned soup and a sis-kebab made with mutton which he proudly assured me was as tough as new leather. The spaghetti was really good. I had a double helping of it. As soon as the Hamuls arrived, I got away, giving as an excuse that I had work to do on the car. I went out to the yard.

The terrace ran along the front and right side of the house, I had noticed a door in the wall beside the garage. There was an orchard of fig trees beyond and I thought it possible that the side terrace might be accessible from there.

The door had no lock, only a latch, but the old hinges were rusty and I used the dip-stick from the car to run some oil into them before I attempted to open it. It swung inwards silently and I shut it behind me. I waited then, not only so that my eyes would get used to the dark, but because the spies had not yet gone into dinner. I could hear their voices faintly. I knew that Tufan would have wanted me to go closer and hear what they were saying; but I didn't. The ground was uneven and I would have to feel my way towards the terrace balustrade. I preferred to do that while they were well away from the terrace and trying to get their teeth into Geven's sis-kebab.

After fifteen or twenty minutes, dinner was served and I edged forward slowly to the terrace. As soon as I reached it and was able to see through the balustrade, I realized that it would be impossible for me to get close enough to the windows of the room they had been using to hear anything. There was too much light coming from them. I suppose one of these daredevil agents you hear about would have concealed himself in the shadows; but that looked too risky for me. Getting to the shadows would have been easy enough; but if Harper and Co. decided to sit outside, as they had done the night before, there would have been no way of getting back without being seen.

I walked on through the orchard until I came to the outer edge of the front courtyard. This was the side which overlooked the Bosphorus and there were no trees to obstruct the view. A low stone balustrade ran along the edge with a statue on a plinth at each end. The first of these statues was over thirty feet from the corner of the terrace, but it was the nearest I could get and still remain in cover. The top of the plinth was chest-high. Using the balustrade as a stepping-stone, it wasn't difficult to climb up. The statue, a larger than life-size Vestal virgin with bird-droppings all over her, seemed quite steady, and I was able to hold on to her draperies. From the plinth I could see over the terrace balustrading and through the windows of the corner drawing-room. It was not much, but it was something. If they did decide to come out on to the terrace, I might even catch a word or two of what they said.

After about twenty minutes, they came back into the room. The bits of it that I could see contained an old leather-topped library table, part of a faded green settee, part of a wall mirror, a low round table and one or two gilt chairs. The only person I could actually see at first was Miller, who took a corner of the settee; but he was talking nineteen to the dozen and waving his hands about, so he obviously wasn't alone. Then Mrs Hamul came in with a coffee tray which she put on the round table, and I saw bits of the others as they helped themselves. Somebody gave Miller a glass of brandy, which he drank as if he needed it; he could have been trying to wash away the taste of his dinner. After a bit, he stopped talking and appeared to be listening, his head moving slightly as he shifted his attention from one speaker to another. Then there was a flash of white in the mirror and his head turned. For a moment, I saw Miss Lipp. She had changed into a green dress, though; the white belonged to a large sheet of paper. Almost immediately it disappeared from view. Miller's head lifted as he began to listen to someone who was standing up. A minute or so went by and then the paper reappeared, as if put aside, on the library table. I could see now that it was a map. At that distance and at that angle it was impossible to tell what it was a map of, but it looked to me like a roughly triangular island. I was still staring at it when Harper moved in and folded it into four.

After that, nothing seemed to happen until, suddenly, Harper and Miss Lipp came out on to the terrace from a window much farther away and walked down the marble steps. There was nothing purposeful about their movements—they were obviously just going for a stroll—but I thought it as well to get out of the way. If they were going to admire the view from the balustrade, I would be in an awkward spot.

I got down from the plinth and moved back into the shelter of the fig trees. Sure enough, they made their way round to the balustrade. When they turned to go back I was only twenty-five feet away from them. I heard a snatch of conversation.

'… if I took over?' That was Miss Lipp.

'He was Leo's idea,' he answered. 'Let Leo take care of him. After tomorrow, he doesn't matter too much anyway. Even Arthur could do the rest of that job.'

She laughed. 'The indignant sheep? With his breath you wouldn't even need the grenades, I guess. You'd get a mass surrender.'

He laughed.

She said: 'When does Giulio's man arrive?'

'Some time today. I didn't wait. Giulio knows…'

I heard no more.

As soon as they were well clear, I went back through the orchard to the yard, and then up to my room. I locked the door. Geven would be free of the kitchen at any moment, and I did not want to be bothered with him.

I had to think about what they had said and it was hard to do so, because all I could think about was her laugh and the words she had used about me. I felt sick. There was another time when it had been like that, too. Jones iv and I had gone up to Hilly Fields to meet a couple of girls we knew. One of them was named Muriel, the other was Madge. Madge didn't turn up because, so Muriel said, she had a cold. So there were just the three of us. Muriel was really Jones' girl, so I was more or less out of it. I tried to pick up another girl, but that was more difficult when you were alone and I didn't have any luck. After a while, I gave up and went back to where I had left the other two necking on a seat under the trees. I thought I'd come up quietly and give them a surprise. That is how I overheard it. She was saying that she had to get home early, for some reason or other, and he was asking her about Saturday night.

'With Arthur, too?' she said.

'I suppose so.'

'Well, Madge won't come.'

'She'll be over her cold by then.'

'She hasn't got a cold. She just didn't want to come. She says Arthur's a little twerp and gives her the creeps.'

I went away and they didn't know that I'd heard. Then I was sick behind the bushes. I hated that girl Madge so much that it was like a pain.

Geven came up and I heard him go into the bathroom. A little while afterwards he came out and knocked on my door. I had taken the precaution of switching out the light so that it wouldn't show under the door and he would think that I was asleep. He knocked again. After a few moments I heard him muttering to himself. Then he went away.

I nearly changed my mind and called him in. I could have done with a drink just then, and someone to talk to. But then I thought of how dirty he was and how the stink of his body would stay in the room—'the perfume of the great unwashed', as my father would have said. Besides, I couldn't be sure of getting rid of him when I wanted to, and I had the eleven o'clock radio call to take.

It came at last.

'Attention period report. Attention period report. Passenger for yacht Bulut arrived Pendik seventeen hundred hours today. Name Enrico, other names unknown so far. Description: short, stocky, black hair, brown eyes, age about thirty-five. Casual observation of subject and hand luggage suggests workman rather than guest of charterer Corzo. Are you able to identify this man? Important that written notes of all conversations, with particular care as to political content, should be made. Essential you report progress. Repeat. Essential.'

The outside of the body can be washed of sweat and grease; but inside there are processes which produce other substances. Some of these smell. How do you wash away the smells of the inside of the body?

CHAPTER EIGHT

T HE MORNING CALL WAS A REPETITION OF THAT OF THE PRE-
vious night, and made no more sense at seven a.m. than it had
at eleven. I got up and went to the bathroom. Luckily, I had had
the sense to remove my towel to my bedroom; but Geven had left
a filthy mess. There was grey scum in the bath and shaving soap in
the basin. Patience was necessary in order to flush the toilet successfully, and he had given up too soon.

Shaved, he looked more bleary-eyed than he had with the three-
day growth, but his mood was one of jovial aggression. Fischer's
complaints about the sis-kebab, it seemed, had been loud and insolent. But the reprisal had already been planned—the spies' dinner
that night would be boiled mutton in yoghourt à la Turque. Fischer
would learn to his cost who was master in the kitchen; and if he
didn't like the knowledge, well, then, the spies could go on eating
pig-swill or find themselves another chef.

I had breakfast, got the car out and drove to the garage for petrol.

Tufan answered promptly. I made my report about the overheard
conversation first, editing only slightly. 'If I took over. He was Leo's
idea, let Leo take care of him. After tomorrow he doesn't matter
too much anyway. Grenades… mass surrender.'

He made me repeat it slowly. When he started to complain that
there wasn't more of it, I told him about the map. I had guessed
that this would excite his interest, and it did.

'You say it looked like a map of an island?'

'I thought so. The shape was roughly triangular.'

'Was it a coloured map?'

'No, black and white.'

'Then it could have been a marine chart?'

'I suppose so.'

He said thoughtfully: 'A boat, the chart of an island, grenades, respirators, guns, surrender...'

'And something that Fischer is to do today,' I reminded him.

He ignored the interruption. 'You are sure this island had a triangular shape?'

'I thought so, but the map wasn't absolutely flat. It was hard to see. It could have been a design for a swimming pool.'

He ignored the frivolity. 'Could it have been kidney-shaped?'

'Perhaps. Would that mean something?'

'That is the shape of the island of Yassiada where certain political prisoners are held awaiting trial. It is only fifteen kilometres from Pendik. Have you heard the name Yassiada mentioned?'

'No.'

'Or Imrali?'

'No. Is that an island, too?'

'It is a town on an island sixty kilometres from Pendik. It is also the place where Menderes was hanged.'

'How is that island shaped?'

'Like the head of a dog. I must have another report from you this evening without fail, even if it is only negative.'

'I will do what I can.'

'Above all, you must search for this chart.'

'How can I?'

'You can search at night. In any case you must obtain a closer look at it.'

'I don't see how I can do that. Even if they bring it out again, I won't be able to get any closer.'

'With binoculars you could.'

'I have no binoculars.'

'On the way back to the villa, stop on the road. The Opel is on surveillance duty today. An agent from the car will give you binoculars.'

'Supposing Harper sees them. How do I explain them?'

'Do not let him see them. I expect a report tonight. If necessary, you will make contact with the surveillance personnel. Is that clear?' He hung up.

I drove back towards the villa. Just outside Sariyer on the coast road I pulled up. The Opel stopped a hundred yards behind me. After a minute or two, a man got out of it and walked towards the Lincoln. He was carrying a leather binocular case. He handed it to me without a word and went back to the Opel.

I put the binoculars on the seat and drove on. They were too big to put in my pocket. I would either have to smuggle them up to my room somehow or hide them in the garage. I was annoyed with myself. I should have known better. Any sort of map is cat-nip to intelligence people. I should have kept quiet about it.

Even without the binoculars, though, I would have been irritated, and I did have sense enough to realize that. The binoculars were only a nuisance. It was really the conclusion he had come to that bothered me.

What he'd wanted to see all along, and, quite evidently, what he now *did* see, was yet another conspiracy against the Committee of National Union, yet another *coup* in preparation. The last attempt to overthrow the Committee had been made by a group of dissident army officers *inside* the country. What more likely than that the next attempt would be made with the help of money and hired terrorists from *outside* the country? What more likely than that it would begin with a daring rescue of officer prisoners awaiting trial? As he had said: 'A boat, the chart of an island, grenades, respirators, guns, surrender.' It all added up so neatly.

The trouble was, as it had been all along, that he didn't know the people concerned. I did. I knew how vile they were, too. In fact, there was nothing I wanted more at that moment than to see them get hell. But they just didn't strike me as the sort of people who would be hired terrorists. I could not have said why. If he had countered by asking me what sort of people *were* hired terrorists and how many I had met, I would have had no sensible answer. All I could have said would have been: 'These people wouldn't take that kind of risk.'

When I got back to the villa, Fischer was standing on the terrace at the top of the steps. He motioned to me to pull up there. As he came down the steps, I remembered, just in time, to shove the binoculars on to the floor by my feet.

'You will not be wanted today, Simpson,' he said. 'We are going on a private excursion. I will drive the car.'

'Very good, sir. It is full of petrol, but I was going to dust it.' I was all smiles above, and all binoculars below.

'Very well.' He waved me off in his high-handed way. 'The car must be here in half an hour.'

'Yes, sir.'

I drove round the courtyard into the garage, and hid the binoculars behind an empty oil-drum before I gave the car a flick over with a wet duster.

Just before ten I drove it to the courtyard and left it there with the ignition key in. Then I went back to the yard, through the door into the orchard, and found a place from which I could see the car without being seen. When they went out, I wanted to make sure that they had all gone—Fischer, Harper, Miss Lipp and Miller.

After forty minutes or so, all four came out and got into the car. As soon as they had gone, I went to the kitchen. Geven was there, chopping meat and sipping brandy. I had a drink myself and let him talk for a while before asking whether they were expected back for lunch. They were not. He would make an omelette *pour le personnel*.

I went upstairs to the bedroom floor. At the head of the back stairs the corridor ran left and right, parallel to the rear wall of the villa. If you turned right, you came to my room and Geven's, among others: if you turned left, you were faced by a pair of double doors. Beyond them were the master bedrooms and guest suites.

The double doors were half-open when I went up. Through the opening, I caught a glimpse of a wickerwork trolley full of dirty linen, and of old Hamul working on the floor of the corridor with a carpet-sweeper. Mrs Hamul was presumably changing the sheets on the beds.

I went to my room, waited an hour, and then strolled back along the corridor.

The door was still open and the Hamuls were still messing about in the bedrooms. I went down to the kitchen and had another drink with Geven. He was busy with the stewpot and another hour went by before he decided to make the omelette. I heard the Hamuls come down at about the same time and go through to the laundry. As soon as I had finished eating, I told Geven that I was going to have a sleep and went upstairs again.

First, I locked my room from the outside in case he looked in to see if I were there; then I went through the double doors and shut them behind me.

What I was looking for was the map, and it was difficult to know where to start. There were about eighteen rooms there, and they were of all shapes and sizes. Some were bedrooms, some sitting-rooms; some were so sparsely furnished that it was hard to tell what they had been. Where there was furniture, it was all in the same bilious-looking French-hotel style. The only things not in short supply were mirrors and chandeliers; every room had those.

I identified Miller's room first, because his suitcase was open on the bed, then Fischer's because of the shirts in one of the drawers. I found no map in either room. Miss Lipp's suite was over the centre portico, with Harper's next to it on the corner. There was a connecting door. I looked through all the drawers and cupboards, I looked inside the suitcases, I looked above and below every piece of furniture. The only maps I found were in a copy of *Europa Touring* that was on Miss Lipp's writing desk, along with some Italian paper-backed novels.

Beyond Harper's suite, and on the side of the building overlooking the orchard, there was a room that had been fitted up as a studio. Architect's drawers had been built along one wall. It seemed a good place to look for a large flat map, and I was carefully going through every drawer when I heard the sound of car doors slamming.

I scrambled through Harper's bedroom, which had windows on to the courtyard, and saw the roof of the Lincoln in front of the portico. Then I panicked. I missed the door which led to the passage and got into his bathroom instead. By the time I had found the right door, I could hear Fischer's voice from the stairs. It was hopeless to try to dodge round through the rooms. I didn't know the way well enough. All I could do was retreat back through Harper's bedroom into the studio and shut the door. From there, there was no other way out, except through the window, but it was the only hiding place I could find.

I heard him come into the room, then a clink of money, then a sort of slap. He was emptying his pockets on to the table. The door didn't latch properly and I could hear every move he made. I knew that he would hear any move I made, too. I froze there.

'My God, that city's worse than New York in August,' he said.

I heard Miss Lipp answer him. The door connecting the suites, which I had shut, must have been opened by her.

'I wonder if Hamul fixed that water. Undo me will you, *Liebchen?*'

He moved away. I tiptoed over to the studio window and looked out. There was a small balcony outside and, a few feet below, the roof of the terrace. If I could get down there, I thought it might be possible to reach the orchard without breaking my neck. The trouble was that I would have to open the french window to get to the balcony. It had one of those long double bolts that you work by twisting a handle in the centre. They can make a clattering noise when they spring open, and this one looked as if it would. I went back to the door.

It sounded as if they were in his sitting-room. I heard her give a soft chuckle.

'Too many clothes on,' she said.

He came back into the bedroom and, then, after a moment or two went into the bathroom. Water began to run. I went to the window again and gingerly tried the handle. It moved easily enough. The bottom bolt slid out and the door sprang inward with a slight thud; but then I saw that one side of the connecting link was broken and that the top bolt hadn't moved. I tried to pull it down by hand, but it was too stiff. I would have to push it down through the slot at the top. I put a chair against the window and looked about for something metal I could use to push with.

The noise of running water from the bathroom stopped, and I stood still again. I tried to think what I had in my pockets that might move the bolt; a key perhaps.

'I will have to do something about my tan when we get back,' said Miss Lipp. She was in the next room now.

'It's holding up.'

'Your hair's wet.'

Silence, then a deep sigh from her and the bed creaked.

For about two minutes I clung to the hope that they were going to have a siesta. Then movements began. After a while I could hear their breathing and it wasn't the breathing of sleep. More minutes went by and there were other sounds. Then the beast with two backs was at work, and soon it was making its usual noises, panting and grunting and moaning, while I stood there like a half-wit, picturing her long legs and slim thighs and wondering how on earth I was going to get out of there without anybody seeing me. I was sweating so much that it was running into my eyes and misting my glasses. I couldn't have seen to get the bolt open just then, even if I had dared to try.

They seemed to go on interminably; but the noisy finales arrived at last. I waited, hopefully, for them to go to their bathrooms, but they didn't. There was just a long silence, until I heard him say, 'Here,' and a lighter clicked. Another silence, until he broke it.

'Where shall we eat tonight?'

'Les Baux. I will have the *feuilleté de ris de veau*. You?'

'Avallon, Moulin des Ruats, the *coq au vin*.'

'With the *Cuvée du Docteur*?'

'Of course. Though right now, frankly, I'd settle for a ham sandwich and a glass of beer.'

'It's not for long, *Liebchen*. I wonder who told Hans that this man could cook.'

'He can cook all right, but he's one of those lushes who has to be wooed. If he isn't, he gets into a white rage and says "The hell with you". Hans doesn't know how to handle him. I'll bet Arthur eats better than we do. In fact, I know damn well he does. Where's the ash-tray?'

'Here.' She giggled. 'Careful!'

'*Merde, alors!*'

'That is not the place for an ash-tray.'

Soon it began all over again. Eventually, when they were exhausted, they did have the decency to go to the bathrooms. While the water was running, I got up on to the chair and worked on the bolt with my room key. By the time he had finished in the bathroom, I had the window unlatched. I had to wait then until they were asleep; though it was not until I heard her voice again that I knew that she had returned to his bed.

'*Liebchen,*' she said drowsily.

'What is it?' He was half-asleep, too.

'Be careful, please, tomorrow.'

'*Entendu.*'

There was the sound of a kiss. I looked at my watch. It was twenty past three. I gave them ten minutes, then carefully edged over to the window and pulled one side open. I did it very slowly because there was a slight breeze outside and I did not want the draught to open the bedroom door while I was still there. Then I edged my way out on to the balcony.

It was a four-foot drop to the roof of the terrace and I made scarcely any noise getting down. I had more trouble at the end of the terrace. I am really not built for climbing, and I tried to use the trellis-work as a step-ladder. It gave way, and I slithered to the ground, clutching at the branches of an espaliered peach tree.

I managed to get to my room without anyone seeing the mess I was in. When I had cleaned up and changed my shirt, I went down to the car and put it away in the garage.

If I had noticed then that the door panels had been taken off, things would have turned out very differently for Harper, Lipp and Miller; but I didn't notice. It didn't even occur to me to look at them. I was still too flustered to do anything except try to behave naturally. Garaging the car was just a way of showing myself outside and on the job.

I went back into the kitchen. There was nobody there. I found a bottle of Geven's brandy and had a drink and a cigarette. When I was quite calm again, I went out and walked down the drive to the road.

The Opel was parked near the fishing-boat pier. I strolled across to it and saw the men inside watching me. As I passed, I said: 'Tufan.'

When I had gone on a few paces I heard a car door open. A moment or so later a man fell in step beside me.

'What is it?' He was a dark, hard-eyed police type in an oatmeal-coloured shirt with buttoned pockets. He spoke in French.

'Something dangerous is to be attempted tomorrow,' I said. 'I do not know what. I overheard part of a conversation. Major Tufan should be informed.'

'Very well. Why did you not drive today?'

'They told me I wasn't needed. Where did they go?'

'To Istanbul, Beyoglu. They drove to a garage by the Spanish Consulate. It is a garage that has spare parts for American cars. The driver, Fischer, remained there with the car for ten minutes. The other two men and the woman walked to the Divan Hotel. They had lunch there. Fischer joined them there and also had lunch. Then they walked back to the garage, picked up the car and returned here. Major Tufan says that you are to report on a chart later.'

'If I can. Tell him I made a search of the bedrooms while they were out, but could not find the chart. I will try to search the living-rooms tonight. It may be quite late before I can report. Will you be here?'

'Someone will be.'

'All right.'

As we turned and walked back towards the Opel, I crossed the road and re-entered the drive. I had something to think about now. From what I had overheard in the courtyard the night before, I knew that Fischer had some special task to perform that day. Had he already performed it, or was it yet to be performed? Driving the car into Istanbul so that he and the others could have some eatable food didn't seem very special. On the other hand, it was odd that I should have been told to stay behind, and odd about that visit to the garage. There was nothing wrong with the car and it needed no spare parts. And why had Fischer not walked to the Divan with the other three? Why had he stayed behind?

It is obvious that I should have thought of the car doors first. I didn't do so for a very simple reason: I knew from personal experience how long it took to remove and replace one panel, and Fischer had not been at the garage long enough to empty one door, let alone four. The possibility that his function might have been to give orders instead of doing the actual work didn't occur to me, *then*. And, I may say, it didn't occur to Tufan *at all*. If it had, I should have been spared a ghastly experience.

Anyway, when I went back through the yard to take a look at the car, my mind was on spare parts. I looked in the luggage compartment first to see if anything had been stowed away there; then I examined the engine. You can usually tell by the smudges and oil-smears when work has been done on an engine. I drew a blank, of course. It wasn't until I opened the door to see if anything had been left in the glove compartment that I saw the scratches.

Whoever had taken the panels off had made the very mistake I had been so careful to avoid; he had used an ordinary screwdriver on the Phillips heads. There were scratches and bright marks on the metal as well as cuts in the leather where the tool had slipped. Of course, nobody would have noticed them on a casual inspection, but I was so conscious of the panels and what I had seen behind them that the slightest mark stood out. I went over all four and knew at once that they had all been taken off and replaced. I also knew, from the different feel of the doors when I swung them on their hinges, that the heavy things which had been concealed inside were no longer there. Presumably, they had been removed in the garage near the Spanish Consulate. Where they were at that moment was anybody's guess.

I wondered whether I should go down to the road again immediately and report to the surveillance car, or wait until I reported later about the map. I decided to wait. If the stuff was still in the garage, it would probably still be there in the morning. If, as seemed more likely, it had already been moved somewhere else, then the damage was done and two or three hours would make no difference. Anyway, I didn't *want* to go back down to the road. I felt that I had run enough risks for one day already; and I still had to go looking for that damned map. I think I did the sensible thing. I can't stand people who are wise after the event, but it must be obvious now that it was Tufan who made the real mistakes, not me.

The trouble with Geven began while we were in the kitchen eating our dinner; or, rather, while I was eating and he was putting away more brandy. It was about seven o'clock, and he had been drinking steadily since six. In that hour he must have had nearly a third of a bottle. He wasn't yet quite drunk, but he was certainly far from sober.

He had made a perfectly delicious risotto with finely chopped chicken livers and pimentos in it. I was on my second helping and trying to persuade him to eat what he had on his plate, when Fischer came in.

'Geven!'

Geven looked up and gave him his wet smile. *'Vive la compagnie,'* he said convivially, and reached for a dirty glass. *'Un petit verre, monsieur?'*

Fischer ignored the invitation. 'I wish to know what you are preparing for dinner tonight,' he said.

'It is prepared.' Geven gave him a dismissive wave of his hand and turned to me again.

'Then can you tell me what it is.' At that moment Fischer caught sight of my plate. 'Ah, I see. A risotto, eh?'

Geven's lip quivered. 'That is for us servants. For the master and his guests there is a more important dish in the manner of the country.'

'What dish?'

'You would not understand.'

'I wish to know.'

Geven answered in Turkish. I understood one word of what he said: *kuzu,* baby lamb.

To my surprise, and to Geven's, too, I think, Fischer answered in the same language.

Geven stood up and shouted something.

Fischer shouted back, and then walked from the room before Geven had time to answer.

Geven sat down again, his lower lip quivering so violently that, when he tried to drain his glass, most of the brandy ran down his chin. He refilled the glass and glowered at me.

'Pislik!' he said. *'Domuz!'*

Those are rude words in Turkish. I gathered that they were meant for Fischer, so I said nothing and got on with my food.

He refilled my glass and shoved it towards me. 'A toast,' he said. 'All right.'

'There'll be no promotion this side of the ocean, so drink up, my lads, bless 'em all!'

Only he didn't say 'bless'. I had forgotten that he had been educated in Cyprus when it was under British rule.

'Drink!'

I drank. 'Bless 'em all.'

He began to sing. 'Bless all the sergeants and W.O. ones, bless all the corporals and their bleeding sons! Drink!'

I sipped. 'Bless 'em all.'

He drained the glass again and leaned across the chopping table, breathing heavily. 'I tell you,' he said menacingly; 'if that bastard says one more word, I kill him.'

'He's just a fool.'

'You defend him?' The lower lip quivered.

'No, no. But is he *worth* killing?'

He poured himself another drink. Both lips were working now, as if he had brought another thought agency into play in order to grapple with the unfamiliar dilemma my question had created.

The Hamuls arrived just then to prepare for the service of the evening meal, and I saw the old man's eyes take in the situation. He began talking to Geven. He spoke a country dialect and I couldn't even get the drift of what he was saying; but it seemed to improve matters a little. Geven grinned occasionally and even laughed once. However, he still went on drinking, and, when I tried to slip away to my room, there was a sudden flare of temper.

'Where you go?'

'You have work to do here. I am in the way.'

'You sit down. You are my guest in the kitchen. You drink noth-ing. Why?'

I had a whole tumbler full of brandy in front of me by now. I took another sip.

'Drink!'

I drank and tried to look as if I were enjoying myself. When he wasn't looking, I managed to tip half the brandy in my glass down the sink. It didn't do much good. As soon as he noticed the half-empty glass, he filled it up again.

Dinner had been ordered for eight-thirty, and by then he was weaving. It was Mrs Hamul who did the dishing up. He leaned against the range, glass in hand, smiling benignly on her while she ladled the loathsome contents of the stewpot on to the service plat-ters. Dinner was finally served.

'Bless 'em all!'

'Bless 'em all!'

'Drink!'

At that moment there was an indistinct shout from the direc-tion of the dining-room. Then a door along the passage was flung open, and there were quick footsteps. I heard Miss Lipp call out 'Hans!' Then Fischer came into the kitchen. He was carrying a plateful of food.

As Geven turned unsteadily to confront him, Fischer yelled something in Turkish and then flung the plate straight at his head.

The plate hit Geven on the shoulder and then crashed to the floor; but quite a lot of food went on to his face. Gravy ran down his smock.

Fischer was still shouting. Geven stared at him stupidly. Then, as Fischer flung a final insult and turned to go, a most peculiar expres-sion came over Geven's face. It was almost like a wide-eyed smile.

'*Monsieur est servi,*' he said. At the same instant, I saw his hand dart out for the chopping knife.

I shouted a warning to Fischer, but he was already out in the passage. Geven was after him in a flash. By the time I got through the door, Fischer was already backing away and yelling for help. There was blood streaming from a gash on his face and he had his hands up trying to protect himself. Geven was hacking and slashing at him like a madman.

As I ran forward and clung on to the arm wielding the chopping knife, Harper came into the passage from the dining-room.

'*Senden illâllah!*' bawled Geven.

Then Harper hit him in the side of the neck and he went down like an empty sack.

Fischer's arms and hands were pouring blood now, and he stood there looking down at them as if they did not belong to him.

Harper glanced at me. 'Get the car around, quick.'

I stopped the car at the foot of the steps and went in through the front of the house. It did not seem to be a moment for standing on ceremony.

Fischer was sitting in a marble-floored washroom just off the main hall. Harper and Miss Lipp were wrapping his hands and arms in towels; Miller was trying to staunch the face wound; the Hamuls were running round in circles.

Harper saw me and motioned to Hamul. 'Ask the old guy where the nearest doctor is. Not a hospital, a private doctor.'

'I will ask him,' muttered Fischer. His face was a dirty grey.

I caught Hamul's arm and shoved him forward.

There were two doctors in Sariyer, he said, but the nearest was outside Bülyükdere in the other direction. He would come to the villa if called by telephone.

Harper shook his head when Fischer told him this. 'We'll go to *him*,' he said. 'We'll give him five hundred lira and tell him you tripped over an electric fan. That should fix it.' He looked at Miss Lipp. 'You and Leo had better stay here, honey. The fewer, the better.'

She nodded.

'I don't know the way to this doctor's house,' I said. 'May we take Hamul as a guide?'

'Okay.'

Harper sat in the back with Fischer and a supply of fresh towels; Hamul came in front with me.

The doctor's house was two miles along the coast road. When we got there, Fischer told Hamul to wait outside in the car with me; so it was not possible for me to walk back and tell the men in the Opel what was going on. Presumably, they would find out from the doctor later on. Hamul fingered the leather of the seat for a while, then curled up on it and went to sleep. I tried to see if I could get out without waking him, but the sound of the door opening made him sit up instantly. After that, I just sat there and smoked. I suppose that I should have written a cigarette packet message about the car-doors and dropped it then—Hamul wouldn't have noticed that—but at that point, I still thought that I was going to be able to make a verbal report later.

They were inside well over an hour. When he came out, Fischer didn't look too bad at first sight. The cut on his face had a lint dressing neatly taped over it, and his left arm was resting in a small sling of the kind that suggests comfort for a minor sprain rather than a serious injury. But when he got closer I could see that both his hands and forearms were quite extensively bandaged, and that the left hand was cupped round a thick pad taped so as to immobilize his fingers. I got out and opened the door for him. He smelt of disinfectant and surgical spirit.

He and Harper got in without a word, and remained silent on the way back to the villa.

Miller and Miss Lipp were waiting on the terrace. As I pulled up into the courtyard, they came down the steps. I opened the door for Fischer. He got out and walked past them into the house. Still, nothing was said. Hamul was already making for his own quarters at the back. Miller and Miss Lipp came up to Harper.

'How is he?' Miller asked. There was nothing solicitous about the question. It was a grim request for information.

'The left hand has seven stitches on one cut, four on another, more stitches on the arm. The right forearm has seven stitches. The other cuts weren't so deep. The doctor was able to tape those up. He gave him some shots and a sedative.' His eyes went to Miss Lipp. 'Where's the cook?'

'Gone,' she said. 'When he woke up, he asked if he could go to his room. We let him. He just packed his things and went off on that scooter of his. We didn't try to stop him.'

He nodded.

'But about Fischer...' Miller began, his teeth showing as if he wanted to eat someone.

Harper broke in firmly. 'Let's go inside, Leo.' He turned to me. 'You can put the car away for now, Arthur, but I may want it again later to drive to Pendik, so you stick around. Make yourself some coffee in the kitchen, then I'll know where to find you.'

'Very good, sir.'

When I got to the kitchen I found that someone, Mrs Hamul no doubt, had washed the dishes and cleaned the place up. The charcoal fires on the range were not quite dead, but I made no attempt to revive one. I found a bottle of red wine and opened that.

I was getting anxious. It was nearly ten-thirty and the radio call was due at eleven; but I didn't so much mind missing another 'Essential you report progress'; it was the undelivered report on the car doors that bothered me. Obviously, Fischer's getting hurt had thrown some sort of spanner into the works and changes of plan were being made. If those changes meant that I was going to be up all night driving Harper to Pendik and back, I would have to deliver the message via a cigarette packet after all. I went into the scullery, in case Harper should suddenly come into the kitchen, and wrote the message—Car doors now empty, check garage near Spanish Consulate—on a piece of paper torn off a shelf-lining. I felt better when I had done that. My other assignment for the night, the search for the mysterious map, didn't worry me at all. In fact, though it may seem funny now, at that point in the proceedings I had completely forgotten about it.

It was after eleven-thirty and I had finished the last of the wine, when there was the sound of a door opening and Harper came through from the dining-room. I got to my feet.

'Sorry to keep you up this late, Arthur,' he said, 'but Mr Miller and I are having a friendly argument, and we want you to help us decide who's right. Come in.'

I followed him through the dining-room and along the passage to the room in which I had seen them the previous night.

It was L-shaped and even bigger than I had thought. When I had looked through the windows, all I had seen had been the short arm of the L. The long arm went all the way to the main entrance hall. There was a low platform with a concert-size grand piano on it. The room looked as if it had been used at some time for 'musical soirées'.

Miss Lipp and Miller were sitting at the library desk. Fischer was in the background, sitting in an armchair with his head thrown back so that he stared at the ceiling. I thought for a moment that he had passed out, but as I came in he slowly raised his head and stared at me. He looked terrible.

'Sit down, Arthur.' Harper motioned me to a chair facing Miller.

I sat down. Miss Lipp was watching Miller. Miller was watching me through his rimless glasses. The toothy smile was there as ever, but it was the most unamused smile I have ever seen; it was more like a grimace.

Harper leaned against the back of the settee.

'It's really two problems, Arthur,' he said. 'Tell me this. How long does it take to get to Pendik at this time of night? The same as during the day?'

'Less, perhaps; but it would depend on the ferry to Uskudar.'

'How often does that run at night?'

'Every hour, sir.'

'So if we missed one it could take us well over two hours?'

'Yes.'

He looked at Miller. 'Two hours to Pendik, two hours to persuade Giulio, two more hours to persuade Enrico…'

'If he would be persuaded,' Miss Lipp put in.

Harper nodded. 'Of course. And then two hours back. Not a very restful night, Leo.'

'Then postpone,' Miller snapped.

Harper shook his head. 'The overheads, Leo. If we postpone, it means abandon. What will our friends say to that?'

'It is not their necks.' Miller looked resentfully at Fischer. 'If you had not…' he began, but Harper cut him off sharply.

'We've been over all that, Leo. Now, why don't you at least give it a whirl?'

Miller shrugged.

Harper looked at me. 'We want to make an experiment, Arthur. Do you mind going over there and standing against the wall with your back against it?'

'Over here?'

'That's right. Your back touching the wall.' He went over to Fischer, picked up a length of thick cord which was lying across the bandaged hands and threw one end of it to me. I saw that the other end was attached to a leg of the settee. 'Now here's what it is, Arthur,' he went on. 'I've told Mr Miller that you can pull that settee six feet towards you just with the strength of your arms. Of course, your back's leaning against the wall, so you can't use your weight to help you. It has to be just your arms. Mr Miller says you can't do it, and he's got a hundred-dollar bill that says he's right. I've got one that says he's wrong. If he wins, I pay. If I win, you and I split fifty-fifty. How about it?'

'I'll try,' I said.

'Very well, begin,' said Miller. 'Your shoulders against the wall, your heels not more than ten centimetres from it and together.' He moved over so that he could see that I didn't cheat.

I have always detested that kind of parlour trick; in fact, I dislike any sort of trial of physical strength. They always remind me of a lot of boys I once saw in the school lavatories. They were standing in a row seeing who could urinate the farthest. Suddenly, they started laughing and then began to aim at each other. I happened to get in the way and it was very unpleasant. In my opinion, rugger is the same kind of thing—just childish, smelly, homosexual horseplay. I always got out of it whenever I could. Today, any sort of exercise brings on my indigestion immediately.

Frankly, then, I didn't think that there was the slightest chance of my being able to pull that heavy settee one foot, much less six. I am not particularly strong in the arms anyway. Why should I be? I have enough strength to lift a suitcase and drive a car; what more do I want?

'Go on,' said Miller. 'Pull with all your strength!'

I should have done as he said and fallen flat on my face. Then Harper would have lost a hundred dollars, and I should have been spared the ordeal. But Miss Lipp had to interfere.

'Just a minute, Arthur,' she said. 'I tried this and I couldn't do it. But you're a man with a good pair of shoulders on you, and I think you *can* do it.'

Even if I had never heard her use the phrase 'indignant sheep' about me, I would have known this heavy-handed guile for what it was. I do *not* have a good pair of shoulders on me. I have narrow, sloping ones. Women who think they can get away with that childish sort of flattery make me sick. I was really annoyed. Unfortunately, that made me go red. She smiled. I suppose she thought I was blushing because of her bloody compliment.

'I'm not much good at this sort of game,' I said.

'The thing is to pull on the cord steadily, Arthur. Don't jerk it. Pull steadily, and when it starts moving keep pulling steadily hand over hand. It's an easy fifty dollars. I *know* you can do it.'

I was getting really browned-off with her now. 'All right, you bitch,' I thought to myself; 'I'll show you!' So I did the exact opposite of what she'd said. I jerked on the cord as hard as I could.

The settee moved a few inches; but, of course, what I'd done by jerking it was to get the feet out of the dents they'd made for themselves in the thick carpet. After that, I just kept on pulling and it slid some more. As it got nearer it became easier because I was pulling up as well as along.

Harper looked at Miller. 'What about it, Leo?'

Miller felt my arms and shoulders as if he were buying a horse. 'He is flabby, out of condition,' he said sourly.

'But he did the trick.' Harper reminded him.

Miller spread out his hand as if to abandon the argument.

Harper took a note from his wallet. 'Here, Arthur,' he said, 'fifty dollars.' He paused and then went on quietly: 'How would you like to earn two thousand?'

I stared at him.

'Sit down,' he said.

I sat down and was glad to do so. My legs were trembling. With two thousand dollars I could buy a Central American passport that would be good for years; and it would be a real passport, too. I know, because I have looked into such matters. As long as you don't actually go to the country concerned, there's no trouble at all. You just buy the passport. That's the way their consuls abroad line their pockets. Of course, I knew it was all a pipe-dream. Even if I did whatever it was they wanted, Harper wasn't going to be in a position to pay me because the chances were that Tufan would have him in jail by then. Still, it was a good dream.

'I'd like that very much,' I said.

They were all watching me intently now.

'Don't you want to know what you have to do for it?' Harper asked.

I wasn't going to let him walk all over me. I sat back. 'What Mr Fischer was going to do, I suppose,' I answered; 'that is, if he hadn't had that little accident this evening.'

Miss Lipp laughed. 'I told you Arthur wasn't as simple as he looks,' she said.

'What else do you know, Arthur?' This was Harper again.

'Only what Miss Lipp told me, sir—that you are all very sensible, tolerant persons, who are very broad-minded about things that the law doesn't always approve of, but who don't like taking risks.'

'I told you all that, Arthur?' She pretended to be surprised.

'It was what I gathered, Miss Lipp.'

Harper smiled. 'All right, Arthur,' he said; 'suppose we just leave it there. We have a deal.'

'I think I'm entitled to know a little more than that.'

'And you will, Arthur. We'll be leaving here tomorrow afternoon around three, bags packed and everything because we won't be coming back. Before we go you'll have a complete briefing. And don't worry. All you have to do is just pull on a rope at the right place and time. Everything else is taken care of.'

'Is this a police matter?'

'It would be if they knew about it, but they don't. I told you, you don't have to worry. Believe me you've taken bigger risks in Athens for a lot less than two thousand.'

'On that subject, sir, I think I am now entitled to have my letter back.'

Harper looked questioningly at Miller and Fischer. The latter began to talk in German. He spoke slowly and wearily now, and I guessed that the sedative had taken effect, but his attitude was clear enough. So was Miller's. Harper turned to me and shook his head regretfully.

'I'm sorry, Arthur, that'll have to wait. In fact, my friends seem to feel that you may be quite a security risk for the next twelve hours or so.'

'I don't understand.'

'Sure you do.' He grinned. 'I'll bet the idea's been churning around in that cute little brain of yours for the last five minutes.

"If two hands on a rope are worth two thousand dollars to these people, what would a tip-off be worth to the police?"'

'I assure you…'

'Of course you do, Arthur. I was only kidding.' His tone was quite friendly. 'But you see the problems. We like to feel safe. Even that letter doesn't mean much here. Do you have the car keys?'

'Yes.'

'Let me have them.'

I handed them to him.

'You see, we wouldn't want you to have second thoughts and maybe walk out on us,' he explained.

'And we would not like him to use the telephone,' said Miller.

'That's right.' Harper thought for a moment. 'Hans is going to need help undressing,' he said, 'and the doctor's given him another antibiotic he has to take. I think it would be best if we made up an extra bed in his room and Arthur slept there.'

'So that he can kill me when I am helpless and get out by the window?' Fischer demanded thickly.

'Oh, I don't think Arthur would do that. Would you, Arthur?'

'Of course not.'

'That's right. But we don't want Hans to be worrying, do we? The doctor says he really needs to sleep. And you should have a good night's sleep, too, Arthur. You won't get any tomorrow night. You wouldn't mind taking a couple of good strong sleeping pills, would you? Or maybe even three?'

I hesitated.

'Oh, they won't hurt you, Arthur.' Miss Lipp gave me a fond smile. 'I'll tell you what. If you'll be a good boy and take your pills, I'll take one, too. We'll all need our sleep tomorrow.'

What could I say?

CHAPTER NINE

M Y HEAD FELT AS IF IT HAD BEEN STUFFED WITH STEEL WOOL. There was even a metallic taste in my mouth. It took me some time to remember where I was. I could hear a loud buzzing noise. When, at last, I managed to open my eyes, I saw Fischer. The buzzing came from an electric shaver which he was holding, awkwardly, in his right hand.

My bed consisted of a mattress on the floor and the blankets from my old room. I rolled off the mattress and got to my feet unsteadily. Fischer gave me a disagreeable look.

'You snore like a pig,' he said.

He had a shirt and slacks on, I was glad to see; Harper or Miller must have helped him. Undressing him, the night before, had been an unpleasant task. It had meant touching him, and I hate touching anyone I dislike—another man especially.

'What's the time?' I asked.

They had taken everything from me after they had made me swallow the sleeping pills, even my watch. All I had been allowed had been my pyjama coat.

'About eleven,' he answered. 'Your clothes have been put in there.' He indicated a door.

I went through and found myself in one of the part-furnished rooms I had seen the day before. My things were piled on a brown, cut-velvet *chaise-longue*. I disposed of a minor anxiety first. The cigarette packet with the message inside it was still in my hip pocket and apparently undetected. I left it where it was. With any luck, I thought, I might be able to add to it. My papers were there. The radio was in its case.

From the bedroom Fischer said: 'I have finished with this bath-room. You may use it.'

'I think I will go and get some coffee first.'

'Then bring all your papers and money in here.'

There was no point in arguing. I did as he said, put some trousers on and found my way downstairs to the kitchen.

Mrs Hamul was there. The sight of the hired driver, unshaven and wearing a pyjama jacket at eleven in the morning must have seemed odd to her. She looked at me as if I were raving mad. I asked her for coffee. She gave me tea, and some of the previous day's bread toasted. The tea wasn't bad. My head began to clear. As I ate the toast, I wondered if I could muster enough Turkish to persuade her or her husband to take a message to the surveillance people on the road. Then Miss Lipp came in, well-groomed and very chic in white with yellow stripes.

'Good morning, Arthur. How do you feel?'

'Good morning, Miss Lipp. I feel terrible, thank you.'

'Yes, you look it, but I expect you'll feel better when you've cleaned up a bit. What's the Turkish for eggs?'

'"*Yumurta*", I think.'

Mrs Hamul heard the word and they began a sign-language conversation about eggs. I went back upstairs.

Miller was helping Fischer to pack. I slipped the empty cigarette packet and a pencil into my shaving kit and went into the bathroom. There was a lock on the door. While my bath was running, I added to the message I had written the previous night. *Am forced replace injured Fischer and closely watched. Event planned for tonight. Details unknown. Miller may be key person.*

The bedroom was empty when I returned to it. I dressed, packed my bag and went back down to the kitchen.

Miss Lipp was supervising the Hamuls' preparations for lunch. She looked up as I came in.

'The others are out on the terrace, Arthur,' she said. 'Why don't you go out there and get yourself a drink?'

'Very well.'

I went through the dining-room into the main hall. There, I hesitated. I was still trying to think of a way of getting down to the road and back without their knowing. As they were on the terrace it was, of course, hopeless to attempt to cross the courtyard. I would have to find some other way round the back and down through the trees. But that might take twenty minutes or more. And supposing Miss Lipp came out to the terrace and asked where I was. I gave up, and decided to rely upon dropping the cigarette packet.

The first thing I saw on the terrace was the cardboard box which Harper had brought back with him from Pendik. It was open and discarded on a chair. Harper, Fischer and Miller were contemplating something laid out across two tables.

It was a block-and-tackle, but of a kind I had not seen before. The blocks were triple-sheaved and made of some light metal alloy. They were so small that you could hold both of them in one hand. The 'rope' was a white cord about a quarter of an inch in diameter and there was a lot of it. On another table there was a thing that looked like a broad belt with hooks at each end, like those you see on dog-leashes.

Fischer looked up and stared at me haughtily.

'Miss Lipp told me to come here and have a drink,' I said.

Harper waved to a table with bottles and glasses on it. 'Help yourself. Then you'd better have a look at this.'

I gave myself some *raki* and looked at the cord of the tackle. It was like silk.

'Nylon,' Harper said; 'breaking strain over a ton. What you have to remember about it is that it's also slightly elastic. There's a lot of give in this tackle. You know how these things work?'

'Yes.'

'Show me,' said Miller. He picked up the belt and hooked it around one of the terrace pillars. 'Show me how you would pull this pillar down.'

I hooked one block to the belt, tied the other to the balustrade and pulled on the tackle.

'Okay,' said Harper, 'that'll do. Leo, I think you'd better carry the tackle. Arthur's too fat. It'll show on him. He can take the sling and the anchor rope. I don't think Hans should carry anything except his gun and the water-flask.'

'It is only because my skin is very sensitive that I object,' said Miller.

'Well, it won't be for long. As soon as you're inside you can take it off.'

Miller sighed irritably but said no more.

'May I know what it is I have to do?' I asked.

'Just pull on this tackle, Arthur. Oh, you mean about taking this gear along? Well, you'll have to carry that sling—' he indicated the belt—'and this extra rope here, wound around that beautiful body of yours under your shirt, so that nobody can see it. It'll be a bit warm for a while, but you'll have plenty of time to cool off. Any other questions?'

I had a dozen and he knew it, but there isn't any sense in asking when you know you're not going to be answered.

'Who is going to carry the bag?' asked Miller.

'You'd better take that, folded in your pocket.'

Miss Lipp came out. 'Lunch in thirty minutes,' she said.

'Lunch!' Miller looked sour.

'You can eat eggs, Leo. You've got to eat something.' She took the drink Harper handed her. 'Does Arthur know that he's going to have to wait for his dinner tonight?'

'I don't know anything, Miss Lipp,' I said calmly; 'but I will say this. I was told that I would be given a briefing today. So far, all I have been given is a bad attack of nervous indigestion. Whether I eat dinner or not, and, for that matter, whether I eat lunch or not, are matters of complete indifference to me.'

She went quite red in the face, and I wondered for a moment if I had said anything offensive; then I realized that the damned woman was trying not to laugh. She looked at Harper.

'Okay,' he said. 'Come in here.' He led the way through a french window into the drawing-room. Only Miss Lipp followed with me. I heard Fischer asking Miller to pour him another drink and Miller telling him that he ought to exercise the hand not pamper it. Then I no longer listened. Harper had walked to the library table, opened a drawer in it and pulled out the 'map'.

'Recognize this place?' he asked.

'Yes.'

It was a plan of part of the Seraglio area and of the roads adjacent to the walls. The triangular shape I had noted was formed by the coastline.

'This is what we are going to do,' he went on. 'When we leave here, we will drive to a garage in Istanbul. Our bags will be in the trunk of the Lincoln. At the garage, Mr Miller, Mr Fischer, you and I will get out of the Lincoln and into a different car which will be waiting there. I will then drive you to the Seraglio Palace. Then, Mr Miller, Mr Fischer and you will get out. The Palace is open to the public until five. The three of you will buy tickets and enter in the

ordinary way as tourists. You will then cross the second courtyard
to the Gate of Felicity. When you are sure that the guides have lost
interest in you, you will go through into the third courtyard and
turn left. You then have a short walk—exactly sixty paces—before
you come to a big bronze gate in a courtyard to the left with a small
door beside it. Both gate and door are kept locked, but Mr Miller will
have a key to the door. Beyond the door is a passage with a stairway
leading up to the roof of the White Eunuchs' apartments'—he
pointed to the plan—'here. Then you lock the door behind you and
wait. Clear so far?'

'Quite clear, except about why we're doing all this.'

'Oh, I thought you'd have guessed that.' He grinned. 'We're just
going to have ourselves a piece of the old Sultans' loot. Just a little
piece, that's all—about a million dollars' worth.'

I looked at Miss Lipp.

'I was being cagey, Arthur,' she said. 'There is some obsidian and
garnet there, and green tourmaline, too. But a lot of that stuff's the
real thing. There are six pigeon's blood rubies in that throne-room
that must be over twenty carats apiece. Do you know what just one
ruby like that is worth, Arthur? And the emeralds on those Koran
caskets! My God!'

Harper laughed. 'All right, honey, I think Arthur has the picture.
Now'—he turned again to the plan—'there are civilian watchmen
on duty, but not very many of them, and the night-shift comes on
at eight. You give them an hour to settle down. At nine you move.
You go up the stairs to the roof and turn left. There are three little
domes, cupolas they call them, on the roof there, and you walk
along to the right of them. After that the roof is more or less flat
until you get to the gate arch. You go around that over the roof of
the audience chamber and on until you see the chimneys of the

SEA OF MARMARA

Ataturk Statue

Seraglio Point

Goths Column

St Irene

Bab-i-Hümayun Gate

St Sophia

Steep rough ground

Terraced ground

N

YARDS
0   100   200   300

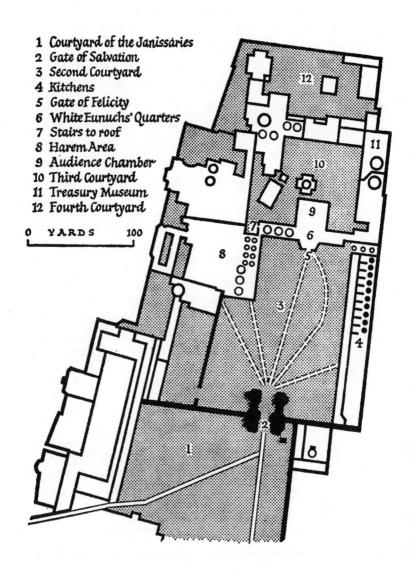

1 Courtyard of the Janissaries
2 Gate of Salvation
3 Second Courtyard
4 Kitchens
5 Gate of Felicity
6 White Eunuchs' Quarters
7 Stairs to roof
8 Harem Area
9 Audience Chamber
10 Third Courtyard
11 Treasury Museum
12 Fourth Courtyard

0 YARDS 100

kitchens on your right. Then you turn left again, cross the roof of the place where they have the miniatures and tapestries. At the end of it there's a three-foot drop on to the roof of the Treasury museum. That's where you have to be careful. The Treasury roof is thirty-five feet wide, but it's vaulted. There is a flat area around the cupola, though, so you climb down there. All quite safe. The cupola is ten feet in diameter and that'll be your anchor for the tackle. Mr Miller'll tie the knots for you. When he's got the sling hooked up, he'll sit in it. Then all you have to do is lower him over the side until he's level with a steel shutter eighteen feet below. He'll do the rest.'

'Mr Miller will?'

He looked at me with amusement. 'You think he's too old for that sort of thing? Arthur, when Mr Miller gets busy he makes a fly look like a man in diving boots.'

'You said there was a steel shutter?'

'You could open it with a toothpick. The wall's four feet thick and solid stone. I guess it'd stand up to a six-inch shell. But the shutters over the window apertures are just quarter-inch plate with ordinary draw bolts on them. They don't even fit properly. And no alarm system.'

'But if this jewellery is so valuable...'

'Have you ever looked through one of those window apertures, Arthur? There's a sheer drop of three hundred feet below. It's quite impossible to get up or down there. That's why we're going in from above. The trick is getting out again. What their security set-up relies on is the fact that the whole area is walled like a fortress. There are gates, of course, and the gates have troops guarding them at night; but gates can be opened if you know how. That'll all be taken care of. You'll walk out of there just as easily as you walked in.' His eyes found mine and held them. 'You see, Arthur, we're professionals.'

I forced myself to look away. I looked at Miss Lipp; but her eyes had the same intent look as his. 'I'm sorry,' I said; 'I'm not a professional.'

'*You* don't have to be,' she said.

'I can't do it, Mr Harper.'

'Why not?'

'Because I'd be too afraid.'

He smiled. 'That's the best thing I've heard you say, Arthur. You had me quite worried for a moment.'

'I mean it.'

'Sure you do. Who wouldn't be scared? *I'm* scared. In a few hours' time I'll be even more scared. That's good. If you aren't a bit scared you don't stay on your toes.'

'I'm not talking about being a bit scared, Mr Harper. I'm talking about being *too* scared. I'd be no use to you.' And I meant it. I was thinking of myself on top of that roof with a three-hundred-foot drop down to the road. I can't stand heights.

There was a silence, and then she laughed. 'I don't believe you, Arthur,' she said. 'You? You with two good arms and hands to hold on with, scared of going where Hans Fischer isn't afraid to go with only *half* a hand? It doesn't make sense.'

'I'm sorry,' I said again.

There was another silence and then he glanced at her and moved his head slightly. She walked out on to the terrace.

'Let's get a couple of things straight, Arthur,' he said. 'All I'm asking you to do is take a little ride and then a little walk, and then handle a rope for twenty minutes. You'll be in no danger. Nobody's going to take pot-shots at you. And when it's done you get two thousand bucks. Right?'

'Yes, but…'

'Let me finish. Now, supposing you chicken out, what do we do?'

'Get someone else, I suppose.'

'Yes, but what do we do about *you*?' He paused. 'You see, Arthur, it's not just a question of getting the job done. You know too much now not to be a part of it. If you're going to be on the outside, well, we'll have to protect ourselves another way. You follow me?'

He could see that I did. I had a choice: I could either frighten myself to death on the roof of the Seraglio, or take a shorter, quicker route to the police mortuary.

'Now go get yourself another drink and stop worrying,' he said; 'just think of the two thousand bucks.'

I shrugged. 'All right. I'm merely telling you how I feel, that's all.'

'You'll be okay, Arthur.' He led the way back on to the terrace.

It was on the tip of my tongue to ask him how okay Mr Miller would be if the height got me down and I passed out while I was handling the tackle; but I thought better of it. If he realized that I really wasn't just being timid, that I really couldn't stand heights, he might decide that I was too dangerous a liability in every way. Besides, I was coming to my senses again now. Tufan's 'politicals' had turned out to be big-time crooks after all. I had been right all along, and he had been hopelessly wrong; but he was still a powerful ally, and I still had a good chance of being able to stop the whole thing. All I had to do was add just three words—*raiding Seraglio treasury*—to the note in the cigarette packet and drop it for the surveillance people. After that, my worries would be over, and Harper's would begin. I had a pleasing vision of the lot of them, rounded up and in handcuffs, watching Tufan hand me a brand-new British passport.

'What are you grinning at, Arthur?' Harper asked.

I was pouring myself the second drink he had prescribed. 'You told me to think of the two thousand dollars, Mr Harper,' I answered. 'I was just carrying out orders.'

'You're a screwball, Arthur,' he said amiably; but I saw a reflective look in his eyes and decided that I had better watch myself. All the same, I couldn't help wondering what he would have said and done if he had been warned, at that moment, that the customs people in Edirne had looked inside the doors of the car, and that every move he had made since had been made with the knowledge and by permission of the security police—if, in other words, he had been told how vulnerable he was. Not that I had the slightest desire to warn him; I hadn't forgotten the caning he had given me in Athens; but if it had been safe to do so, I would have liked to have told him that it was my lousy out-of-date Egyptian passport that had done the job. I would have liked to have seen the bastard's face. I still would.

Hamul shuffled out and made signs to Miss Lipp that lunch was served. She glanced at me. 'Bring your drink in with you, Arthur.'

Presumably I was being promoted to eating with the gentry so that they could keep an eye on me.

Miller was a gloomy feeder, and made the omelette less appetizing than it could have been by talking about infectious diseases all the time. How did they grow virus cultures in laboratories? Why, in eggs, of course! He discussed the possible consequences at length. The others took no notice; evidently they were used to him; but it got me down. I hadn't felt much like eating anyway.

When the fruit came Harper looked across at me. 'As soon as the Hamuls have cleared away,' he said, 'you had better start getting the bags down. They think we're going to Ankara for a couple of days, so it doesn't matter if they see us. The important thing is that we leave ourselves time to clean up the rooms.'

'Clean them up?'

'For fingerprints. With any luck we'll never be connected with this place. The rent was paid in advance and the owner couldn't care less if we don't show up again. The Hamuls will dust off most of it automatically. They're great polishers, I've noticed. But things they could miss, like window handles and closet mirrors, we should take care of ourselves—just in case.'

By two o'clock I had all the bags down and asked Harper if I could go to my old room to clean up there. He nodded. 'Okay, Arthur, but don't be too long. I want you to give Mr Fischer a hand.'

I hurried upstairs. In the bathroom, I completed the cigarette packet message. Then I went through the motions of 'cleaning up'— Tufan already had *my* fingerprints—and returned to Fischer's room.

At a quarter to three Harper drove the car from the garage to the courtyard and I loaded the bags. There wasn't room for all of them in the luggage compartment, so some had to go on the floor by the back seat.

At three, Harper, Miller and I went up to Miller's room. There, Miller and I took our shirts off and swathed ourselves in the tackle, Harper assisting and rearranging things until he was satisfied that nothing would show. I had the spring hooks of the sling hanging down inside my trouser-legs. It was dreadfully uncomfortable. Harper made me walk up and down so that he could see that all was in order.

'You look as if you've wet your pants,' he complained. 'Can't you walk more naturally?'

'The hooks keep hitting one another.'

'Well, wear one higher and one lower.'

After further adjustments, he was satisfied and we went downstairs to be inspected by Miss Lipp. She had fault to find with

Miller—he had developed the same trouble with the blocks as I had with the hooks—and while they were putting it right I managed to transfer the cigarette packet from my hip to my shirt pocket, so that it would be easier to get at when the time came.

Fischer was getting edgy now. The bandages prevented his wearing a wrist-watch and he kept looking at Miller's. Miller suddenly got irritated.

'You cannot help, so do not get in the way,' he snapped.

'It is time we were leaving. After four-thirty, they count the people going in.'

'I'll tell you when it's time to leave,' Harper said. 'If you can't keep still, Hans, go sit in the car.'

Fischer sulked, while Miller returned to his bedroom for final adjustments. Harper turned to me.

'You're looking warm, Arthur. Better you don't drive with all that junk under your shirt. You'll only get warmer. Besides, Miss Lipp knows the way. You ride in the back.'

'Very well.' I had hoped that I might be able to drop the packet while I was making a hand signal; but I knew it was no use arguing with him.

At three-thirty we all went out and got into the car. Miller, of course, was first in the back. Harper motioned me to follow, then Fischer got in after me and Harper shut the door. So I wasn't even next to a window.

Miss Lipp drove with Harper beside her.

From where I was sitting, the driving mirror did not reflect the road behind. After a minute or two, and on the pretext of giving Fischer more room for the arm that was in the sling, I managed to make a half-turn and glance through the rear window. The Peugeot was following.

Miss Lipp drove steadily and very carefully, but there wasn't much traffic and we made good time. At ten to four we were past the Dolmabahçe Palace and following the tramlines up towards Taxim Square. I had assumed that the garage Harper had spoken of would be the one near the Spanish Consulate, and within walking distance of the Divan Hotel, which I had heard about from the surveillance man. It looked at that point as if the assumption were correct. Then, quite suddenly, everything seemed to go wrong.

Instead of turning right at Taxim Square, she went straight on across it and down the hill towards Galata. I was so surprised that I nearly lost my head and told her she was going the wrong way. Just in time, I remembered that I wasn't supposed to know the way. But Miller had noticed my involuntary movement.

'What is the matter?'

'That pedestrian back there—I thought he was going to walk straight into us.' It is a remark that foreigners driving in Istanbul make every other minute.

He snorted. 'They are peasants. They deny the existence of machinery.'

At that moment, Miss Lipp turned sharply left and we plunged down a ramp behind a service station.

It wasn't a large place underground. There was garage space for about twenty cars and a greasing bay with an inspection pit. Over the pit stood a Volkswagen Minibus van. In front of it stood a man in overalls with a filthy rag in his hand.

Miss Lipp pulled the Lincoln over to the left and stopped. Harper said: 'Here we are! Out!'

Miller and Harper already had their doors open, and Harper opened Fischer's side as well. As I slid out after Miller, I got the cigarette packet from my shirt pocket into the palm of my hand.

Now Harper was climbing up into the driving seat of the van.

'Move yourselves,' he said, and pressed the starter.

The other door of the van was at the side. Miller wrenched it open and got in. As I followed, I pretended to stumble and then dropped the cigarette packet.

I saw it land on the greasy concrete and climbed on in. Then, the door swung to behind me and I heard Fischer swear as it caught him on the shoulder. I leaned back to hold it open for him, so I was looking down and saw it happen. As he put out his good hand to grasp the hand-rail and climb in, his left foot caught the cigarette packet and swept it under the van into the pit. It wasn't intentional. He wasn't even looking down.

Miller shut the door and latched it.

'Hold tight,' Harper said and let in the clutch.

As the van lurched forward, the back of my legs hit the edge of a packing case and I sat down on it. My face was right up against the small window at the back.

We went up to the top of the ramp again, waited a moment or two for a bus to go by, and then made a left turn on down towards the Galata Bridge. Through the window, I could see the Peugeot parked opposite the garage.

It was still there when I lost sight of it. It hadn't moved. It was waiting, faithful unto death, for the Lincoln to come out.

CHAPTER TEN

F OR A MINUTE OR TWO I COULDN'T BELIEVE THAT IT HAD happened, and kept looking back through the window expecting to see that the Peugeot was following after all. It wasn't. Fischer was swearing and massaging his left shoulder where the door had caught him. Miller was grinning to himself as if at some private joke. As we bounced over the tram-lines on to the Galata Bridge, I gave up looking back and stared at the floor. At my feet, amid some wood shavings, there were torn pieces of an Athens newspaper.

Of the six packing cases in the van, three were being used as seats. From the way the other three vibrated and slid about they appeared to be empty. From the way Miller and Fischer were having to hold on to steady themselves on the corners, it looked as if their cases were empty, too. Mine was more steady. It seemed likely that the case that I was sitting on now held the grenades, the pistols and the ammunition that had come from Athens inside the doors of the car. I wished the whole lot would blow up then and there. It didn't even occur to me, then, to wonder how they were going to be used. I had enough to think of with my own troubles.

As Harper drove past Aya Sophia and headed towards the gate in the old Seraglio wall, he began to talk over his shoulder to us.

'Leo goes first. Hans and Arthur together a hundred yards behind him. Arthur, you pay for Hans so that he doesn't have to fumble for money with those bandages on. Right?'

'Yes.'

He drove through into the Courtyard of the Janissaries and pulled up under the trees opposite St Irene.

'I'm not taking you any nearer to the entrance,' he said. 'There'll be guides hanging around and we don't want them identifying you with this van. On your way, Leo. See you tonight.'

Miller got out and walked towards the Ortakapi Gate. He had about a hundred and fifty yards to go.

When he had covered half the distance, Harper said: 'Okay, you two. Get ready. And, Arthur, you watch yourself. Leo and Hans both have guns and they'll use them if you start getting out of line in any way.'

'I will think of the two thousand dollars.'

'You do that. I'll be right behind you now, just to see that you make it inside.'

'We'll make it.'

I wanted to appear as co-operative as I could just then, because, although I was sick with panic, I had thought of a way of stopping them that they couldn't blame on me—at least in a dangerous way. I still had my guide's licence. Tufan had warned me against attracting attention to myself as a guide in case I was challenged and had to show it. He had said that, because I was a foreigner, that would cause trouble with museum guards. Well, trouble with museum guards was the one kind of trouble I needed at that moment; and the more the better.

Fischer and I began to walk towards the gate. Miller was within a few yards of it, and I saw a guide approach him. Miller walked straight on in without a glance at the man.

'That's the way,' Fischer said and began to walk a little faster.

The hooks began to thump against my legs. 'Not so fast,' I said; 'if these hooks swing too much they'll show.'

He slowed down again immediately.

'You needn't worry about the guides,' I said, 'I've got my licence. I'll be your guide.'

As we got near the Gate, I began to give him the set speech, all about the weekly executions, the block, the fountain, the Executioner who was also the Chief Gardener.

The guide who had approached Miller was watching us, so I raised my voice slightly to make sure that he heard me and knew what I was up to. What I hoped was that he would follow us and complain about me to the guard at the gate. Instead, he lost interest and turned away.

It was disappointing, but I had another plan worked out by then.

Just inside the gate-house there is the counter where you pay to go in. When I got to it, I handed the man three separate lira and said: 'Two tickets, please.' At the same time I showed him my guide's licence.

From his point of view I had done three wrong things. I had shown a guide's licence, and yet, by asking for two tickets, revealed that I didn't know that guides were admitted free; I had given him three lira, which a real guide would have known was enough to buy six tickets; and I had spoken to him in English.

He was a haggard man with a small black moustache and a disagreeable expression. I waited for trouble. It never came. He did absolutely nothing but glance at the licence, push across one ticket, take one of the lira and give me sixty kurush change. It was maddening. I picked the change up very slowly, hoping he would start to think.

'Let's go,' Fischer said.

Out of the corner of my eye I could see Harper approaching the gate. There was nothing for it but to go on. Usually there are one or two guides touting for customers inside the Second Courtyard. In fact, it had been there that I had been challenged three years previously. *That* episode had ended up in my being jailed for the night. I could only count on the same thing happening again.

Of course, the same thing did *not* happen again. Because it was the last hour of the museum day, all the courtyard guides were either out with parties of suckers completing tours of the palace, or cooling their fat arses in the nearest café.

I did my best. As we walked on along the right side of the Second Courtyard, I gave Fischer the set speech on the Seraglio kitchens—all about the Sung, Yuna and Ming porcelains—but nobody as much as looked at us. Miller had already reached the Gate of Felicity and was standing there gawking at it like a tourist. When he heard our footsteps behind him, he walked through into the Third Courtyard.

I hesitated. Once we were through the gate, the Audience Chamber and the Library of Ahmed the Third would screen us from the buildings across the courtyard that were open to the public. Unless a guard came out of the manuscript library, and there was no reason why one should, there would be nothing to stop us getting to the door to which Miller had the key.

'Why are you stopping?' Fischer asked.

'He said that we were to stop here.'

'Only if there were guides watching.'

There were footsteps on the paving stones behind us. I turned my head. It was Harper.

'Keep going, Arthur,' he said; 'just keep going.' His voice was quite low, but it had an edge to it.

He was only about six paces away now, and I knew suddenly from the look on his face that I dare not let him reach me.

So I went on with Fischer through the Gate of Felicity. I suppose that obedience to Harper had become almost as instinctive with me as breathing.

As he had said, the walk was exactly sixty paces. Nobody stopped us. Nobody noticed us. Miller already had the door open when Fischer and I got there. All I remember about the outside of the door was that it had wood mouldings on it arranged in an octagon pattern. Then, with Fischer behind me, I was standing in a narrow stone passage with a vaulted ceiling and Miller was re-locking the door.

The passage was about twenty feet long and ended in a blank wall with a coiled fire hose inside a glass-fronted box fastened to it. The spiral stairway to the roof was of iron and had the name of a German company on it. The same company had supplied the fire hose. Miller walked to the bottom of the staircase and looked up at it appreciatively. 'A very clever girl,' he said.

Fischer shrugged. 'For someone who interpreted air photos for the Luftwaffe it was not difficult,' he said. 'A blind man could have seen this on the enlarged photo she had. It was I who had to find the way to it, and I who had to get a key and make all the other arrangements.'

Miller chuckled. 'It was she who had the idea, Hans, and Karl who worked out the arrangements. We are only the technicians. They are the artists.'

He seemed to be enjoying himself thoroughly, and looked more wolfish than ever. I felt like being sick.

Fischer sat on the stairs. Miller took off his coat and shirt and unwound the tackle from about his skinny waist. There didn't seem any point in being uncomfortable as well as frightened, so I unbuttoned, too, and got rid of the sling and anchor rope. He attached them to the tackle. Then he took a black velvet bag from his pocket. It was about the size of a man's sock and had a draw string at the top and a spring clip. He attached the clip to one of the hooks on the sling.

'Now,' he said, 'we are ready.' He looked at his watch. 'In an hour or so Giulio and Enrico will be on their way.'

'Who are they?' I asked.

'Friends who will bring the boat for us,' said Miller.

'A boat? How can a boat reach us?'

'It doesn't,' said Fischer. 'We reach the boat. You know the yards along the shore by the old city wall, where the boats land the firewood?'

I did. Istanbul is a wood-burning city in winter. The firewood yards stretch for nearly a mile along the coast road south-east of Seraglio Point, where the water is deep enough for coasters to come close inshore. But we were two miles from there.

'Do we fly?'

'The Volkswagen will call for us.' He grinned at Miller.

'Hadn't you better tell me more than that?'

'That is not our part of the operation,' Miller said. 'Our part is this. When we leave the Treasury we go quietly back over the kitchens until we come to the wall of the Courtyard of the Janissaries above the place where the cars park during the day. The wall is only twenty feet high and there are trees there to screen us when we lower ourselves to the ground with the tackle. Then...'

'Then,' Fischer broke in, 'we take a little walk to where the Volkswagen will be waiting.'

I answered Miller. 'Is Mr Fischer to lower himself to the ground with one hand?'

'He will seat himself in the sling. Only one hand is needed to hold on to the buckles.'

'Even in the outer courtyard we are still inside the walls.'

'There will be a way through them.' He dismissed the subject with an impatient wave of his hand and looked about him for a place to sit down. There was only the iron staircase. He examined the steps of it. 'Everything here is very dirty,' he complained. 'That these people do not all die of disease is incredible. Immunity, perhaps. There was a city here even before Constantine's. Two thousand years or more of plague are in this place—cholera, bubonic, *la vérole*, dysentery.'

'Not any more, Leo,' said Fischer; 'they have even cleaned the drains.'

'It is all waiting in the dust,' Miller insisted gloomily.

He arranged the nylon rope so as to make a seat on the stairs before he sat down. His exuberance had gone. He had remembered about germs and bacteria.

I sat on the bottom step wishing that I had an irrational anxiety like his to occupy my mind, instead of the real and immediate fears that occupied my lungs, my heart and my stomach.

At five o'clock, bells were sounded in the courtyards and there were one or two distant shouts. The guards were herding everyone out and closing up for the night.

I started to light a cigarette, but Miller stopped me. 'Not until it is dark,' he said. 'The sun might happen to illuminate the smoke before it dispersed above the roof. It is better also that we talk no more. It will become very quiet outside and we do not know how the acoustics of a place like this may work. No unnecessary risks.'

That was what Tufan had said. I wondered what he was doing. He must, I thought, already know that he had lost everyone and everything, except Miss Lipp and the Lincoln. The Peugeot would have radioed in. The question was whether the surveillance people had remembered the Volkswagen van or not. If they had, there would be a faint possibility of Tufan's being able to trace it, using the police; but it seemed very faint. I wondered how many thousand Volkswagen vans there were in the Istanbul area. Of course, if they had happened to notice the registration number—if this, if that. Fischer began to snore and Miller tapped his leg until he stopped.

The patch of sky at the top of the staircase turned red and then grey and then blue-black. I lit a cigarette and saw Miller's teeth gleaming yellowly in the light of the match.

'What about flashlights?' I whispered. 'We won't be able to see a thing.'

'There will be a third-quarter moon.'

At about eight there was a murmur of voices from one or other of the courtyards—in there it was impossible to tell which—and a man laughed. Presumably, the night watchmen were taking over. Then there was silence again. A plane going over became an event, something to think about. Was it preparing to land at Yesilköy airport or had it just taken off?

Fischer produced a flask of water with a metal cup on the base, and we each had a drink. Another age went by. Then there was the faint sound of a train pulling out of the Sirkeci station and chugging round the sharp curve at Seraglio Point below. Its whistle sounded shrilly, like a French train, and then it began to gather speed. As the sound died away, a light glared almost blinding me. Miller had a penlight in his hand and was looking at his watch. He sighed contentedly.

'We can go,' he whispered.

'The light a moment, Leo,' Fischer said.

Miller held the light up for him. With his good hand, Fischer eased a small snub-nosed revolver from his breast pocket, worked the safety-catch and then transferred the thing to a side pocket. He gave me a meaning look as he patted it.

Miller got up, so I stood up, too. He came down the steps with the tackle and looped it around one shoulder like a bandolier. 'I will go first,' he said. 'Arthur will follow me. Then you, Hans. Is there anything else? Ah yes, there is.'

He went and relieved himself in the corner by the fire hose. When he had finished Fischer did the same thing.

I was smoking. 'Put that out now,' Miller said. He looked at Fischer. 'Are you ready?'

Fischer nodded, then, an instant before the light went out, I saw him cross himself. That is something I don't understand. I mean, he was asking a blessing, or whatever it is, when he was going to commit a sin.

Miller went up the stairs slowly. At the top he paused, looking all round, getting his bearings. Then he bent his head down to mine.

'Karl said that you may have vertigo,' he said softly; 'but it is all quite simple. Follow me at three paces. Do not look sideways or back, only ahead. There is one step down from this ironwork. Then there is lead sheet. I will step down, go three paces and wait a little so that your eyes can adjust themselves.'

I had been so long in the darkness that the intermittent glare of the pen-light had been almost painful. Outside on the roof, the moonlight seemed to make everything as bright as day; too bright for my liking; I was certain that someone would see us from the ground and start shooting. Fischer must have had the same feeling. I heard him swear under his breath behind me.

Miller's teeth gleamed for an instant; then he started to move forwards past the three cupolas over the quarters of the White Eunuchs. There was a space of about five feet between the cupolas and the edge of the roof. Staying close to the cupolas and looking only ahead as Miller had instructed me. I had no sensation at all of being on a high place. For a while, my only problem was keeping up with him. Harper had compared him to a fly. To me he looked more like an earwig as he slithered round the last of the three cupolas and scuttled on, leaning inwards over the slight hump in the centre of the roof. He stopped only once. He had crossed the roof of the Audience Chamber, to avoid what looked like three large fanlights over the Gate of Felicity, and was returning to the Eunuchs' roof when another fanlight appeared and the flat surface narrowed slightly. The way across was only about two feet wide.

I saw the ground below and started to go down on my knees—I might just have been able to crawl across by myself, I suppose—when he reached back, gripped my forearm and drew me after him. It was done so quickly that I had no time to get sick and lose my balance. His fingers were like steel clamps.

Then we were level with the kitchens and I could see the conical bases of their ten squat chimneys stretching away to the right. Miller led the way to the left. The flat space here was over thirty feet wide and I had no trouble. There was a four-foot rise then, which brought us over the big room with the exhibition of miniatures and glass in it. Ahead, I could see the whole of one cupola and, beyond it, the top of another smaller one. The smaller one, I knew, was the one on the roof of the Treasury Museum.

Miller began to move more slowly and carefully as he skirted the big cupola. Every now and again he stopped. Then I saw him lower himself over a ledge. When his feet found whatever there was below, only his head and shoulders were showing.

I was following round the big cupola, and had started to move away from it towards the ledge, when Miller turned and beckoned to me. He had moved a yard or two towards the outer edge of the roof, so I changed direction towards him. That is how it was that when I came to the ledge I saw too much.

There was the vaulted roof of the Treasury, and the cupola with a flat space about four feet wide all around the base of it. That is where Miller was standing. But beyond him there was nothing, just a great black emptiness, and then, horribly far away below, the faint white hairline of a road in the moonlight.

I felt myself starting to lose my balance and fall, so I knelt down quickly and clung to the lead surface of the roof. Then I began retching. I couldn't help it; I've never been able to help it. From what I've heard from people who get sea-sick, that must be the same sort of feeling; only my feeling about heights is worse.

I had nothing in my stomach to throw up, but that didn't make any difference. My stomach went on trying to throw up.

Fischer began kicking me and hissing at me to be silent. Miller reached up and dragged me by the ankles down over the ledge, then made me sit with my back against the side of the cupola. He shoved my head hard between my knees. I heard a scuffling noise as he helped Fischer down off the ledge, then their whispering.

'Will he be all right?'

'He will have to be.'

'The fat fool.' Fischer kicked me as I started to retch again.

Miller stopped him. 'That will do no good. You will have to help. As long as he gets no nearer the edge it may be possible.'

I opened my eyes just enough to see Miller's feet. He was laying out the anchor rope round the cupola and presently he pulled one end of it down between my back and the part I was leaning against. A moment or two later, he crouched down in front of me and began knotting the rope. When that was done, he slipped on the upper block of the lifting tackle. Then he brought his head close to mine.

'Can you hear me, Arthur?'

'Yes.'

'If you didn't have to move, you'd feel safe here, wouldn't you?'

'I don't know.'

'You *are* safe now, aren't you?'

'Yes.'

'Then listen. You can handle the tackle from here. Open your eyes and look up at me.'

I managed to do so. He had taken his coat off and looked skinnier than ever. 'Hans will be at the edge,' he went on, 'and with his good hand will hold my coat in place there. In that way the ropes will run smoothly over it and not be cut. You understand?'

'Yes.'

'And you will not have to go near the edge—only let out rope and pull in when you are told.'

'I don't know. Supposing I let it slip?'

'Well, that would be bad, because then you would have only Hans to deal with, and he would certainly make sure that you slipped, too.'

The teeth, as he smiled, were like rows of gravestones. Suddenly, he picked up a coil of rope from the lead beside him and put it in my hands.

'Get ready to take the strain,' he said, 'and remember that it stretches. I don't mind how slowly I go down or how quickly I come up. Hans will give you the signals to lower, stop and raise.' He pointed to a ridge in the lead. 'Brace your feet against this. So.'

The day Mum died, the Imam came and intoned verses from the Koran: *'Now taste the torment of the fire you called a lie.'*

Miller slipped the end of the rope around my chest and knotted it firmly. Then he hauled in the slack. 'Are you ready, Arthur?'

I nodded.

'Then look at Hans.'

I let my eyes go to Fischer's legs and then his body. He was lying on his right side with his shoulder on Miller's coat and his right hand on the tackle ready to guide it. I dared not look any nearer the edge. I knew I would pass out if I did.

I saw Miller put a pair of gloves on, step into the sling, then crouch down and move out of sight.

'Now,' Fischer whispered.

The strain didn't come suddenly; the stretch in the nylon had to be taken up first. My hands were slippery with sweat and I had looped the rope round the sleeve of my left arm to give me more purchase. When the full strain came, the loop tightened like a tourniquet. Then the pressure fluctuated and I could feel Miller bouncing in the sling as the tackle settled down.

'Steady.' Fischer held his right hand palm downwards over the tackle.

The movement in the block by the anchor rope beside me ceased.

'Lower slowly.'

I let the rope slide round my arm and the bouncing began again.

'Keep going, smoothly.'

I went on paying out the rope. There was less bouncing now, just an occasional vibration. Miller was using his feet to steady himself against the wall as he descended. I watched the coil of rope beside me growing smaller and had another terror to fight. The end of the rope was tied round my chest. I couldn't untie it now without letting go. If there were not enough rope in the coil to reach the shutter below, Fischer would make me move nearer to the edge.

There were about six feet left to go when he raised his hand.
'Stop. Hold still.'

I was so relieved that I didn't notice the pain in my arm from
the tightened loop; I just closed my eyes and kept my head down.

There were slight movements on the rope, and, after a moment
or two, faint clicking sounds as he went to work on the metal shutters. Minutes went by. My left arm began to go numb. Then there
was another sound from below, a sort of hollow tapping. It only
lasted a moment, before Fischer hissed at me. I opened my eyes
again.

'Lower a little, very slowly.'

As I obeyed I felt the tension in the rope suddenly slacken. Miller
was inside.

'Rest.'

I loosened the rope on my arm and massaged it until the pins-
and-needles began. I didn't try to massage them away. They kept
my mind on my arm and away from other things, such as the day
the games master had made me dive. When you got into the cadet
corps you had to be able to swim, and, once a week, all the boys
in each squad who couldn't do so were marched to the Lewisham
Public Baths to take lessons. When you had learned to swim you had
to dive. I didn't mind the swimming part, but when my head went
under water I was always afraid of drowning. For a time I didn't
have to, because I kept telling the games master that I had bad ears;
but then he said that I would have to get a doctor's certificate. I tried
to write one myself, but I didn't know the proper words to use and
he caught me out. I expected him to send me with a note to The
Bristle, but instead he made me dive. I say 'dive'. What he did was
pick me up by one arm and a leg and throw me in the deep end; and
he kept on doing it. Every time I managed to get out, even while I

was still choking up water, he would throw me in again. One of the attendants at the Baths had to stop him in the end. He was married, so I wrote a letter to his wife telling her how he messed about with certain boys in the changing cubicles and pestered them to feel him. I was careless, though, because I used the same handwriting as I had used on the certificate, and he knew for certain it was me. He couldn't prove it, of course, because he had torn up the certificate. He took me into a lobby and accused me and called me an 'unspeakable little cad'; but that was all he did. He was really shaken. When I realized it, I could have kicked myself. If I had known that he actually had been messing about with boys in the cubicles, I could have put the police on to him. As it was, I had simply warned him to be more careful. He had thin, curly brown hair with an officer's moustache, and walked as if he had springs on the soles of his feet. The term after that he left and went to another school.

Fischer hissed at me and I opened my eyes.

'Take the strain.'

I wrapped the rope round my waist this time so that I could use my weight to push away from the edge if necessary.

'Ready?'

I nodded and held on tight. There was a jerk as Miller got his weight into the sling again. Then Fischer nodded.

'Up.'

I started to pull. The friction of the rope against the coat on the edge of the roof made it terribly hard. The sweat ran into my eyes. Twice I had to stop and knot the rope round my waist so that I could wipe my hands and ease the cramp in my fingers; but the coil got larger again and then Fischer began to use his good hand on one of the ropes in the tackle.

'Slow... slower... stop.'

Suddenly, the tackle ran free and Miller, grinning, was crawling across the roof towards me. He patted my leg.

'Merci, mon cher collègue,' he said.

I shut my eyes and nodded. Through the singing in my ears I could hear him reporting to Fischer as he gathered in the tackle.

'All those we counted on and a few more to garnish the dish. I even fastened the shutters again.'

I felt him untying the rope from my chest. When I opened my eyes he was clipping the velvet bag to his belt. Fischer was fumbling with the knots in the anchor rope. I crawled over and began to help him. All I wanted was to get away, and I knew that they would have to help me.

Fischer with his injured hand needed help to get back on to the upper roof level. Then Miller somehow managed to heave me up high enough for me to claw my way over the ledge. I crawled then on my hands and knees to the shelter of the big cupola. By the time Miller reached me, I was able to stand up.

We started back, as we had started out, with Miller in the lead. This time, however, there was no turn to make. We left the White Eunuchs' quarters on our right and went on over the kitchen roofs to the wall by the Gate of Salvation. There was one awkward place—for me, that is—by the old water tower, but I somehow got past it on my hands and knees. Then we were on the wall overlooking the Courtyard of the Janissaries.

There was a row of tall plane trees close to the wall, and Miller used an overhanging branch as an anchor for the tackle. He lowered Fischer first, in the sling, and then me; but he wouldn't use the sling himself, because that would have meant leaving the tackle in the tree. It was not the tackle itself he cared about, he said; he didn't want to leave any traces behind of how the job had been done. He got off the wall by looping the anchor rope over the branch and sliding down it. Doubled like that, it wasn't quite long enough to reach the ground, so he dropped the last six feet, pulling one end of the rope with him. He landed as lightly as a cat and began gathering in the rope. After all he had done, he wasn't even out of breath.

Fischer took over the lead now, and headed for the outer wall on a line parallel with the road the tourist cars used during the day. Miller walked behind me. After a minute or two, we could see the lights of the guard-room beside the huge Bab-i-Hümayun Gate and Fischer slowed down. We had been walking in the shadow of a row of trees, but now they came to an end. Fifty yards across the road to the right was the bulk of St Irene; ahead the road forked, the right prong going to the gate, the left prong narrowing and curving inwards down the hill towards the sea.

Fischer stopped, staring at the gate.

It was no more than fifty yards away and I could see the sentry. He had his carbine slung over his shoulder and was picking his nose.

Fischer put his mouth to my ear. 'What time is it?'

'Five to ten.'

'We have time to wait.'

'Wait for what?'

'We have to go left down the hill. The guard changes in five minutes. It will be safer then.'

'Where are we going to?'

'The railroad—where it bridges the wall.'

A section of the railway ran along the shore-line just inside the big wall for about three-quarters of a mile; but I knew that there were guard posts at both ends of it. I said so.

He grinned. 'Guard posts, yes. But no gates.'

Miller hissed a warning.

An oblong of light glowed as the door of the guard-room opened. For an instant two men were outlined in the doorway. Then, as the business of changing sentries began, Fischer touched my arm.

'Now.'

He moved forward out of the shadow of the trees and cut across a patch of rough grass to the road. It descended sharply and narrowed to little more than a track. Within thirty seconds the top of the slope hid us from the sentries. Fischer glanced back to see that we were with him, and then walked on at a more leisurely pace.

Ahead was a strip of sea and beyond it the lights of Selimiye and Haydarpasar on the Asian side. Other lights moved across the water—a ferry and small fishing-boats. In the daylight, tourists with ciné-cameras waste hundreds of feet of film on the view. I suppose it's very beautiful. Personally, I never want to see it again—in any sort of light.

After a couple of minutes' walking we came to another track, which led off to the right towards the outer wall. Fischer crossed it and went straight on down over a stretch of waste land. There were piles of rubble from archaeological diggings, and part was terraced as if it had at some time been cultivated as a vineyard. At the bottom was the railway embankment.

There was a wooden fence running alongside it, and Miller and I waited while Fischer found the damaged section which he had chosen on an earlier reconnaissance as the best way through. It was about thirty yards to the right. We clambered over some broken boards to the side of the embankment and walked along the drainage ditch. Five minutes later it was possible to see the big wall again. We walked on another hundred feet, and there the embankment ended. If we were to go any farther we had to climb up and walk along the track over the bridge.

Fischer stopped and turned. 'What is the time?'

'Ten-fifteen,' said Miller. 'Where is the guard post exactly?'

'On the other side of the bridge, a hundred metres from here.'
He turned to me. 'Now listen. A train will be coming soon. When
it starts to cross the bridge we go to the top of the embankment.
As soon as the last wagon has passed us we start to follow along the
tracks at walking speed. When we have gone about twenty metres
we will hear a loud explosion ahead. Then we start to run, but not
too fast. Have you ever smelt tear-gas?'

'Yes.'

'You will smell it again, but do not worry. It is our tear-gas, not
theirs. And there will be smoke, too, also ours. The train will have
just gone through. The guard post will not know what is happening. They may think the train has blown up. It does not matter. The
tear-gas and the smoke will make it hard for them to think, or see.
If any of them tries too hard he will get a bullet or a plastic grenade
to discourage him. In the confusion we run through. And then, as
I told you, the Volkswagen will be waiting for us.'

'What about our confusion?' I said. 'How do we see where to
go with tear-gas and smoke?'

Miller nodded. 'I asked the same question, my friend. We should
have had respirators. But Karl's argument was good. With so much
to conceal, how could we carry respirators, too?'

'I made the experiment,' Fischer said defensively. 'I tried to take
a respirator in. They stopped me because of the bulge in my pocket.
They thought I was trying to smuggle a camera into the Seraglio.
They are strict about that, as you know. It was embarrassing.'

'How did you explain it?' Miller asked.

'I said I was a doctor.'

'They believed you?'

'If you say you are a doctor, people will believe anything. We need not worry where to go. We simply follow the rail tracks and leave everything to Karl. We have done our work for this evening. Now we only wait for our train.'

We waited twenty-five minutes.

It was a mixed train, Fischer said, carrying newspapers, mail-bags, local freight, and a few passengers, to the small towns between Istanbul and Pehlivanköy. It chuffed towards the bridge as noisily and importantly as the Orient Express. There was a slight off-shore breeze blowing. The thick black smoke from the engine rolled along our side of the embankment and engulfed us.

'*Los! Vorwärts!*' Fischer shouted, and, coughing and spluttering, Miller and I scrambled after him up the embankment.

For half a minute we stayed there with the train wheels clacking over a join in the rails about three feet from our noses. Then the last axle-box went by.

'*Los!*' said Fischer again, and we were stumbling along the side of the tracks between the jutting ends of the sleepers and the parapet of the bridge.

We must have been about seventy yards from the guard post when the concussion grenade went off, and even at that distance the detonation made my ears sing. In front of me Fischer began to trot. Almost immediately he tripped over something and fell. I heard him gasp with pain as his left arm hit a sleeper; but he was on his feet and moving again before I got to him.

There was shouting ahead now, and I could hear the plunking, sizzling noise of tear-gas and smoke grenades detonating. The train smoke was still billowing around, but a moment later I got the first whiff of chemical smoke. Three yards more and I saw the white bandage on Fischer's right hand go to his forehead. Then I was in the tear-gas, too, and the first excruciating reaction of the sinuses began to spread into my eyes. I blundered on, choking. As the tears began to blind me, another concussion grenade went off. Then a shape loomed up out of the smoke and a respirator goggled at me; a hand gripped my arm and steered me to the right. I had a vague, tear-blurred impression of a lighted room and a man in uniform with his hands above his drooping head leaning against a wall. Then the arm belonging to the hand was supporting me as I stumbled down a long flight of steps.

I was out of the smoke now and I could just see the door of the Volkswagen van. The arm shoved me towards it. I almost fell inside. Fischer was already there, hawking and coughing. More grenades were exploding on the bridge above as Miller scrambled in after me. Then there was a sound of running feet and the men in the respirators piled in. Someone pressed the starter. A moment later the van was on the move. I was crouched on the floor against one of the empty packing cases and somebody was treading on my feet. The stink of tear-gas was everywhere. I heard Harper's voice from the front passenger seat.

'Everything okay, Leo?'

Miller was coughing and chuckling at the same time. 'The dogs have fed and clothed themselves,' he wheezed.

CHAPTER ELEVEN

THERE WERE FIVE MEN BESIDES HARPER IN THE RESPIRATORS, but my eyes were still so painful that I didn't see any of their faces well enough to be able to identify them. One of them was named Franz and he spoke German as well as Turkish. I know, because I heard him use both languages—the German to Fischer. The other four only spoke Turkish, I think. I can't be certain because I was only with them a few minutes, and I was coughing most of the time.

The van must have gone about three miles when it slowed down, made a wide U-turn and stopped.

Harper opened the door from the outside.

Miller was nearest the door and he got out first. I followed, with Fischer behind me. The other men just moved enough to make way for us. Then Harper shut the door again and the van was driven off.

'This way,' Harper said.

We were opposite one of the big wood yards by an unloading pier and some beached caïques. He led the way along the pier. I was beginning to see well enough again now to recognize Giulio standing up in the *Bulut*'s outboard dinghy. We climbed down into it. I heard Giulio ask who I was and be told that he would find out later. Then the motor started, and we shot away from the pier.

The *Bulut* was anchored a quarter of a mile away, and a man on deck, Enrico presumably, was at the small gangway waiting to help us on board. I followed the others to the saloon.

By the time I reached the bottom of the narrow companionway that led down to it, Harper was already untying the drawstring of

Miller's velvet bag, while the others crowded round to look. I saw the glitter of dozens of green and red stones and I heard Giulio draw in his breath. The stones didn't look all that large to me; but of course, I am no judge of such things.

Harper was grinning his head off. 'Nothing but the best, Leo,' he said. 'You're a great man.'

'How much?' said Fischer.

'Better than a million and a half,' Harper replied. 'Let's be on our way as soon as we can, Giulio.'

'*Pronto.*'

Giulio brushed past me and went up the companionway. There were sandwiches and drinks set out at the other end of the table. While they drooled over the stones, I poured myself a large whisky.

Harper looked across at me. 'Aren't you interested in the loot, Arthur?'

I had a sudden desire to hit him. I shrugged indifferently. 'I'm not interested in counting chickens,' I said. 'I'll settle for two thousand dollars, cash on the barrel.'

They all stared at me in silence for a moment. The deck began to vibrate as the boat's diesels started up.

Harper glanced at Miller. 'I take it Arthur behaved himself this evening.'

'He was a damned nuisance,' Fischer said spitefully.

Harper ignored him. 'Well, Leo?'

'He was afraid,' Miller answered; 'but what he did was enough. Under the circumstances I think he did well.'

Harper looked at me again. 'Why the cracks, Arthur? What's the problem?'

'How do you imagine you're going to get away with it?'

'Oh, I see.' He relaxed again, all smiles. 'So our Arthur's worried that the bloodhounds are going to start snapping at his butt, is he? Well, forget it. They won't. All they know so far is that a bunch of armed men in a Volkswagen van roughed up one of their guard posts. So the first thing they'll do is set up blocks on all the roads leading out of the city and look for the van. They'll find it, abandoned, over in Galata. Then they'll start the usual routine—Who's the owner? Where is he? What did he look like?—and get no place. By then, though, they'll have done some thinking, too, and some big brain will be starting to wonder why it had to be that particular post and why nobody got killed—why a lot of things. He may even think of checking out the Treasury Museum and so come up with the right answer. When he does, they'll double up on the road-blocks and throw out the dragnet. Only we won't be inside it. We'll be going ashore at a little place sixty miles from here and two hours' easy driving from Edirne and the frontier.' He patted my arm. 'And where we go ashore, Arthur, Miss Lipp will be waiting to pick us up.'

'With the Lincoln?'

'What else? We wouldn't want to walk, would we, or leave without our bags?'

I had to laugh. I couldn't help it. And it didn't matter, because Harper thought that it was the beauty of his plan that I found so amusing, and not the bloody great hole in it. I thought of the customs inspector's face when the Lincoln drove up for clearance—if Tufan allowed it to get that far—and when he saw me again. I laughed so much that Fischer began to laugh, too. It was the best moment I had had in days. I ate some sandwiches and had another drink. There was garlic sausage in the sandwiches, but I didn't even have a twinge of indigestion. I thought my worries were over.

The place we were to go ashore was a port called Serefli, a few miles south of Corlu. Harper said that it would take five hours to get there. I cleaned off the filth I had collected from the Seraglio roof as best I could and went to sleep in the saloon. The others used the cabins. Giulio and Enrico ran the boat between them. I found out later that they had sent the boat's regular crew ashore at Pendik for an evening on the town, and then slipped out of the harbour after dark. The patrol boat that was supposed to be keeping an eye on the *Bulut* missed it completely.

It was getting light when voices in the saloon woke me. Harper and Miller were drinking coffee, and Fischer was trying to make his dirty bandages look more presentable by brushing them. He seemed to be having some sort of discussion with Harper. As it was in German I couldn't understand. Then Harper looked at me and saw that I was awake.

'Arthur can use a screwdriver,' he said, 'if you just show him what to do.'

'Which door?' Fischer asked.

'Does it matter? How about the right rear?'

'We were talking about a safe place for the loot,' Harper said to me. 'Inside one of the car doors seems a good place for the customs people to forget about.'

'Arthur would not know about such things,' Miller said waggishly.

They had a good laugh over that gem of wit, while I tried to look mystified. Luckily, Enrico came in just then and said that we would be entering port in ten minutes.

I had some of the coffee and a stale sandwich. Harper went up to the wheel-house. Half an hour later, the sun was up and we were moored alongside a stone jetty.

Fishermen are early risers and the harbour was already busy. Cuttlefish boats were unloading the night's catch at the quayside. Caïques with single-cylinder engines were chugging out to sea. A port official came aboard to collect dues. After a while, Harper came down and said that he was going ashore to make sure that Miss Lipp was there. He left the velvet bag with Fischer.

He returned fifteen minutes later and reported that the Lincoln was parked in a side street beside a café-restaurant on the main square. Miss Lipp was in the restaurant eating breakfast. The side street was a quiet one. Fischer and I could get busy on the door. We would be allowed half an hour to complete the job.

Fischer borrowed a screwdriver from Enrico and we went ashore. Nobody seemed to take any notice of us, probably because we looked so scruffy. I couldn't see the Opel or the Peugeot anywhere about, but that didn't worry me. I knew that one or other of them would be on tap. We found the car without difficulty and I started on the door. It was an ordinary screwdriver I had to work with, but the earlier removals of the panel had eased the screws and I didn't do any more damage to the leather. It took me ten minutes to take the panel off, five seconds for Fischer to wedge the velvet bag in clear of the window mechanism, and fifteen minutes for me to replace the panel. Then Fischer and I got into the back seat. Two minutes later, Miss Lipp came out of the restaurant and got behind the wheel. If she had slept the previous night it could only have been at the inn in Corlu; but she looked as fresh as she always did.

'Good morning, Hans. Good morning, Arthur. The others are just coming across the square now,' she said.

They arrived a moment after. Harper got in the front seat with her, Miller sat on my left. She said good morning to Miller, and drove off the moment she heard the door close.

From Serefli to Corlu, where we would join the main Istanbul-Edirne road, there are twelve miles of narrow secondary road. The first mile or so is winding, and I waited until we got to a straighter part before I risked a look back.

The Peugeot was there, and I caught a glimpse of another car behind it. The Opel was on the job as well.

Harper had started telling Miss Lipp about the night's work and the size of the haul. Miller was putting in his word, too. There was a lot of mutual congratulation. It was like being in the winning team's bus. I wasn't needed in the conversation, and didn't have to listen to it either. I could think.

There were several possible explanations for the two cars being there. Miss Lipp had probably driven straight to Corlu from the garage, after dropping us the previous afternoon. By the time she had left the Istanbul area, Tufan must have been told that the men were no longer in the car, and realized that his only hope of re-establishing contact lay in keeping track of the Lincoln. The Opel could have been sent to make sure that there were no further mistakes. Or it may have been to compensate for lack of radio communication outside the Istanbul area. The two cars could talk to one another; if an urgent report became necessary, one car could stop and reach Istanbul by telephone while the other continued the surveillance. Then a third possibility occurred to me. Tufan must have been told about the attack on the guard post. As soon as he heard the details—smoke, tear-gas, concussion grenades, six men in respirators—he would know that the attack and the Lincoln were related. If he also knew that the *Bulut* had left Pendik and that the Lincoln had stopped at Corlu, he might have decided that reinforcements were necessary in that area.

The only certainty, I decided sourly, was that Tufan would not be the 'big brain' who would think of checking the Treasury Museum.

He would still be off on his political wild goose chase. Well, he would have some surprises coming.

At that moment Miss Lipp said sharply: 'Karl!'

Miller had been in the middle of saying something and he broke off abruptly.

'What is it?' Harper said.

'That brown car behind us. It was behind me yesterday when I drove out from Istanbul. I thought then that I'd noticed it before, earlier in the day. In fact, I was so sure that when I stopped at Corlu I waited to get a look at it. When it didn't show up I figured it had turned off somewhere and thought no more about it.'

'Don't look around, anyone,' Harper said. He swivelled the driving mirror so that he could look behind. After a moment, he said: 'Try slowing down.'

She did so. I knew what would happen. The Peugeot would keep its distance. After about a minute, Harper twisted the mirror back into position. 'Do you think you could lose it?' he said.

'Not on these roads.'

'Okay. Just keep going. Doesn't look like a police car. I wonder…'

'Franz!' Fischer said suddenly.

'All set for a little hi-jacking operation, you mean?'

'Why not?'

'He could have done that better last night when he had us in the van,' said Miller.

'I'm not so sure,' said Harper. 'He might have figured that it would be safer to wait until we were all outside the city.'

'But Franz didn't know this end of the plan,' Miss Lipp objected.

'If he put a tail on you,' Fischer said, 'he could have guessed.'

'Well, we'll soon find out,' Harper said grimly. 'There are only two of them in that car. If it's Franz we're dealing with, that probably means that he's set up an ambush somewhere ahead with his other two mugs. That makes five. We only have three guns, so we'd better take care of this lot first. We'll pick a spot with some trees and then pull off the road. Okay?'

'May I look round at this car?' I asked.

'Why?'

'To see if I recognize it.'

I knew that I had to do something. If they started shooting at Turkish security agents, Turkish security agents were going to start shooting back—and they weren't going to stop to ask questions or worry about who got hit.

'Okay,' he said; 'but make it casual.'

I looked back.

'Well?' he asked.

'I don't recognize the brown one,' I said; 'but there's another one behind it, a grey Opel.'

'That's right,' Miss Lipp said; 'it's been there some time. But so what? The road's too narrow for passing.'

'I'm almost sure it was outside that garage yesterday afternoon.' I tried to sound like a really worried man. It wasn't very difficult.

'There are many grey Opels,' Miller said.

'But not with such a very long radio aerial. That is why I noticed it.'

Harper had swivelled the mirror again and was peering into it. 'You'd better look, too, Leo,' he said grimly. 'See the antenna?'

Miller looked and swore. 'It could be a coincidence,' he said.

'Could be. Do you want to take a chance on it?'

'No,' said Fischer.

'I agree,' said Miller; 'but what do we do about them?'

Harper thought for a moment. Then he asked: 'How much farther to Corlu?'

'About three kilometres,' Miss Lipp answered.

'Then he must have it set up somewhere between Corlu and Edirne.'

'So?'

'So, instead of turning left at Corlu and going to Edirne, we change our plans and turn right.'

'But that would take us back to Istanbul,' Miller objected.

'Not all the way,' Harper said; 'only as far as the airport and the first plane out.'

'Leaving the car behind?' asked Miss Lipp.

'Don't worry, sweetie. We'll all be able to buy fleets of Lincolns when we cash in this pile of chips.'

Suddenly, they were all smiles again.

I tried to think. It was barely seven-thirty and the run from Corlu to the Istanbul Airport at Yesilköy would take little more than an hour. It was Wednesday, which meant that the Treasury Museum would normally stay closed until the following day. Unless the big brain had already started working, or unless Tufan had decided to stop uncovering non-existent terrorist plots and let the police know what was going on, there was every chance that, within a couple of hours, Harper and the rest would be out of the country. In that case, if anyone were going to stop them it would have to be me. The question was—did I *want* to stop them? Why didn't I just go along with them and collect my two thousand dollars?

I was still tired and confused or I would have remembered that there could be only one answer to that—my passport was not valid and an airline would not carry me. But instead of the answer, another stupid question came into my mind; and, stupidly, I asked it.

'Am I included in this?'

Harper turned right round in his seat to face me, and gave me the cold, unpleasant smile I liked least.

'Included, Arthur? Why? Did you have something else in mind—like making a quick deal with Franz, for instance, or even the police?'

'Of course not. I just wanted to be certain.'

'Well that makes five of us who want to be certain. Don't you worry, Arthur. Until we're on that plane with the loot all safe and sound, you're not even going to the can by yourself. That's how much you're included.'

Fischer and Miller thought that hilariously amusing. Miss Lipp, I noticed, was keeping her attention divided between the road ahead and the cars behind.

We came to Corlu and turned right on to the main Istanbul road. Harper began to organize the change of plan.

'The first thing is to get the stuff out of the door. Hans, you'd better change places with Arthur. He can get busy now.'

'He can't,' Fischer said. 'There are seven screws on the rear doors. With the door shut he cannot get at them. The door has to be open.'

'All the way open?'

'Nearly.'

Harper looked at the heavy doors. They were hinged at the rear, and would swing open against the wind. We were doing over sixty. It was obviously out of the question to take the panel off while we were on the move. He nodded. 'All right. Here's what we'll do. As soon as we get to the airport, Elizabeth and Leo will take all the passports and get busy buying tickets and filling out passport cards and customs forms for all of us. Right?'

They nodded.

'Then I follow them inside just to check on the flight number and boarding time so that we all know what the score is. As soon as

I have that, I return to the car and Arthur drives us to the parking lot. There, we open the door and get the stuff. When it's out, Hans gets porters and we unload the baggage. We leave the car on the park. Any questions?'

'You could unload the baggage first,' said Miller, 'while the car is in front.'

'Maybe. If we have plenty of time. If we don't have too much, I'd sooner make sure of the loot first.'

'We must have some baggage for the customs,' Miss Lipp put in. 'People without baggage get a personal search.'

'All right. We'll unload just the stuff from inside the car and leave the rest until later.'

There was a murmur of agreement. Miller asked: 'If there are two flights available within a short time, which do we take?'

'If one of them flies over a lot of Turkish territory—say to Aleppo or Beirut—we take the other. Otherwise, we take the first.'

They went on discussing which city they would prefer as a destination. I was wondering what would happen if I told them about my passport. From Harper, I decided, there would be only one reaction; if they could not take me with them, yet dared not leave me because I knew too much, I would have to be eliminated from the picture altogether. There would be a corpse on the floor of the car they left behind them. On the other hand, if I waited until the passport was challenged at the airport, there wasn't much they could do. I could yell my head off, demand to see a security official and tell him to contact Tufan. True, the three men had guns; but even if they managed to shoot their way out of the place, I would stand a better chance of coming out of it alive.

'Any more problems?' Harper asked. 'No? Okay, then, let's have the passports.'

I nearly threw up, but managed to cough instead.

Fischer asked me to get his out of his inside pocket for him. Miller passed his over and Harper flipped through the pages. I gave him Fischer's.

Miss Lipp said: 'My bag is on the floor, if you want to put them in it now.'

'Okay. Where's yours, Arthur?' *Has any boy not handed in his homework?*

I handed the wretched thing to him and waited.

He lingered over my vital statistics. 'Know something, Arthur? I'd have said you were a good three years older. Too much *ouzo* and not enough exercise, that's your trouble.' And then, of course, his tone changed. 'Wait a minute! This is over two months out-of-date!'

'Out-of-date? But it can't be!' *I know I handed in my work with the rest, sir.*

'Look at it!' He leaned over and jammed it under my nose.

'But I had no trouble coming in. You see, there's the visa!'

'What difference does that make, you stupid slob? It's out-of-date!' He glowered at me and then, unexpectedly, turned to Miss Lipp. 'What do you think?'

She kept her eyes on the road as she answered. 'When you leave here the immigration people are mostly interested in seeing that the exit cards are properly filled in. He'll get by there. It's the airline counter check that matters. They are responsible at the port of disembarkation if papers are not in order. We'll have to write in a renewal.'

'Without a consular stamp?'

She thought for a moment. 'There's a Swiss airmail stamp in my purse, I think. We could use that. Ten to one they won't look at it closely if there is writing across it. Anyway, I'll keep them talking.'

'What about where we land?' asked Miller. 'Supposing they catch it there?'

'That's *his* worry,' Harper said.

'Not if they send him back here.'

'They wouldn't trouble to do that. It's not that serious. The airport police would hold him until the airline could get the Egyptian Consul to come out and fix the renewal.'

'He has been nothing but a nuisance from the beginning.' This was Fischer, of course.

'He was useful enough last night,' remarked Miss Lipp. 'By the way, that renewal had better be in his handwriting. Would it be in Arabic?'

'French and Arabic, both.' Harper stuck the stamp on the renewal space. 'Okay, Arthur. Here you are. Write across the centre of the stamp. *"Bon jusqu'au,"* let's see—make it April ten of next year. Then do it in Arabic. You can, I suppose?'

I did as I was told—as ever—and handed the passport back to him.

I didn't know *where* I stood now. If the plane went to Athens I might be able to get away with it; I still had my Greek *permis de séjour* to fall back on. But if I went to Vienna, or Frankfurt, or Rome, or (hideous thought) Cairo, then I'd be completely up the creek. I would have to wait until I knew whether they were going to Athens or not before I decided whether I would go along or try to stay. If I wanted to stay, though, it would be more difficult now. With Harper and Fischer keeping their eyes on me, and no official to single me out because of my invalid passport, yelling for help wouldn't do much good. A quick clip on the jaw from Harper and some fast talking—'So sorry. Our friend tripped and hit his head on a suitcase. He'll be all right in a moment. We'll take care of him.'—would be the end of *that*. I would have to rely upon the surveillance cars. The only trouble was that before they regained direct contact with Tufan we would be at the airport. I would have to give the men in the cars time to draw the right conclusions and issue the necessary orders.

I could only think of one way of causing a delay. When I had finished putting back the door panel, I had slipped the screwdriver into my pocket. There wasn't another one in the car, I knew.

While we were going through Mimarsinan, fifteen minutes or so away from the airport, I managed to ease the screwdriver from my pocket and let it slide back on the seat until I was sitting on it. A minute or two later, I pretended to stretch my legs and stuffed it deep down behind the seat cushion and below the back of the seat. If I wanted to go, I could 'find' it; if I wanted to delay I could look for it in vain on the floor. That way, I thought, I would at least have some sort of control over the situation.

And then Miss Lipp began to worry again about the Peugeot and the Opel.

'They're still tailing us,' she said. 'I don't get it. Franz must have guessed where we're heading for by now. What does he think he's going to do?'

'Supposing it isn't Franz?' Miller said suddenly.

'If it isn't Franz, who is it?' Fischer demanded irritably. 'They can't be police or they would have stopped us. Could it be Giulio?'

'That is an imbecile suggestion,' Miller retorted. 'Giulio is of our company. You are not. If you were, you would not say such a stupid thing.'

I have a unique capacity for self-destruction. I said, helpfully: 'Perhaps it is Franz. Perhaps he thinks that we are going back to the villa. If we were, we would still be on this road.'

Harper looked back. 'When will he know better, Arthur?'

'Not until we turn right for the airport.'

'How far is the turn-off?'

'About six miles.'

'How far then?'

'A mile and a half.'

He looked at Miss Lipp. 'Do you think you could lose them so that they wouldn't see us make the turn?'

'I could try.'

The Lincoln surged forward. Seconds later I saw the red speedometer needle swing past the ninety mark.

Harper looked back. After a minute, he said: 'Leaving them cold.'

'We're going too fast for this road,' was all she said. It didn't seem to be worrying her unduly, though. She passed two cars and a truck going in the same direction as if they were standing still.

I already knew that I had made a bad mistake, and did my best to retrieve it. 'There's a bridge a mile or so ahead,' I warned her. 'The road narrows. You'll have to slow down for that.'

She didn't answer. I was beginning to sweat. If the surveillance cars lost us, that was really the end as far as I was concerned.

She beat a convoy of army trucks to the bridge by fifty yards. On the other side, the road wound a little and she had to slow down to seventy; but when I looked back there wasn't a car in sight. As she braked hard and turned right on to the airport road, Harper chuckled.

'For that extra ounce of get-up-and-go,' he announced facetiously, 'there is nothing, but *nothing,* like a Lincoln Continental.'

There's nothing like feeling a complete bloody half-wit either. When we drove up outside the airport building, my legs were quivering like Geven's lower lip.

Miller was out of the car and into the building almost before the car had stopped. Miss Lipp and Harper followed while Fischer and I handed the bags inside the car, mine included, to a porter.

I couldn't help looking back along the airport approach road and Fischer noticed. He smiled at my lily-livered anxiety.

'Don't be afraid. They are on their way to Sariyer by now.'

'Yes.' I knew that at least one of them would be; but I also knew that the men in the cars were not incompetent. When they failed to pick up the Lincoln again, the second car would turn back and try the airport road. How long would it take them to get the idea, though? Five minutes? Ten?

Harper came out of the building and hurried to the car.

'There's an Air France jet to Rome,' he said. 'Seats available. Boarding in twenty minutes. Let's get moving.'

I drove to the car-park, a chain-fenced area just off the loop of road in front of the building and beyond the taxi rank. There were only a few cars already there and, on Harper's instructions, I backed into an empty space between two of them.

'Where is the screwdriver?' Fischer asked.

'On the floor.' I was still backing the car and could see that he was already searching for it.

'It must have rolled under one of the seats,' Harper said impatiently. 'Okay, Arthur, that'll do. Let's get the doors open so we can see.'

I pulled up, got out and immediately began trying to peer under the seats. With a Lincoln there is not much to see. The seats are snug against the floor.

'Oh, for God's sake!' Harper said angrily. Suddenly, he grabbed at my jacket. 'You must have put it in your pocket.' He started slapping them to find out.

'I put it on the floor.'

'Well, it isn't there now,' Fischer said.

Harper glanced at his watch. 'It must have been pulled out with the baggage.'

'Shall I go back and look?'

'No, get one out of the tool-kit.'

'There isn't one there,' Fischer said. 'I noticed that before.'

'Okay, see if it's on the ground back there.' As Fischer hurried off, Harper looked at the next car to us, a Renault, and tried the front doors. They were locked, of course. Then he tried the front luggage compartment. To my horror, it opened. The next moment he had a tool-roll in his hand and was taking a screwdriver from it.

He grinned. 'If the owner comes back, we'll buy it off him as a souvenir,' he said, and quickly went to work on the door panel of the Lincoln.

I was utterly desperate or I could never have done what I did; but as I stood there gaping at him I became aware of the sound of the engine running. I hadn't finished backing the car into line with the others when he had made me stop. Then I had simply forgotten to switch off.

The door to the driving seat was open and so were both back doors. He was crouched over the panel of the right-hand one on the opposite side of the car from me.

I glanced at the car-park entrance to make sure that Fischer wasn't coming back, and then I moved. I went to the door by the driver's seat, leaned across it as if I were going to switch off the engine and looked across the back of the seat.

Harper was bending down to undo one of the screws by the hinge.

I slid in to the driving seat gently so as not to rock the car, and eased the transmission lever from 'Park' to 'Drive'. The car gave a slight jerk. At the same moment I stamped on the accelerator.

I heard a thump as the door sent him flying, then I spun the wheel and was heading for the car-park entrance.

About twenty feet from it, I jammed on the brakes and the two rear doors swung shut with a slam. Through the rear window I could see Harper scrambling to his feet. As I closed the door beside me I accelerated again and went through on to the road. A moment later I was half way round the loop. Another car ahead slowed me for a moment. In the driving mirror I saw Harper running towards the taxi rank. I leaned on the horn ring and the car in front swerved. Then I was out of the loop and on the approach road.

I had gone about a mile when the Opel passed me, going in the opposite direction. I waved frantically, but kept on going. I didn't care whether they thought I'd gone mad or not. All I wanted was to get away from Harper.

I went on driving fast towards Istanbul until I saw in the mirror that the Opel was behind me. Only then did I stop.

It wasn't my fault that they took all that time to catch up with me.

CHAPTER TWELVE

'THE DIRECTOR IS NOT PLEASED WITH YOU,' TUFAN INFORMED me.

It was on the tip of my tongue to tell him what the Director could go and do to himself; but I managed to keep my temper. 'You got the stuff back,' I reminded him sharply; 'you have the names and descriptions of the people who took it. You know what was done and how it was done. What more do you want?'

'The woman and the three men,' he snapped.

The nerve of it! 'It wasn't I who let them get on that plane to Rome,' I said.

'It was your stupidity that did. If you hadn't panicked, if you had stopped immediately you saw the Opel instead of driving off like a madman, they would be in prison now. As it was, they got a close enough look at my men to realize their mistake. We had had no information from you. By the time we were able to re-establish contact with you, naturally they had gone.'

'They can be arrested in Rome. You can extradite them.'

'Not without a case strong enough to justify extradition proceedings.'

'You have it. I've told you what happened.'

'And what do you think your evidence would be worth in an Italian court?' he demanded. 'You smuggled the explosives in. Who is there to confirm your story of the subsequent robbery? They would have your record from Interpol to discredit you. Is the court to extradite four persons on your unsupported word that you have told the truth? They would laugh at us!'

'What about Giulio and Enrico?'

'Very sensibly, for them, they are saying nothing useful. They chartered a yacht. They decided to go for a night cruise. They were hailed by some men in a caïque who said that their motor had broken down. They took them to Serefli and put them ashore. Is that a crime? Tomorrow the police will have to let them go. There is nothing we can do. Your mistake, Simpson, was in not carrying out orders.'

'What orders, for God's sake?'

'The orders I gave you in this very room. You were told to report. You failed to do so. It was unfortunate that the packet you dropped in the garage was overlooked, but you had other opportunities. You could have reported at Serefli. You could have dropped your guide's licence at the guard post as you were taken through. There was want of imagination. We have no choice but to abandon the inquiry.'

'Including the inquiry about the attack on the guard post?'

He looked more po-faced than ever. 'That has already been officially described to the newspapers as an unsuccessful attempt by dissident elements to blow up a train.'

There was no polite comment I could make on that one, so I just shrugged and looked over his head at the picture of Abdul Hamid being deposed.

He stood up, as if to end the discussion, and smoothed down the front of his tunic. 'Luckily for you,' he said, 'the Director is not entirely dissatisfied with the affair. The Bureau has recovered the proceeds of a serious robbery which the Criminal Police did not even know about. It shows that *we* are not at the mercy of events, but in charge of them, that we anticipate. You were not entirely useless to us. As a result the Director has authorized the payment to you of a bonus.'

'So I should think. How much?'

'Five thousand lira, together with permission to sell them for foreign exchange, dollars or pounds sterling, at the official rate.'

For a moment I thought he must have made a mistake.

'Lira, Major? You mean dollars, don't you?'

'I mean Turkish lira,' he said stiffly.

'But that's only five hundred dollars—two hundred pounds!'

'Approximately. The fact that your suitcase and other personal belongings were lost has also been taken into consideration. In addition, arrangements are being made to have the various smuggling charges against you withdrawn. A favourable report on you will be made to Interpol. I think you will agree that you have been generously treated.'

A kick in the stomach couldn't have been more generous.

I opened my mouth to tell him that I wished now that I had taken my chance in Rome; but then I gave up. These policemen are all piss and wind anyway. Why add to it?

'You were going to say something?' he asked.

'Yes. How do I get out of this country?'

'The Director has persuaded the British Consul-General to issue to you a travel document good for one journey from here to Athens. I may say that it was not easy. The Consul agreed in the end only as a personal favour to the Director. In addition, an air passage has been reserved for you on the five o'clock Olympic Airways flight to Athens. A representative from the Consulate-General will meet you with the travel document at the Olympic Airways office by the Hilton Hotel at three-thirty. If you will tell me in what currency you would like the bonus paid, a representative from the Bureau will also be there to give you the money.'

'I'll take it in dollars.'

'Very well. That is all, I think. You do not seem as pleased as you should be.'

'What is there to be pleased about?'

He shrugged. 'Perhaps you think you would have been better off in Rome. You wouldn't, you know. If those jewels had left the country, we would have known enough to get them back, and you would have been the first to be arrested. Why not consider yourself lucky?'

'Aren't you forgetting that Harper still has a certain letter of mine?'

'Why should he send it now?'

'To get his own back on me, of course.'

He shook his head. '*You* are forgetting. He can never be sure now how much you found out about them and how much you told us. Even I cannot be quite sure of that. As far as he is concerned, the less you see of policemen the better.' He smiled slightly. 'You see, you both have an interest in common.'

'Very gratifying.'

'You might even consider becoming an honest man.'

Work, Simpson, for the night cometh.

I ought to have blown the smug bastard a raspberry; but I was afraid he might call off the bonus if I did. Even a crumb is better than no bread. So I just gave him an imitation of Harper's most unpleasant grin, and tried to let him see how much I despised him. I don't really think I succeeded. He had a hide as thick as an elephant's.

There was a sergeant on duty this time to escort me back to the guard-room gate. He watched me all the time as if he thought I might try to steal one of the pictures. Then, when I got outside there were no taxis. You never can get a taxi from outside the Dolmabahçe Palace. I had to walk a mile before I found one, and that made me angrier still.

The representative from the Bureau looked like a plainclothes policeman. He watched me carefully as I signed for the money and kept his fingers on the paper all the time in case I snatched it away. There were no flies on *him*. He knew how careful you had to be when dealing with crooks.

The representative from Her Britannic Majesty's Consulate-General in Istanbul was a snotty-nosed clerk who made me sign a paper saying that I understood that the granting of the travel document did not constitute recognition of any claim I had made or might make to United Kingdom citizenship. When I had signed it, I told him what he could do with it.

But on the way back to Athens in the plane, it gave me an idea.

I had been thinking about Nicki and wondering whether I would stop on my way to the flat and buy her a stone marten stole. She'd been hankering after one for a long while, and I thought that with the American notes I had I might get a good fur really cheaply—for thirty or forty dollars perhaps. I would be 'papa' for at least a month. That is, if she hadn't moved out while I had been away. I was deciding that I had better make sure of that first when the stewardess stopped by my seat.

'Your nationality, sir?'

'British,' I said.

She handed me a passport control card to fill in and moved on to the next seat.

I had said 'British' without thinking. Why? Because I consider myself British, because I *am* British.

I took out the travel document and looked at it carefully. It, too, said I was British. And yet they had made me sign a paper which said in effect that I wasn't. Therefore, the travel document could be considered an admission of my claim. The paper was unimportant because I had signed that under duress. You cannot take away a man's nationality by refusing to recognize his right to it. The 1948 Act is quite clear. The only way you can lose British nationality is by renouncing it. I haven't renounced mine at any time. Specifically, I did not renounce it by taking that Egyptian passport. Since the Egyptians say that my Egyptian naturalization is null and void because I made false statements, then it *is* null and void—*all* of it.

The British Government can't have it both ways. Either I am Egyptian or I am British. The Egyptians say I am not Egyptian and never have been. *I* say that I am not Egyptian and never have been. My father was a British officer. I am British.

That is why I have been so completely frank and open. I am not asking to be loved. I am not asking to be liked. I do not mind being loathed, if that will make some pettifogging government official happier. It is a matter of principle. If necessary, I shall take my case to the United Nations. They caned the British after Suez; they can cane them again for me. Sheep I may be; and perhaps certain persons find my breath displeasing; but I am no longer merely indignant. I am angry now.

I give the British Government fair warning. I refuse to go on being an anomaly. Is that quite clear? I *refuse!*

Also Available

PASSAGE OF ARMS

'A taut and extraordinary piece of writing'
Sunday Times

Some men take to gun-running because they have a longing for danger and adventure. Girija Krishnan, an Indian clerk, is not one of them. Deep in the Malayan jungle, Girija stumbles on a cache of arms hidden during the communist insurgency. Selling the arms will help Girija achieve his lifelong dream of founding a transport company.

Two American tourists in the Far East find more adventure than they bargained for when they get entangled in Girija's plans. Greg and Dorothy Nilsen had wanted to go on an adventurous trip; so when Mr Tan in Hong Kong asks Greg to travel to Singapore to help with a business deal, Greg is surprisingly receptive. All he has to do is sign some papers and collect a handsome fee – but this is Greg's first step into the dangerous world of post-colonial rebellions, Chinese gun smugglers and Islamic revolutionaries.

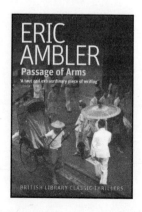